Before We Ever Spoke

Dan Largent

ISBN-10: 0692130667
ISBN-13: 978-0692130667

DEDICATION

For my children, Brooke, Grace, and Luke. Dream BIG and know that YOU are my greatest accomplishment. I started writing this book *before* you were born… I finished writing it *because* you were born.

For my wife, April, who lets me chase all of my dreams - as crazy as they usually are. YOU are my "Cara Knox".

For my mother, Anne Cole, who has always been my creative role model, my greatest supporter, and the one who taught me how to love unconditionally.

For my late father, Jeffrey Largent, who instilled a love of literature in me from a young age simply by letting me lay next to him as he read books every night.

ACKNOWLEDGMENTS

In 2016, I decided that I would finally finish the book I began writing in 2005. I wanted to show my children that even when life gets in the way that you can still follow your dreams and finish the job. Whether it was typing in a hotel lobby during my daughter's volleyball tournament or while sitting in an IHOP outside Columbus, I stayed the course for the next two years and finally finished it in May of 2018.

It has been a true labor of love.

There are so many people to thank, and I could not have done this without their help and support:

Kathy Meadows and Terri Tantanella, for constantly encouraging me to write the book that they believed I had in me.

Every single teacher and professor who encouraged me to believe in myself.

My editor, Dominque, who helped clean up a LOT of punctuation errors.

Daniel E. John, for designing the book cover.

The team at CreateSpace, for providing me with the platform to publish my first novel.

Dr. James Gorman, my favorite college professor, for providing guidance on this novel.

All of my friends and colleagues, who encouraged me along the way and never made me feel anything but supported.

My wife and children, for enabling me to chase this dream down and make it a reality.

1

"Wescott, room 1100!" yelled Stucky as he handed a box to a young woman, barely in her twenties.

"Wescott penthouse? Wow, what's the name on it?" she asked.

Beneath her cap, pulled low over her piercing blue eyes, lies a face that needs no makeup. Aside from her eyes, there is nothing about her appearance that is particularly unique. She is average height and has an athletic build. Her skin is slightly bronzed due to her guilty pleasure of visiting a tanning bed once a week, and her shoulder-length brunette hair is typically pulled back in a ponytail covered by a ball cap.

Cara Knox would best be described as a girl you may not notice in a crowd, but if you were lucky enough to bump into her, you may never be able to forget her.

"Madison," he replied. "Must be a big-timer to live on the 11th floor of the Westcott."

"Which usually means a lousy tip. Why is it the rich ones usually tip less than the average guys, Stuck?" Cara questioned.

"Most of them grew up with money, I suppose. Probably never learned the value of a buck or what it means to someone's income," replied Stucky. "Hurry back now, kiddo, I got three orders coming up for the Federal Building and you don't keep *those* guys waiting!"

Stucky, a short, stocky man in his early fifties, is the proud owner of Stucky's Place, a takeout restaurant on the corner of East

9th Street and St. Clair in downtown Cleveland. Most people who have worked downtown over the past 14 years have likely eaten food from Stucky's, at least once, and loved it. Offering a wide menu selection, they are open from breakfast until midnight, daily.

Most of his customers are corporate grunts who only have time for a quick meal to be delivered to their cubicles so they could eat while they worked. However, he also had a lot of business from the nearby hotels. Stucky, always shrewd, had garnered a deal with a few of the closest hotels when he first opened in the early 1990's. In exchange for putting a Stucky's Place menu in each room, he would send food over to each manager once a week at lunch. A small price to pay, he always said, for the business those menus brought in.

Cara walked out of Stucky's back door, which faced an alley behind the building. Only employees could use this door, which was ideal for Cara because she could hop right on her Vespa motor scooter without having to deal with the traffic on St. Clair. The motor scooter was Stucky's, but he let Cara take it home and use it around the city because it was her only means of transportation. Stucky used to work at the plant with Cara's father, and he always tried to look out for her as best he could.

After securing the box of food on the back of the scooter, Cara headed for the Westcott.

2

The Westcott Hotel was about three blocks from Stucky's. It had been in Cleveland for over a century and was the epitome of class. It was fully updated in the mid-nineties, but still had the feel of a 1900's turn-of-the-century hotel.

Many businessmen visiting Cleveland stay at the Westcott, and that means a lot of business for Stucky. However, some businessmen also lived there during the week in suites that looked more like luxury apartments.

Room 1100 is the penthouse suite of the Westcott. Calling it a suite would be an injustice as it was more like a 3,000 square foot house on top of a hotel.

Cara parked her scooter out front where Henry, the doorman, could watch over it for her. Cara knew every doorman in the city by name, and they would do anything for her. She was always pleasant to them and even brought them free food from time to time.

Cara has a way of making everyone she meets feel like they matter. That's why she does so well at her job and is also why Stucky is dreading the day that he has to say goodbye to his best employee when she graduates from college in nine months as a member of the Cleveland State University Class of 2007.

"Penthouse level please," Cara asked the elevator operator with a smile.

"No problem," said the operator, whose name tag read "Manny".

It was an old-fashioned elevator, the kind with a brass handle that actually requires an operator to run. Inside, soft music played in the background while Cara and the operator shared pleasantries.

"Good luck..." said the operator as Cara exited the elevator.

"Thanks...?" Cara responded, caught off guard by his warning veiled as words of encouragement. Before she could ask what he meant, the doors had already closed.

It wasn't a long walk from the elevator to the front door of the penthouse, just long enough for Cara to grasp how beautifully decorated the exterior was. She could only imagine the interior.

When she pressed the doorbell button she could hear gentle sounds similar to that of a grandfather clock notifying the occupant that a visitor was at the door. As she waited, Cara wondered what type of person lived in such a magnificent place. Was it the president of a bank? A big-shot businessman? An actor?

The door cracked open, but not far enough to see inside.

"How much do I owe you?" asked a deep voice with a slight southern drawl from the other side of the door.

Without missing a beat, Cara replied, "Twenty-eight dollars and seventy-five cents."

She had been in the food delivery business too long to be surprised by someone not opening the door all the way. Naked men and women, drag queens, and even a dwarf dressed up like Abraham Lincoln were just a few of the crazy things that Cara had seen when the door opened on past deliveries.

"Here, take this and the rest is yours. Please just set the food down outside the door," said the voice as a fifty-dollar bill slid through the crack.

"Are you sure you don't want any change?" Cara asked as the door was shutting.

There was no reply.

Cara put the food down in front of the door and walked toward the elevator. She had received big tips before, but they always came at the holidays or when office parties signed off on the bill using the company charge card. This was just a random tip on a random day.

Why the big tip? New money, she figured. They are always the most generous, but also the first to end up broke. Was he in the mafia and afraid to show his face? Witness protection?

Inside the elevator, Cara asked the operator if he knew anything about the man in the penthouse.

He gave her an odd look as if he was waiting for a punchline. When he realized she was being sincere, he broke the awkward silence.

"You must not be a big baseball fan."

"Not really. Does he play for the Indians?"

"No, but he used to play against them sometimes," he chuckled as the elevator doors opened.

"What's so funny?" Cara prodded.

"Listen," he whispered, "I shouldn't even be saying anything about a tenant, but what I can tell you is that he was the best pitcher in baseball until he lost it. It was really sad, too, watching a guy fall apart like that. Can't blame him, though. I blame the coach for letting him play so soon after…"

The elevator operator stopped short, realizing that talking about a tenant was a violation of the one rule that could get him fired, even though what he was about to reveal to the delivery girl was common knowledge to anyone who watched SportsCenter in the fall of 2005.

As she exited, he continued, "Look, as far as who he is, or was, talk to any baseball fan and you'll hear more about Cooper Madison than you ever wanted to know."

It bothered her a little that while his name sounded familiar she still didn't know anything about him. Cara, too, was an athlete in high school. She earned all-conference honors her senior year at Berea High School in basketball and track, but she had never been much of a baseball fan. Too slow - not enough action.

Stucky's was so busy the rest of the night that she forgot all about asking Stucky or one of the other guys who Cooper Madison was. Besides, when she went home Cara shifted her attention to Statistics 390, the class she had a midterm on the following Monday.

3

Looking through the peephole on the door, he saw her board the elevator. As the door shut behind her, he wondered why a girl who looked like *that* was delivering food in downtown Cleveland.

Probably the owner's daughter?

That had to be it. She just didn't fit the mold of the typical delivery people that he had seen since arriving in Cleveland.

He slowly opened the door, looking out to make sure the elevators weren't on their way up before picking up the food and shutting the door. He punched in his code on the alarm system keypad.

It was kind of pointless, he thought, looking at the elevators. Aside from a visit from his best friend in June, the only people that had visited him in the three months that he lived there were those delivering food and mail. Of course, he never invited anyone, either.

That doesn't mean that there weren't uninvited guests. Namely, reporters, who once they found out that Cooper Madison was holed up in the Wescott in Cleveland, Ohio of all places, tried every trick in the book to gain access to the 11th floor.

Luckily for Coop, the Wescott took their tenant's privacy very seriously. The doormen and even the elevator operators could sniff out a fraud in no time, like the one time a reporter from the Times tried delivering flowers to suite 1100.

Unfortunately, for the reporter, Henry Wilson knew every delivery person in town.

Henry, the Wescott's daytime doorman for the better part of two decades, is also an imposing figure as a former defensive end who played two years of college football at the University of Michigan before dropping out of school. He and his girlfriend at the time had a baby girl, and he needed to provide for both of them. Henry's father was never in the picture, and he wanted to ensure that would never be the case for his daughter - even if it meant giving up the dream of becoming a college graduate or playing in the NFL.

Henry was also one of the few people, along with the other doorman and elevator operators, who had even seen Cooper Madison in the few months since he moved in. Henry, always one to practice complete discretion, never talked to Coop about baseball. However, he did divulge the story of the Times reporter and his half-assed attempt to deliver Coop flowers.

"I knew he was a fraud, Mr. Madison, because he had roses, and you seem like more of a carnation guy," Henry joked, even getting a chuckle out of Coop that early morning in August.

Coop was wearing his typical disguise of sunglasses, a Buckeyes hat, and workout clothes. He would occasionally sneak out for an early morning stroll and felt an immediate connection with the doorman when they first were introduced.

He also appreciated the fact that Henry, while always professional, wasn't afraid to bust his balls a little bit like only a former athlete would feel comfortable doing to a relative stranger. Coop missed that camaraderie most of all these days, and would even play along a bit in his brief encounters with Henry.

"Well, if you must know, I prefer lilies… they're more delicate, like a Michigan Wolverine…" Coop teased.

"Here we go again, I'll have you know we beat your precious 'Suckeyes' my sophomore year!" Henry replied. This was where almost every conversation ended up between the two former athletes.

"I know, you remind me EVERY time I see you," Coop mocked, "and I always tell you that blind squirrels find acorns, too."

The two would always laugh off the insults, just as anyone who has ever spent time in a locker room would expect them to, and table the battle for another day.

He laughed about that encounter as he opened the two orders of Chicken Parmesan, garlic bread, minestrone, and cheesecake inside the bag. He would soon find out that Stucky's made a mean Chicken Parm. He had always been a big eater, and this time just one of the entrees was more than enough for him. He would definitely order from Stucky's again.

4

After eating, Coop plopped down on his leather recliner, which was parked in front of a 50-inch plasma television with the latest satellite technology that 2006 had to offer. It was the ultimate bachelor pad. In addition to the recliner and television, the den was furnished with a slate pool table, full-service wet bar, matching leather sofas, and three full-sized arcade games.

The kitchen was the size of a studio apartment and was equipped with stainless steel appliances and marble countertops. Possessing a knack for cooking, he actually used the kitchen in a way that would make Emeril proud, except for the fact that he only cooked for one. He would get groceries delivered twice a week, and would often try to duplicate a recipe from one of the many celebrity chefs that he enjoyed watching.

The living room was obviously decorated for show, just in case he built up the strength to have a visitor come by. However, it had not been used by anyone yet, even him. Ironically, the penthouse also had a wonderful guest bedroom.

The exercise room was state-of-the-art by all means imaginable but had been used sparingly over the last few months. The lack of use was beginning to show in his gut for the first time in his life.

The master bedroom was elegant, yet masculine. It had solid oak dressers and cabinets, a huge walk-in closet, and a plush king-sized bed. With the push of a button, another flat-screen television would appear from the wall and the blinds would close.

Each of the three bathrooms had a marble foundation, but the bathroom off of the master bedroom was the most magnificent. A large standing shower graced the far corner, while an enormous Jacuzzi sat next to a window that overlooked the city's shoreline. Lake Erie, though historically the butt of jokes, could look quite majestic on a sunny day.

5

It was amazing that she never got tired of the food; Cara thought to herself after finishing off a Stucky Club that she took home for dinner. Besides the decent tip money, the motor scooter, and flexible schedule, Stucky's Place also provided Cara with free food at every meal. Stucky knew that it was tough enough for her to pay for her tuition and board, so he let her take food home when she needed it.

"Home" these days was a small dorm room located on the 5th floor in Viking Hall, a dormitory at Cleveland State. Since she was a senior, it wasn't tough for her to get her own room. Cara never minded having a roommate, but it was nice to have a place of her own.

Growing up in Brook Park, a suburb of Cleveland, she learned to appreciate privacy. After all, 3 older brothers don't always make life easy on a little sister. Her parents, still married after 27 years, both worked at the Ford plant in Brook Park. Her father had worked his way up to foreman on one of the assembly lines, while her mother was a second shift office cleaner.

The daily routine was the same growing up. Her mother would be there in the morning to get them off to school, and her father would be there when she got home since he worked the third shift.

Money had become tight the years leading up to Cara's high school graduation. Her father was forced to take early disability retirement stemming from an accident on the job.

Between his pension and her mother's wages, there was more than enough to get by, but nowhere near enough to send her to college.

Through grants, student loans, her wages at Stucky's, and the small amount her parents could provide, Cara was on pace to be the first four year college graduate in her family. Even though she would have a degree in business, she still wasn't sure what it was she would actually do with that degree.

As she turned out the light, all she knew was that she wouldn't settle for anything less than a salary position. She was going to be through with time clocks the day she graduated.

6

The sun had set long ago over the lake, and Cooper Madison was sitting on his private balcony. It was early September 2006, and summer was just beginning to succumb to autumn. The days were still plenty hot, but at night you could see your breath.

This was Coop's favorite time of year for many reasons. As a high school student, it meant the beginning of the high school football season, when students everywhere spoke of the upcoming season being the year their team won it all. By the end of September, most of those dreams had already been dealt a crushing blow, and chants of, "Next year, we'll get 'em," filled locker rooms and hallways around the country.

From 1992 to 1996, Cooper Madison never had to talk much about "next year" while starring in three sports at Pass Christian High School in Pass Christian, Mississippi. In all, Cuppah, as it pronounced south of the Mason-Dixon, won 5 state titles in four different sports while playing for the Pirates.

He led his team to two baseball championships and quarterbacked the football team to one his senior year. As a freshman, which would be the only year he wrestled, he won the state title at 171 pounds. After lots of nagging by the basketball coach, Cooper went out for the basketball team his sophomore year and shot his team to the title as a swingman the following season as a junior. He had already committed to Ohio State for football before his senior year, so he chose not to risk injury on the basketball court his senior year, much to the basketball coach's dismay.

Everyone in the country knew, though, that Cooper would never play a down for Ohio State. The only reason he even committed there was as a backup plan, and the fact that he always loved watching the Buckeyes play hard-nosed football. Cooper's father, Jeffrey Madison, was a transplant from Ohio who bled scarlet and gray and Coop knew that it made him a very proud man to say that his son was a Buckeye.

Football, and almost everything else, always took a backseat to baseball, his passion. Coop was 6'5" and 220 pounds as a senior at Pass High, as it is referred to by locals, and his perpetual southern tan accented his light brown hair. He ran the 40-yard dash in 4.5 seconds. As a right-handed pitcher his fastball topped out at 98 miles per hour and he had a slider that made high school batter's knees buckle like a belt. It was no secret that he was going to be the first pick of the 1996 Major League Baseball draft and soon would be on a fast track for the majors.

Coop, now feeling like a 28-year-old resident at his own version of a retirement home, thought back to those days as if they happened to a stranger.

He also thought about what it must have been like for his father, Jeffrey Madison, on the day that they became closer through grief.

7

It had been 12 years since he moved from Cleveland to "The Pass", but Jeffrey Madison felt like he had lived in the pleasant surroundings of the Gulf Coast his entire life. Everything was different from life "The North", where everyone always seemed like they were in a hurry.

However, things were moving even slower than normal for Jeff on that spring day in 1990. Jeff could barely remember who had just talked to him a minute earlier. How could he? His wife of 14 years had just passed away after a long battle with breast cancer. She was only 36 years old; and now Jeff, 37, would have to know life as a single parent, not to mention a lonely one.

People Jeff had known his entire life were visibly apprehensive to talk to him. What do you say to someone that has lost his closest companion?

Jeff's wife, Kelsey, was a southern belle that he had met up in Cleveland while she attended Baldwin-Wallace College as a sophomore education major in the spring of 1974. It was a long way from home for her to attend college, but since her uncle was the Dean of Admissions at B-W, she was able to attend for free. Besides, she liked the feeling of being up north where the seasons actually changed more than once a year. "Nobody ever filmed a Christmas movie in Mississippi," she loved to say.

Jeff and Kelsey met a Delta Zeta sorority mixer that spring. Jeff was a junior at B-W, majoring in physical education. In a time when it wasn't unusual for a college athlete to compete in more than one sport, Jeff was the starting quarterback for the football team and a catcher on the baseball team.

Jeff finally convinced Kelsey Lemieux to be his bride on the day after her graduation from college, in 1976. They traveled down to Mississippi and married later that summer in a nice southern wedding, but were back in Cleveland after a short honeymoon in Florida. Jeff already had a job up in the Cleveland area as a gym teacher and coach at North Olmsted High School, his former rival, and Kelsey had just been hired to teach second grade in nearby Strongsville.

When Kelsey discovered that she was pregnant in the summer of 1977, she knew that she wanted to be back home in Mississippi. Jeff, who was moving up the coaching ranks in both football and baseball, needed some convincing, though. They eventually agreed to wait until the following summer to make the move, giving Jeff enough time to find a job down in Mississippi. He wasn't so sure how the folks down there would react to a "Yankee" yelling at their boys during a game.

Jeff, standing just under six feet tall, coached the way he played football: with a chip on his shoulder. The main reason for his demeanor was due to the fact he wasn't recruited to play ball for a bigger school, namely Ohio State. He had grown up worshipping the Buckeyes and Woody Hayes but just didn't have the size to play for the Bucks.

As an All-Ohio quarterback at Olmsted Falls High School, just southwest of Cleveland, Jeff garnered a lot of attention from college scouts. However, all were reluctant to give a scholarship to a kid whose build was a dime a dozen. That's how Jeff ended up at B-W, as a big fish in a small pond. After a stellar collegiate career, Jeff knew that his playing days were over, so he decided to do the next best thing: Coach.

Kelsey's father, James, had a friend who was on the Pass Christian school board, and through him arranged an interview for Jeff that June when they moved down to Mississippi. There was a PE job available, along with assistant coaching opportunities for football and baseball. The district was impressed with his resume, and feeling the need for a fresh face in the sleepy Gulf town, hired Jeffrey Madison for what would be the beginning of a very long tenure coaching the Pirates.

"Hey Champ," said Jeffrey as he poked his head into his son's bedroom, "You mind if I come hang out in here with you for a while? I'm tired of talking to people." Jeff's Midwestern dialect had morphed over the years into what his friends in Mississippi referred to as a "Yankee Drawl".

Cooper, tired from all the tears he had shed over the last few days, had been holed up in his bedroom ever since returning home from the funeral that morning.

Cooper made room on his bed for his father to join him. As Jeff sat down, Cooper, now 12 years old, sensed something from his father he had never encountered before. It was defeat.

Sure, his father had lost almost as many as he won, but he always had a poise about him that gave off the aura of confidence, even when on the losing end of a battle. There was no confidence in his eyes today.

Jeff looked into his son's wet eyes, wanting to tell him that everything would be back to normal shortly and that this was just a bump in the road. He'd made a living out of inspiring teams after a tough loss, then leading them to victory the next week. However, he could tell, looking at this boy who would soon be a man, that he wasn't fooling anybody.

"I'm scared, Daddy," Cooper quivered.

Jeffrey always got a chuckle out the fact that boys down south would call their fathers "Daddy", even as they became adults. However, at this moment, he cherished the moniker.

Jeffrey opened his mouth to speak, but nothing came out. He started to tremble, and tears ran down his face.

Cooper reached over and hugged his father as if he was the parent, holding Jeffrey's head close to his chest. Cooper had never seen his father cry like that before. His father had been a pillar of strength for his mother since the day she found out about her cancer. Even when Kelsey was in her final days, Jeffrey had never let on that things wouldn't work out in the end. Cooper was beginning to realize just how strong his father's resolve had been.

The two of them sat there until late that night, mourning the loss of the only woman either of them had ever loved. They took turns crying, while also telling their favorite stories about a mother and wife who passed well before her time.

Cooper had never felt so close to his father in all his life.

8

Donald "Skip" Parsons stared blankly at the plaque on the wall of his office bearing his name. He spit a stream of tobacco juice into a water bottle that was empty with the exception of a tissue wadded up at the bottom to absorb a steady stream of nervous energy.

When he would gaze at the 1994 Minor League Manager of the Year Award he sometimes would chuckle to himself that the name on the plaque, Donald S. Parsons, was never used when addressing him that entire season.

Donald Parsons was only known as 'Skip' in the ballpark. Baseball managers were often referred to as "Skip" or "Skipper" because their job was much like that as a boat captain. A good skipper knew how to train his crew and motivate them to perform as a team. Skip Parsons was one of the most underrated the game had ever seen for the better part of two decades.

Skip was in his twelfth year as manager of the Chicago Cubs. After spending 18 seasons as a minor league coach in the system that drafted him in 1973, he was finally given the chance to be a major leaguer, something he had never done as a player.

They say that catchers often make the best managers, and Skip Parsons knew shortly after his arrival in the minor leagues that his only chance of ever being a big leaguer was as a coach. He bounced around between A and AA ball for five seasons before being cut loose. The only reason he had made it five years in the minors, to begin with, was the fact that he knew how to call a great game behind the plate, and the pitchers loved him.

A career .189 hitter in the minors, Skip knew when he was called in to speak to management during spring training of 1978 that his playing days were over. He figured he'd try to catch on with a high school team somewhere as a coach and make ends meet.

Management, however, was about to offer Skip Parsons a job that would change his life forever.

When he walked out of that meeting into the hot Florida sun Skip had a mix of emotions that he had never felt before. He was still sad over the fact that his playing days were over, but was giddy at the same time over the fact that the Chicago Cubs had thought enough of him to offer him a job as a catching instructor for their Rookie league team.

Known as a player's coach who could also run a tight ship, the Cubs held on to him year after year, eventually making him a minor league manager in 1986. After managing the AAA Iowa Cubs to the championship in 1994, Skip got the nod to finally move up to the big leagues.

In his first season, the Cubs were atrocious. Skip almost considered quitting because he wasn't used to dealing with spoiled players who were usually more concerned about their next contract than winning ball games.

That winter he told management that he wanted to have more control over personnel moves so he could build a winner with *his* guys. Not wanting to lose another manager, the Cubs brass decided to grant his wish on one condition: Win or you're gone. They gave him a three-year timetable to build a winner.

9

As Donald "Skip" Parsons recalled walking into the war room for the 1996 MLB draft after being given the power over all personnel decisions, he knew that there was only one guy to pick with the number one overall pick in the draft.

The kid was dynamite on the hill. Unflappable. His father was a coach and a former collegiate catcher. He lost his mother to cancer but came out stronger. Whatever the kid tried, he excelled at. He had won more championships in high school than some entire schools ever won. He even had a full-ride to play football at Ohio State, but he soon would have a few million reasons not to.

The scouts that saw him pitch couldn't stop talking about him. He was the real deal. Better than Clemens was at his age. Better than Ryan, some even said. Could be a major league hitter, too, many speculated.

It didn't hurt the kid that he was also from the Gulf Coast. Skip was born and raised not far away in Fairhope, Alabama, a sleepy town along Alabama's coast. Skip was certain that they'd probably have a lot of the same stories, and with any luck, the same Southern Grit that helped him persevere through the grind of professional baseball.

Skip Parsons dialed the number that led to a phone in Pass Christian, Mississippi.

"Madison residence," the voice answered on the other end.

"Cooper?" asked Skip.

"Yessir," answered Coop, hands trembling.

"Son, are you watching TV right now?"

"Yessir."

"Well, I suggest you turn up the volume a bit so everyone can hear what's about to be announced."

"Yessir." Cooper motioned to any one of the thirty-five people that were crowded in his home for the draft party to turn up the volume on the television. It was well-known that the Cubs wanted Cooper with the first pick, but nothing in life is certain, and Cooper had been on pins and needles all day waiting for a phone call.

Coop had even put-off hiring an agent because if he wasn't selected high enough, he wanted to make sure that his NCAA eligibility would still be intact.

The crowded house grew deftly silent as they watched the MLB commissioner stride to the podium on the Madison family television. The worst-kept secret in professional sports was about to be revealed.

The commissioner addressed the microphone looking like a man who knew the name he was about to announce had the possibility of being the new face of baseball. In recent years, the MLB had taken a hit in the public eye due to a player strike that ended the 1994 season early, and the young hurler from Mississippi was going to be the shot in the arm that baseball needed. It was time baseball had its own Michael Jordan or Joe Montana.

"With the first pick in the draft," the commissioner announced, "the Chicago Cubs select Cooper Madison, pitcher, Pass Christian High School."

A roar exploded in the Madison household, likewise in every sports bar on Chicago's North Side.

The "expert" television baseball analysts immediately shared their opinions on whether or not they thought it was a good pick in the background, though nobody in the raucous gathering could hear them.

Jeffrey Madison, after giving his son a congratulatory bear hug, took a step back to collect himself and watch the spectacle unfolding before him. He thought about how proud Kelsey would've been of her boy, and at the same time hoped she was proud of the job he had done without her.

As Skip Parsons turned his thoughts back to present day and the end of the 2006 season, he wished that it would have turned out differently for Cooper Madison, and himself.

10

Cara was snapped out of her slumber by the unwelcoming ring of her telephone. It was two o'clock in the morning and she immediately began to feel panic that something bad must have happened.

"Hello," she answered, preparing for the worst. When she heard a familiar slurred voice on the other end of the line she was relieved, but only to an extent.

"Hey, baaabbby! What's up?" the voice managed to ask, "You mind if I come over for a bit? I miiisss you, baaabbby!"

"For the love of God, Kenny, you scared me to death! I thought something happened to my dad!" she hissed into the receiver.

"I don't want to drive drunk, 'cause I'm a little bit home…and I'm only a couple blocks away," Kenny continued, totally unaware of his jumbled words.

"Kenny, I might consider it if you ever called me when you *weren't* drunk. The last time I let you stay over you didn't call me for two weeks! Besides, WE BROKE UP, Kenny!" she yelled as she hung up before Kenny could say anything else.

She was tired of his act. He was in his fifth year at CSU and wasn't on track to graduate for another two years, at least.

When they met, Cara was a freshman and Kenny was sophomore business major in her economics class who was also on the basketball team. At first, she was infatuated with his careless attitude towards life, and it didn't hurt that he was tall, athletic, and handsome. She had never been with someone like that before. In fact, her only boyfriend in high school lasted about two weeks, and she even missed prom for a regional track meet.

Cara always put school and sports first, but Kenny Stevens had a way of bringing her out of a shell that she had been in for four years of high school.

The good times were great, Cara thought in regards to Kenny. She shared many firsts with him. First real kiss. First beer. On the anniversary of their first date, they made love. She always thought that she would have waited until marriage, but she was in love with someone for the first time in her life. Besides, Kenny was still somewhat under control and Cara made sure that he was going to class.

The second anniversary, though, turned out to be a lot less romantic. Kenny, who had been kicked off the basketball team before that season, was over two hours late to pick her up.

When he finally showed up, he was completely blasted. His friends decided at the last minute to have a kegs and eggs party that morning, and Kenny was out of control.

Cara was crushed.

The next day, she broke up with Kenny. School was no longer going to share time with any guys, and she held true to her word, except for the few times she let a typically drunk Kenny stay at her place - mostly because she was afraid he'd do something stupid if she didn't. Occasionally, like the last time, she just wanted to feel loved.

After Kenny's wake-up call, Cara found herself unable to fall back asleep so she pulled herself out of bed and logged-in to her computer. After checking her email she sat at her desk for a few minutes, blankly staring at the screen.

She'd been here before. Numerous times. In addition to Kenny's antics, she had also lost a lot of sleep over her impending graduation and what she would do after that day came.

As she was about to shut her computer down, she glanced up at the bulletin board above her desk. It was a shrine, of sorts, to happier times. The pictures on the board, which were symmetrically arranged in chronological order and held up by clear push-pins - she hated when people used random colors - were mostly from her childhood.

In the top-left corner of the board was a faded Polaroid of her as a newborn baby, laying on her mother Joanne's chest in the delivery room. Her mother was beaming with joy, like any woman who finally got her wish to have a daughter would be.

The next picture was of Cara and her three older brothers when she was about six months old.

Jason, the oldest and 16 years her senior, was on the far left. He was so much older than her that he never really felt like a sibling. His smile in the picture resembled that of a proud uncle. Jason was the reason Cara's parents got married at the age of 18, and also the reason that it would be another 10 years before they could afford to have another child.

In the middle was Christopher, who was 6 when she was born, and he was straight out of central casting if you were looking for a classic "middle-child". This was evident by the scowl on his face in the picture. He had a very hard time when his baby brother was born because he looked up at Jason as if he was a god whom he did not want to share. As hard as it was to share Jason with a younger brother, that paled in comparison to the day his baby sister Cara was brought into this world.

Jason loved playing the part of a protective big brother, and it didn't hurt his luck with the ladies at Berea High when he would bring Cara along to hold in the stands of a basketball game.

"The babes love a guy with a baby," he used to say to his friends, who often would jokingly ask if they could "borrow" Cara for a while in hopes of the same success.

This new role left Christopher on the outside, at least in his mind, and he resented Cara for the first decade of her life. It wasn't until he discovered girls himself that he finally seemed to tolerate her.

On the other side of Christopher, barely able to stand-up on his own, was Cara's "youngest" older brother, Jonathan. Cara and Johnny were "Irish Twins", as they were only 11 months apart.

Cara's mother, Joanne, had always wanted a girl. Ironically, she finally got her wish in the form of a surprise pregnancy when Johnny was two months old. Joanne was forced to take 6 years off of work, as the cost of childcare far outweighed her wages cleaning offices at the Ford plant. She picked up extra income under the table watching the neighbor's two children, who were close in age to Cara and Johnny. It also helped that Christopher had started kindergarten the year Cara was born, and Jason was almost an adult.

In the top right of the bulletin board was Cara's favorite picture. She was eight years old and standing next to her father after her first basketball game. She was missing her top two teeth, but those piercing blue eyes were still there.

Her father, Charlie, was beaming with his arm securely around his daughter. He loved having a "Tomboy-Princess", as he called her. She could mix it up with the boys, thanks to her older brothers roughhousing her on a daily basis, but also looked like a beauty pageant contestant.

Charlie and Cara had a bond that every mother would want to see her daughter have with her father. Charlie brought Cara flowers to every recital, concert, and performance she ever performed in during elementary school. He would take her out on "Daddy-Daughter Dates" at least once a month.

Charlie would say that he wanted her to know how a girl should be treated so that one day she would make a good choice for a partner. Even as Cara entered her teen years, she always gave her dad a hug and kiss goodbye, even if friends were around.

It wasn't until his accident before her junior year in high school that the relationship they both cherished was forever changed.

11

Kenny's late-night interruption brought back memories of the knock on the dormitory door that changed her life forever. Cara and three of her high school basketball teammates were fast asleep, exhausted from the first day of the 2001 Wooster Fighting Scot Basketball Camp, when they were jolted awake.

Each summer, the players and coaches would spend four days living like college students in the dorms and play at least two basketball games against other schools in attendance each day. The trip was great for basketball but even better for bonding, and Cara looked forward to it each year.

"Cara...open up...girls...I need to speak to Cara...it's urgent…" came from the other side of the door. The voice belonged to the head coach of the Berea Braves, David Paul, who was trying to be both loud and quiet at the same time. Coach Paul was about to knock on the door again when it opened up.

"Is something wrong?" Cara asked as she looked at her coach, even though she knew the answer. Nothing could be right about a 2 a.m. wake-up call from her coach, who stood before her in a pair of red basketball shorts and a 2000-2001 Pioneer Conference Champions basketball t-shirt.

"Your mom called. Something happened at the Ford plant, and your dad was hurt. He was taken to Metro by helicopter."

Coach Paul tried to break the news to Cara the way he knew she would want it: Directly.

"Is he alive?" Cara asked before she could stop herself, but that was the way she was built. She needed to know before she could possibly process anything else.

"Yes, but I'm not going to lie, from the sound of things he is hurt pretty badly. Your mom asked if I would take you to the hospital, so get dressed and grab your things."

It was a 45-minute drive from Wooster to MetroHealth Medical Center, simply known as Metro to Clevelanders, which was recently ranked the top Level I trauma center in the country.

Cara felt numb as she rode in the passenger seat of one of the two large school vans that the team was driven to Wooster in. On the way to camp, the vans were a picture of joy and excitement, filled with giddy teenagers ready for a week of basketball and bonding. That seemed like a distant memory to Cara as she stared out the window.

Metro Health Medical Center architecture resembles that of twin smokestacks. The cylindrical buildings house some of the best trauma doctors and nurses in the world. In a city like Cleveland, there was always a steady stream of gunshot wounds, horrific car accidents, stabbings, and failed suicide attempts coming through the doors.

Workplace accident victims were also common customers at Metro, and Cara would soon learn that Charles Knox had just experienced one of the worst accidents ever to occur at the Ford Motor Company's Brook Park Engine Plant.

Coach Paul pulled the school van alongside the curb opposite the hospital parking garage. The van was too big for the parking garage, and he would have to find parking elsewhere after dropping Cara off. It was just past 3:30 am, which meant that visitors were required to enter via the MetroHealth Police Station entrance.

Coach Paul told Cara he would meet her inside after parking the van and to wait for him if she wanted. He already knew Cara well enough to know that she wouldn't, but offered regardless.

Cara, who up until this point had remained pretty calm, was visibly shaking as she exited the van. She barely nodded to him while her eyes stared straight ahead at the steel door at the bottom of a short flight of concrete steps. Metro was a county hospital and the outdoor decor that greeted Cara as she descended the concrete steps had a prison-like feel to them, save for a few shrubs and gingko trees.

12

Coach Paul watched Cara make her way down the steps towards the after-hours entrance. She had been quiet the entire ride, and he knew better than to attempt small-talk.

He had been in her shoes before at the age of 18 when his own father, Douglas, collapsed of a heart attack while golfing with his only son. They were in Hilton Head, South Carolina at the prestigious Sea Pines Resort Golf Club, home to the Harbour Town Links, when it occurred. It was the father-son trip that they had been planning for years, and a celebration of David's graduation from high school and subsequent basketball scholarship to Cleveland State University.

They had just finished the 13th hole, which was a par 4 hole with a green that features a "Mickey Mouse Ears" bunker which drops down to about 4 feet below the surface of the green.

The father and son made their way along the edge of the bunker towards their golf cart, with Douglas closest to the bunker. David noticed that as his father was recapping his son's beautiful approach shot that his words started to trail. Douglas had abruptly stopped walking, and as David turned back he saw his father slightly bent over with his hands on his knees.

"Dad? You okay?!" David asked as his father dropped to one knee and then toppled over into the deep bunker, rolling lifelessly down the sandy slope. David tried to grab him by the arm, but his father was just out of reach.

"Dad!" David cried as he jumped down into the bunker to his father's side, who was face-down in the sand. As he rolled him over to his back he realized that his father was not breathing and his eyes were rolled back in his head.

David did his best to wipe the sand off of his mouth as he simultaneously looked up for help, hoping someone else was close. He started to scream for help as loud as he could and even started to try and perform CPR on his father. He had never been certified to give CPR, but he had an idea and decided it was better than doing nothing.

Luckily, one of the course rangers witnessed his father fall into the bunker from the next hole over and was already using the walkie-talkie on his golf cart to radio the clubhouse for help as he drove towards them.

The ranger, who David would later learn was a retired fire chief from Rochester named Max, hopped out of his cart and took over. He told David to keep an eye out for the ambulance, which was already on its way. David felt as if he was having an out-of-body experience as he watched Max perform chest compressions and give resuscitation breaths to his father.

David always used to think it was cliché when people said a few minutes seemed like a lifetime. He was a very pragmatic young man, a trait which would help him become a very successful leader as a teacher and coach.

As David shifted his eyes back and forth from his father to the cart path in search of an ambulance he realized that the old cliché was, in fact, a reality. The ten minutes it took for an ambulance to arrive seemed like an eternity. An eternity where David had never felt more helpless and scared.

When the ambulance arrived the EMT's jumped into action, relieving a much winded Max, who had been continuously performing CPR on Douglas. Max had unfortunately seen this happen more than once during his first two years at Harbour Towne, as the course was typically filled with out-of-shape snowbirds often trying to play 36 holes in the hot and humid climate of the Carolina Coast.

Max watched as the EMT's worked on Douglas and loaded him onto the gurney and into the ambulance, which had pulled right up to the bunker on the 13th hole. He was always impressed by the coordinated efforts of a rescue squad, despite having witnessed so many in his own career. David joined his father in the back of the ambulance, and Max made his way back to his Ranger cart.

As he sat in the cart, drained, he said a prayer for both of them. He knew that despite his efforts, the outcome was going to be a coin-flip. He had seen enough of both sides of that coin to know that predictions were futile.

David will never forget the feeling of hope he had watching his father open his eyes in the back of that ambulance for the first time since he collapsed, even though he knew his father was probably scared and disoriented.

"Dad, it's David. Keep your eyes open Dad...I'm right here Dad," David said repeatedly from his spot in the back of the ambulance as it pulled into Hilton Head Regional Hospital.

Douglas Paul survived his heart attack that day, and as David parked the van he prayed that Cara would be as lucky as he was 20 years earlier.

13

Cara was met as she entered the ER by Ed Delaney, one of her father's co-workers at the Ford plant who was also the president of UAW Local 1250. He was also Cara's godfather and her father's best friend.

Ed was a hulking figure of a man, which definitely didn't hurt him at the negotiation table as he represented one of the biggest labor unions in the country. He typically dominated every room he entered, both with his stature and personality. He was well-liked by everyone, including the executives at Ford that he often went to battle with, mainly because he was able to separate business relationships from personal ones. He could play 18 holes on a Sunday with three guys that he'd be putting the screws to over a labor issue on Monday and then leave it in the room.

"Carebear, I'm so glad you made it. Your family is in the waiting area just over there," Ed said as he wrapped Cara up in his enormous frame. Cara loved Ed's hugs second only to those given by her father.

Every emotion Cara had kept at bay during her trip from Wooster to the hospital erupted out of her as Ed pulled her tight to his chest. As she wept she felt her legs going numb and nearly collapsed, but Ed was easily able to support her petite frame.

"It's okay Carebear, your dad's a tough cookie. He's going to pull through," Ed reassured his goddaughter.

Cara was as close as Ed, who was 52 years old at the time, would ever get to being a father. He prayed that he wasn't lying to her with those words.

Ed and his ex-wife, Linda, were never able to conceive prior to their split in 1999 after 27 years of marriage. Ed's job as president of Local 1250 had become his "mistress", as Linda put it, and she left him for a guy she met in an AOL online chat room during one of her many lonely nights at home.

"What the hell happened?" Cara was able to muster to Ed.

"It was an accident, Carebear. Your dad was doing a routine inspection over in Plant 1, and one of the tow motor operators backed into a steel rack, knocking it over...and, well, Charlie got the brunt of it. That's about all I know…" Ed replied, hoping that Cara would believe his lie.

He knew more, but he didn't want to make an awful situation worse. He knew that his best friend, if he made it, would be in bad shape. The steel rack that typically held engines had landed across Charlie's lower back and legs weighed thousands of pounds, even when empty.

As Charlie fought for his life, Ed led Cara over to where her mother and two of her brothers were sitting. Joanne's eyes painted a picture of frantic worry and grief as she looked up and saw her only daughter.

"Oh, Cara…" Joanne mustered as she stood up and embraced her crying daughter. The two of them remained in a tearful embrace as Cara's older brothers joined in.

Jason, now 32 years old, was the first to attempt comforting his baby sister. However, as he put his arms around her he failed to find any words, let alone the right ones. Instead, he just squeezed tighter.

Johnny, a senior at Berea High, mirrored his big brother's embrace. He had just returned home from football practice when Ed showed up at the house to break the news and take them to the hospital.

Absent was Christopher, now 23, who was overseas in Yokosuka, Japan. He had joined the Navy right out of high school and served at the Naval Computer and Telecommunications Station. Word had already reached him, and he was due to arrive back in the states in a couple days.

Also present was Jason's family. His wife, Erica, and their nine-month-old baby daughter, Gabriella, who was sound asleep in her baby carrier. Cara loved being an aunt and promised her big brother that she would be as amazing to Gabby as he was to her.

Seven of Charlie's coworkers at the Ford plant were there, as well. Cara knew most of them by name, and they took turns making sure that there was plenty of coffee and food on hand for the family.

Coach Paul had also joined the group after parking the van and would remain there until later the next day.

Over the next 5 hours, Charlie's family and friends nervously sat in the waiting room as they were given periodic updates by the hospital staff. Charlie had been in surgery since his arrival, as the doctors knew that time was of the essence if they were going to have any chance of saving his legs, let alone his life.

Cara would never forget the extreme range of emotions that she felt when the surgeon who had performed the operation came out to update the family.

"While he's not out of the woods, yet, I am confident that Charlie will survive and begin the recovery process. Unfortunately, he sustained numerous broken bones in his spine and legs. That, along with severe nerve damage, will make the likelihood of him having the use of his legs very unlikely going forward," Dr. Belal Hamadi said as compassionately and directly as possible.

"But, he's going to make it, right?" Cara's mom asked, pleadingly.

"As of right now, I would say the chances are very high that he will survive, but the next few days and weeks will be crucial, especially since he will have to undergo more operations, and with that comes the risk of infections," replied the surgeon, who at the young age of 36 was already regarded as one of the best trauma surgeons in the country.

"But, he's never going to walk again?" Jason said, in a mixture of statement and questioning.

"Is he going to be in a wheelchair?" Johnny piggybacked.

"It's too early to tell at this point, and I have seen far too many miraculous recoveries in my time as a surgeon to ever rule out the possibility of a full recovery. However, at this time, I would say it's highly unlikely that he will be able to walk again. I know that is hard to hear, and trust me it's hard to say, as well, but right now we all need to focus on the fact that Charlie is very lucky to be alive. He is going to need all the support he can get over the next days, weeks, months, even years…" Dr. Hamadi replied.

His words, especially the last sentence, would be prophetic. Charlie was lucky to survive the accident, and he would be a patient at Metro for the months to come, enduring 11 surgeries in all. None of which were able to restore the use of the lower half of his body, essentially leaving him paralyzed from the waist down.

While Charlie had round-the-clock care and support from his wife, children, and friends during his recovery, there was another injury that could not be fixed. Some would say that the worst injury Charlie Knox sustained wasn't physical, at all, because it's impossible to repair a broken spirit, especially if the patient has given up on trying.

Over the next few years, Charlie improved physically, but he would never walk again. He came to think of his motorized wheelchair as a prison, and he often referred to himself as "half a man".

He received a disability check each month, and also a sizeable settlement from Ford and the UAW. Ed made sure of that. Unfortunately, for a man that always equated his value as a man to what he was physically capable of providing, there was no amount of money that would restore that feeling.

While the money helped, it definitely did not do much more for the family after all of the medical expenses and modifications to the house were made. Which is why Cara's job at Stucky's became a necessity for her two years later when she enrolled at Cleveland State.

14

The scrolling screensaver brought Cara back from her thoughts about the accident. Looking at those pictures always seemed to put her in a trance, reflective of both the good and bad times from her adolescence.

She looked over at her alarm clock, which read 2:32 am. She wondered how she would ever get back to sleep. As she was about to get up from her desk, she caught sight of the Chief Wahoo bobblehead doll that she was given at an Indians game in 1997, the year that the Tribe choked away Game 7 of the World Series.

The game they attended was one of the many Daddy-Daughter Dates that Cara and Charlie went on. Cara didn't care much for baseball, but she really wanted a bobblehead doll. Charlie took her down to Jacob's Field early, making sure that she was one of the first 15,000 fans through the gates to get one.

The thought of that day at the ballpark made Cara smile. It also jogged her memory that she wanted to learn more about the mysterious baseball player that she delivered food to earlier.

Cara moved her mouse so that the screensaver disappeared, and she opened up her internet browser search engine. One of the perks of living on-campus at CSU was that Viking Hall had high-speed internet lines in every dorm room.

Cara typed in "COOPER MADISON BASEBALL" and hit enter on her keyboard. The screen said that her search returned 54,027 results. One of the first was a Wikipedia page. Wikipedia, a relatively new online encyclopedia website in 2006, was fast-becoming a favorite of college students everywhere - including Cara.

She clicked on the link to Cooper Madison's Wiki page and was greeted by an entry that had his vital statistics at the top of the screen and a picture of him in a Chicago Cubs baseball uniform in the top right corner.

"Hell-low" she found herself muttering as she stared at the picture. Not only did he look every bit the part of a professional baseball player, he also looked like he could model for J. Crew. He was tall with a muscular, yet lean, build. He had a tanned complexion with brown hair barely visible under his baseball hat, a chiseled jaw-line with just the right amount of stubble, and his unique eye color was best described as steely-grey.

Cara now really wished that he had opened the door all the way when she delivered him food earlier. She never had a "type" in reference to men, but she was pretty certain that she did now.

After taking in the photo for another minute or so, she directed her attention to the rest of the Wiki page. He was born and raised in a town called Pass Christian, Mississippi, which explained the drawl she thought she heard.

He was about 6 years older than her, and as she read the section on his "Early Life" she learned about his mother's death, his amazing athletic feats, and the fact that he was the number one pick of the 1996 MLB Draft. His signing bonus was $1.9 million dollars, which was a record at the time. The thought of having that much money at any point in her life, let alone at the age of 18, was dumbfounding to Cara.

She continued on to his "Professional Career" section and learned that he breezed through the Minor Leagues in just two seasons and made the Cubs major league roster at the age of 21. Cooper made his first of five All-Star games the next season and went on to win three Cy Young Awards. He even helped the Cubs reach the playoffs in 2003.

Cara noticed as she scrolled down that the next section was "Personal Life", and she learned that he had dated the former Miss Mississippi from 1997-2002 and that they were even engaged in 2001. According to the Wiki page, she broke off the engagement in 2002 because she had moved to Hollywood to break into acting and the long distance relationship was a casualty, along with her acting career apparently because Cara had never even heard of her before.

The rest of the section was kind of a letdown, Cara thought, as she only read about two more romances - both of which were short-lived. One was a sideline reporter for ESPN, and the other was a publicist who used to work for the Cubs. She was certain that there had to be more. A guy that good-looking would have no problem finding a girlfriend even if he worked at a fast-food restaurant.

The thought of Cooper Madison taking her order at a drive-thru window made her chuckle as her eyes scanned down to the next section: "Tragedy and Early Retirement". She clicked on the section and immediately recognized the date mentioned in the first sentence: August 29, 2005. As she made the connection between the date and its significance, her heart sank.

15

The Chicago Cubs were in the middle of a long nine-game homestand in late August 2005 when the warnings first came. Cooper Madison immediately called his father, Jeffrey, after he saw a news report on the clubhouse television before a morning workout.

"You board up the house yet?" Cooper asked. "They're saying this is going to be as bad as Camille."

"Yessir, last night," Jeffrey responded in typical southern fashion, even though his drawl was adopted. "It'll probably miss us, though. You know the drill…"

"I don't know," Cooper replied, "I don't like what they're saying on TV. Calling for evacuations. Where you goin? We're in the middle of a homestand, why don't you catch a flight up here and crash with me?"

"I appreciate that, son, but I'll probably go hole-up in the high school with Butkus. My office is safer than any hurricane shelter," Jeffrey said, referencing his office deep in the bowels of the Pass Christian High School locker room and surrounded by windowless cinder block walls. Butkus, just like in the movie "Rocky", was a fawn colored Bullmastiff - and his closest companion since Cooper went north.

Cooper wanted to be more persistent in requesting that his father evacuate "The Pass" altogether, but he knew that his father was probably right. Most hurricanes that are referred to as the "Next Camille" usually turn away from the coast prior to being downgraded to a tropical storm. Hurricane season always seemed to be an exercise in futility.

Still, he couldn't remember a time when the warnings to evacuate the gulf coast seemed so persistent. Even if it did turn away, Hurricane Katrina was going to be one big storm.

"I'm fixin to go throw a bullpen in a minute. Keep your phone on you," Cooper advised, "and give Butkus a hug for me."

"Yessir, will do, son," Jeffrey said before ending the phone call as he typically did, "I'm so proud of you. I love you, Cuppah."

"Yessir, love you, too, Daddy," Cooper said as he hung up.

Cooper chuckled as he imagined his father and Butkus, who he bought for Jeffrey his first Christmas as a professional, huddling in his dad's smelly office. Butkus, along with a new pick-up truck and the balance of his father's mortgage, were not just gifts, but rather the result of a promise he made himself if he was ever able to afford it.

Jeffrey had always loved the movie "Rocky" and the main character's big tan dog. He also loved pick-up trucks but was never able to afford a brand new one on his teacher salary.

Cooper cherished the memory of seeing his dad's face as he led him outside on that December morning in 1997. Sitting in the passenger seat of the brand new, full-sized crew cab pickup truck, was an 8 week old Butkus. Taped to the steering wheel was the deed to his father's house.

Jeffrey had always told his son that he didn't want a dime of his son's money. He knew that if something happened to Cooper's arm, God forbid, that he'd have to live off of his signing bonus. He didn't want Cooper falling into the trap that so many young athletes experiencing money for the first time often did. He even set Cooper up with a financial advisor that he trusted, as he was one of his former college teammates that made it big managing the portfolios of professional athletes.

All that aside, Jeffrey knew that his son was trying to give him the gifts every kid dreams of giving their parents one day. He made Cooper promise that would be the last of the extravagant gifts, hugged him, and took Butkus for a quick spin down the street in what would be the first of his many rides in the new truck.

When Coop watched his dad pull away in that shiny new truck with Butkus by his side, he remembered feeling a sense of accomplishment that he was never able to obtain on a baseball diamond.

16

On Sunday, August 28, 2005, the Chicago Cubs played host to the Florida Marlins in front of 38,763 fans for a Sunday day game. Carlos Zambrano pitched a gem, going 8 innings and scattering 3 runs on 6 hits.

The Cubs, thanks to an 8 run 7th inning, cruised to a 14-3 victory. Leadoff batter and center fielder Jerry Hairston had a career-day at the plate, going 3 for 5 with 4 RBI.

Coop, who took a "No Decision" the day before in a 2-1 Cubs loss to the very same Marlins, didn't get to see much of Zambrano's outing. Or Hairston's big day at the plate.

He was too busy in the clubhouse, cell phone in hand, ice on the arm, watching the news on one of the clubhouse TV's, while keeping an eye on the Cubs blowout.

The news stations were keeping a worried watch on Hurricane Katrina, which seemed to be on a collision course for Mississippi and Louisiana.

Coop managed to get ahold of his father that morning. Despite all of the warnings to evacuate, Jeffrey did not seem very worried.

"It'll turn, son," Jeffrey insisted, "CNN won't get many viewers if they said otherwise, though…"

"Daddy, please, just drive north to Jackson. I'll even book you a room. Just to be safe," Cooper replied.

"Cuppah, you listen closely, now," Jeffrey said in a voice that showed more love than admonishment, "I have lived through more hurricane scares than you've had candles on a cake. I'm going to be just fine. Besides, Butkus wouldn't let nothing happen to me."

"I know, but…"

"But, nothing, boy!" Jeffrey interrupted, changing the subject, "What has me more scared than anything was your ball to strike ratio in yesterday's game..."

"Blue was squeezin' me all night! You could've fit his strike zone inside a Coca-Cola bottle…" Cooper replied, somewhat relieved that his dad had changed the subject.

"Well, I guess you need to get better!" Jeffrey said, in his typical fashion. He hated excuses, and he was certain that part of his son's success was because he never let him make them without consequence.

"Yeah, well... so does he!"

"Alright, son, I gotta let you go. I'm fixin to run some necessary supplies to the school."

"Let me guess - a case of Corona, some limes, chips, and salsa? And couple pig's ears for Butkus?" Cooper guessed. Down south, it wasn't uncommon for people to throw "Hurricane Parties" during the storm.

"You know me well, son!"

"Yessir!" said Cooper.

"Son?" Jeffrey spoke, his voice down an octave.

"Yessir?" Cooper replied.

"I love you very much, Cuppah. You know I'm proud of you, right?" asked Jeffrey, even though he already knew the answer.

"I love you, too, Daddy," said Cooper, "Please be safe."

"Always…" replied his dad.

As Coop pressed "end" on his cell phone, he peeked back up at the television. The circular storm was being animated by a computer that was showing all of the possible scenarios for landfall. All of them looked scary. One of them looked unimaginable.

He thought back to when his parents took him to New Orleans, or "Nawlins" as it's pronounced by most of its inhabitants. He remembered his parents having him walk towards the water, along with the bank of the Mississippi River just outside the French Quarter. He remembered that he thought it was cool that there were concrete steps that actually went down into the water. He remembered his father telling him to turn around and look back at the city.

That's when he realized for the first time that parts of New Orleans are actually an average of 6 feet below sea level. The French Quarter itself is actually above sea level by about 5 feet, but as he looked further upon the horizon he could tell that the city looked almost like it was sinking.

His father told him about the levees that were in place to prevent flooding in the event of a hurricane.

"So the levee walls will block all the water, Daddy?" 8-year-old Cooper asked, looking for reassurance.

"That's the idea, but they say if the storm's bad enough, the whole city could disappear under water," Jeffrey replied.

"Jeffrey Madison! Stop scaring our boy!" Cooper's mom, Kelsey interjected, "Cuppah, they've been telling that old wives tale for hundreds of years. Nawlins ain't goin nowhere, baby."

"Never say never, Momma!" Jeffrey replied in a way that showed he had accomplished his objective of riling his wife up. "C'mon y'all, let's go get some beignets while we still can!" he said as he used a tone that indicated the end was near.

As they walked away towards the world-famous Cafe Du Monde for their traditional New Orleans breakfast of the messy-yet-delicious beignets, Cooper couldn't help but imagine the whole city underwater.

Sensing this, his father put his arm around him and said, "Cuppah, you know your Momma's always right, and this is no different. Don't let it ruin your breakfast, now..."

"Yessir," Cooper replied, as they made their way to breakfast.

The sound of clubhouse attendant, Louis Isaacs, snapped Cooper out of his daydream.

"I can't believe I'm saying this, but this is the first time in my life that I am glad I am NOT in Nawlins... Your daddy got out of there, right, Coop?" Louis asked.

He grew up outside of Baton Rouge, Louisiana before his father moved he and his family to Chicago as a young teenager. Even though he had been in Chicago for more years than the south, he still had a bit of a drawl and knew the power that these hurricanes could bring.

"No sir, he sure did not," Cooper replied, showing his frustration, "He's staying with Butkus at the high school."

Louis, who always liked the way Cooper treated him with respect, sensed this and tried to calm his fears, "I'm sure your daddy is gonna be fine, Coop. He's been through worse… had to raise your ass!!"

Cooper laughed, as the joke wasn't expected, but very much appreciated.

17

Jeffrey Madison and his Bullmastiff, Butkus, rode out what he had assumed was the worst of the storm inside his office at Pass Christian High. Early in the morning on Monday, August 29th, 2005 he felt safe inside his concrete fortress.

The last reports had Katrina heading straight for New Orleans, and while they had predicted possible 25-foot storm surges, Pass Christian sat high enough above sea level that it would likely be out of their reach.

Even though he did not have access to any weather reports, internet, or phone service of any kind, he figured it was probably safe to venture out and survey the damage. The high winds had caused some windows at the school to break throughout the night, and he tried to help Butkus avoid the glass as they made their way to the front of the school.

As he stepped through what was left of the main entrance door frame, he noticed an ominous sky that could only be described as angry with wind gusts that he estimated to be 65-70 mph.

Jeffrey and Butkus quickly made their way to his truck, as he had parked it right against the outer wall of the school where the wind was going to be least likely to cause damage to it. As they approached, Jeffrey noticed that while the windows had all been blown out, it looked pretty much intact still.

He brushed the shards of glass of the passenger seat so Butkus could hop in, and then he followed suit on the driver's side.

He breathed a sigh of relief as he turned the key and the engine came to life.

It was 7:55 am when Jeffrey turned the radio on and scanned for any updates on Katrina. Luckily, it seemed that every station that was still able to broadcast a signal on the Gulf Coast was doing just that.

Unfortunately, they were also contradicting his belief that the worst of the storm had passed. In fact, they were reporting that Katrina had made a late turn east of New Orleans and that the Mississippi coast was receiving the brunt of the storm as it made landfall.

Levees in and around New Orleans had already been breached, and flooding was imminent throughout the entire coastal area. In addition, tornados were being reported, adding to the misery of the Category 5 storm.

Jeffrey knew that he had to get north and fast. He had underestimated the storm and he wasn't going to let his ego get in the way again.

As he headed out of the Pass High parking lot onto E. North Street, Jeffrey started to say a prayer. The high winds and lack of windows in his truck, combined with an extreme lack of visibility, were making it almost impossible to drive. On top of that, there were toppled trees and power lines to navigate.

All of the streets that he tried to use as an avenue towards I-10, which he wasn't sure was even open, were proving to be impossible due to debris and/or flooding. He would have to make his way south to Highway 90, and then hope to outrun the storm while heading east until he could find a highway that would take them northbound to safety.

The wind gusts seemed to have doubled in force during the few short minutes he had been on the road, and he felt as if his full-size pickup truck was about to be lifted off the ground.

As he approached Pass Christian Middle School while trying to make his way to Highway 90, he came to the realization that it probably would have been better if he had just stayed at the high school. There was no doubt in his mind that trying to drive north was going to be a death sentence.

He pulled his truck right along the front of the middle school, and he and Butkus made their way in through the entrance, which like the high school, was basically a metal frame.

Jeffrey had never experienced wind like this before. During his short time in the truck, the radio station reported that winds could reach 150 mph and that a large storm surge was expected to batter the Mississippi coast shortly.

Even though Pass Christian Middle School sat lower than Pass High, making it less safe from flooding, Jeffrey figured that trying to head back to the high school would have been too dangerous. He decided that he and Butkus would take shelter in the school's auditorium, as there were no windows along the walls.

Butkus, who had been pretty calm for most of the night, was whining and shaking in a way that Jeffrey had never seen before. As they walked down the hallway toward the auditorium, Butkus pressed so closely to his owner's leg that he almost knocked him over with each step.

The two of them huddled together between the last two rows of auditorium seats, laying flat so that they would be somewhat protected from any flying debris.

The building began to shake, and Jeffrey swore that he felt it lift off the ground. Water also began to pour in down the sloped floor of the auditorium. It sounded as if a train was on top of the building.

Jeffrey pulled his cell phone out. It was 8:47 am, and due to lack of service, his phone had become a glorified clock. He prayed for just one minute of service, so he could call his son.

He would tell him that he loved him. That he was proud of him. That he was sorry he didn't listen.

18

As Cara scrolled further down the Wikipedia page's entry titled "August 29th. 2005", she felt her eyes well up as she read about Cooper Madison's father:

Jeffrey Madison's body was found floating near Henderson Avenue, on August 29th, 2005. It is believed that he had taken shelter inside Pass Christian Middle School, as his Bullmastiff's body was found amongst the debris. His truck, which had sustained major water damage, was also located nearby. The storm surge from Hurricane Katrina had produced winds that exceeded 130 mph and a wall of water that was nearly 30 feet high ripped through the entire Pass Christian area. More than 1800 people are believed to have lost their lives during the storm.

"He's an orphan…" she felt herself say.

Her internal conversation was interrupted by the sound of the Viking Hall fire alarm.

"You have GOT to be KIDDING ME?!" Cara yelled as the alarm modules screamed and flashed.

She knew it was probably just a stupid freshman paying a drunk prank, as they happened about once a week. However, if she failed to evacuate and was caught by the fire department hiding in her dorm room she could face a fine and possible charges.

After she threw her sweatshirt on, she shut her computer down and made her way outside via the stairway. A crowd of sleepy and annoyed coeds had already filled the area just outside the entrance to Viking Hall when Cara arrived to join them in their misery.

"I swear to GOD, if I find out who did this, I'm going to set them on fire myself!" one of Cara's old roommates, Mallory Perriman, said as she saw Cara approach. Mallory, like Cara, was one of the few seniors still living at Viking Hall. She also had an exam and was none too amused by the false alarm.

"I wish I could say I was sleeping," Cara replied.

"You were awake?" Mallory countered, "Don't tell me...Kenny, again?"

"Bingo! Well, that, and I was trolling a professional baseball player on Wikipedia," Cara admitted.

"Since when have you ever liked baseball?" asked Mallory.

"Since I delivered him food to his penthouse yesterday…" Cara said in a way that she knew she was leading Mallory along.

"Oh my God! An Indians player? Please tell me it was Grady Sizemore. Did he give you a big tip?" Mallory, wide-awake now, inquired.

"Nope. He played for the Cubs. I think he's retired now," Cara said, "but, he did give me a huge tip!"

"The Cubs? What on EARTH is he doing living here, then? And retired? He must be old…" Mallory replied, with less excitement in her voice than when she thought it was Grady.

"Actually, he's still in his 20's. He was really good, I guess, too. Have you ever heard of Cooper Madison?" Cara asked.

"You delivered food to COOPER MADISON?!" Mallory exclaimed so loud that everyone within earshot perked up.

"Why does everyone else seem to know him except me?" Cara replied, using a hushed voice in hopes Mallory would tone it down.

"Cara. Girl. Seriously? He's like the BEST pitcher ever. Not to mention, he's a total babe. Maybe even better than my Grady. Please tell me you got his autograph. Can you take me there? Did he ask you out? Does he know Grady?" Mallory's stream of questions was coming out faster than Cara could answer them.

"Slow down, Mal...Relax! I didn't even see his face. Well, I did when I went online, but not in person," Cara managed to respond.

"Does he have a butler or something?" Mallory pressed.

"No, actually it was really kind of strange. He came to the door and only opened it a crack. Then he told me to leave the food and handed me a bunch of money and said keep the change," Cara replied.

"That is weird. Well, I heard he kinda had a nervous breakdown or something. Did you know his dad died in Katrina?" Mallory asked.

"Yeah, that's what I was just reading as the alarm went off. So sad. And his mom died when he was young of cancer, too," Cara responded.

"So, I'm assuming you never saw the video from last year?" Mallory asked, already knowing the answer.

"What video?" Cara replied.

"Girl, you really are oblivious. I'm sure it's on YouTube still. It'll help explain why he's not playing anymore. And probably why he's hiding out here in Cleveland. It was really kinda sad the way he fell apart," Mallory said, her voice changing as she spoke.

As she spoke, the students were given the "all-clear" to return to their rooms. Mallory told Cara to get some rest and walked off towards the elevators.

Cara chose the stairs, as she didn't want to wait in line for the elevator, and wished Mallory luck on her exam.

Upon returning to her room, she realized that she only had a few hours to sleep before class, and she crawled into bed. As she closed her eyes, she started to count backward from ten.

She never made it to five.

19

Cooper Madison did not sleep the night of August 28, 2005. He couldn't. He had not been able to get ahold of his father, Jeffrey, since Sunday afternoon, and the weather reports looked awful for where his dad was planning on riding out the storm.

Coop, like most of the world with family down south, was glued to the television in his upscale four bedroom Chicago condo on the morning on August 29th. Cell phone in one hand, home phone in the other. Waiting. Praying.

As much as he kept trying to convince himself that his father would call any moment, he could not shake the feeling that he was in grave danger.

The video feeds coming into all of the major news networks showed massive waves and flooding from Louisiana to Alabama.

For the first time ever, tiny Pass Christian, Mississippi was the focus of national news outlets all over the world. Reports flowing in ranged in everything from horrible to unimaginable.

To make matters worse, people kept calling Cooper to see if his father was okay. While he appreciated their concern, he also was worried he'd miss a call from his dad.

Around lunchtime, Skip Parsons, manager of the Cubs, stopped over with food. Coop thanked him for coming over, and the two picked at a world-famous Giordano's pizza while watching the news and waiting for updates.

As luck would have it, Monday was an off-day for the Cubs, and the manager tried to take his star player's mind off of whatever dark places it might have been headed towards throughout the course of the afternoon. There were so many scenarios in which his father could be okay and just unable to make a phone call. After all, phones and electricity had been down for almost 24 hours.

Coop kept bringing up the fact that early reports said that Pass Christian High School, while flooded, was still standing.

"Thank God he was at the high school and not the middle school, Coop," Skip said when an aerial shot of the middle school was shown on the television. At least what was left of the middle school, that is, which appeared to be completely washed away.

"Let's hope he got out of there altogether," Cooper replied.

Minutes passed by as if they were hours, and as nighttime fell, Coop wasn't sure if he should be feeling relieved that he hadn't received a call, or terrified.

Skip stayed until 6 o'clock but had to leave to watch one of his sons play in a flag football game. It was rare that he was ever able to attend any of his kids' activities during the season, and Coop encouraged him to go.

As he had done about a hundred times throughout the course of the day, Coop dialed his father's cell phone number. Just like the hundred times before, it went straight to voicemail.

He also tried calling his dad's friend Clinton James, who was the Sheriff of Pass Christian. Jeffrey and Clinton became close when they played softball together shortly after Jeffrey moved south. Clinton was just a deputy at that point but had worked his way up over the years to Sheriff.

Unfortunately, it was the same result: straight to voicemail.

At around 10:45 that evening, Cooper's cell phone lit up. The caller ID read "Clinton James".

"Finally!" Coop said as he took a breath and answered, "Hello?"

"Cuppah, it's Clinton. I'm sorry I haven't called you sooner, but we are just getting cell service back up around here," the Sheriff spoke.

"Yessir, I understand, Sheriff," Cooper replied, "Have you heard from my daddy?"

The Sheriff could be heard taking a deep breath on the other end, and when he did Cooper's heart sank.

"Cuppah… we found your daddy… and Butkus… I'm sorry, Cuppah… they're both gone…" Sheriff James spoke, his voice cracking.

Cooper heard the words, but couldn't manage a response.

"It seems that your daddy went to the middle school with Butkus at some point during the storm. A lot of us thought the worst was over when it hit. I've never seen anything like this…" Sheriff James continued, hoping to fill the void, "Cuppah? You still there?"

Cooper again heard the words, but instead of responding he clicked "end" on his phone.

He then dropped to his knees.

20

Early in the morning of Tuesday, August 30th, Skip Parsons tried calling his star pitcher's cell phone, just as he did twice the night before. Just like the previous two calls, there was no answer. However, this time it went straight to voicemail. He tried the house phone next.

Busy.

He figured that Coop just was too exhausted last night to answer, but now that his phone wasn't even ringing, Skip became worried. Enough so that he made a detour on his way to Wrigley Field and stopped at Cooper's place.

Skip hit the button to Cooper's condo and waited to be buzzed in.

Nothing.

He tried again.

Nothing.

And again.

Same result.

As Skip walked away from the building's entrance back towards his SUV, he hoped that maybe Cooper had just gone to the park early to get out of the house. While he could've walked to Wrigley from Coop's condo, he instead drove and parked in his usual spot in the employee lot and headed inside the historic stadium.

As he made his way through the belly of the stadium towards his office, he was approached by a nervous-looking staffer, who he only knew as Evan.

"Good morning, Skip, umm Mr. Parsons, I mean...umm did you hear the news report on the radio on your way in today, sir?" Evan asked.

"Skip is fine, son. I try to stay away from listening to people bash me first thing in the morning, so you'll need to fill me in," Skip replied.

"Apparently, umm… they found Cooper Madison's father late last night," Evan said.

"Alive?" Skip replied.

"Unfortunately...no…" Evan said.

"Dear God… he must know… I tried to stop by his condo this morning, but nobody answered. He hasn't answered his phone, either…" said Skip.

"We actually sent an officer over this morning to do a 'welfare check' on Cooper when we heard, but nobody was home. One of his neighbors said that they think they heard him leaving in his car around two in the morning," Evan explained.

"He's probably doing what any of us would, and that's heading down there," Skip asserted.

Approximately 540 miles away from Wrigley Field, Cooper Madison was at a rest stop gas station along I-57 South filling up his Chevy Tahoe with gas. He decided to leave Chicago and head south towards Mississippi shortly after hearing of his father's death. It was a little over 900 miles, which typically took Coop about 14 hours. Today, he was on pace to make it in under 13.

He had his cell phone, which was fully charged, with him. However, he kept it turned off. He needed to be alone with his thoughts. He always felt awkward when people would tell him they were sorry that his mom had died, and he knew that these circumstances would lead to feelings he didn't want to deal with, yet.

After he grabbed a coffee and some beef jerky from inside the service station, he continued on his journey towards his hometown. Or, at least, what was left of it.

He wasn't sure what he would do when he arrived there. He did know that he wanted to see his father and Butkus, as hard as it was going to be. He also knew that he wanted to help his hometown in any way that he could.

21

The alarm clock blaring in Cara's room seemed distant at first, but then louder and louder as she started to come to her senses. As she hit the snooze button, the world began to come back into focus after her short night's sleep thanks to the fire alarm.

Per her morning ritual, Cara sat down at her computer to check her email. She would always give herself until the snooze on the alarm went off again to check her email and surf the web before she started her day.

The newest email message that greeted her was from her old roommate Mallory, and on the subject line it read, "Video Link".

Cara - here's the video I told u about. -Mal

Cara clicked the link and it directed her to YouTube. As it buffered, she noticed that it had 12.7 million views. Her heart sank as she heard the Cubs play-by-play announcers voice pick up the action.

It's the top of the first here at Wrigley Field, and as we are about to get underway all eyes are on Cooper Madison as he toes the rubber for the first time since the tragic loss of his father nearly two weeks ago. He will have to face the 1st place Cardinals as their leadoff man Roberto Valez steps in the box. Valez is batting .289 since being called up from AAA in late June and has settled in nicely. Madison appears to be his usual stoic self on the mound, and manager Skip Parsons said that he would not want to be a Cardinal batter today... Madison starts his wind-up and delivers...STRIKE ONE!!...97 miles per hour right down the chute... Mr. Valez, meet Mr. Madison... right back to work, Madison deals and...STRIKE TWO!!... 101 mph!!... Wow folks, he seems to be really locked in... He usually doesn't get to triple digits until at least a few innings in... 0-2 is the count on the rookie, who has yet to take the bat off of his shoulder... and here's the 0-2 offer... Just a bit outside... Madison does not like the call... He's giving home plate umpire Vance Hightower a glare... I'm sure that Madison's emotions are running awfully high today... Here's the 1-2 pitch... BALL TWO!!... Oh, my, and Cooper Madison is giving the umpire a piece of his mind... Hightower is a veteran crew chief... he is letting him go a bit... He knows he must be feeling all sorts of mixed emotions on the mound today... Madison makes his way back to the rubber... Winds and delivers... BALL THREE!!... and now Madison is pointing and yelling at Vance Hightower, who is looking off into the Cubs dugout at Skip Parsons as if to say, "Hey you need to step in here!"... and here comes Parsons trotting out and getting in between his star pitcher and the home plate umpire... Oh my, NO, Madison has tossed his manager aside and here comes his catcher Josh Adams to try and grab him... Madison is REALLY steamed at Hightower who has to be asking himself what on EARTH did he do to deserve this... Parsons appears to still be struggling to get up off the ground after Madison tossed him like a rag doll... and now Madison has started to back away... Adams is escorting him away from Hightower... But, WAIT! Madison is now CHARGING at Hightower and... Oh no... he just landed a vicious right hand to the umpire's face and Hightower is DOWN... Oh my! And now we have police officers and players from both sides running onto the field and two of the officers just tackled Madison who is fighting with them now... I have never seen ANYTHING like this in all my years Cubs fans...

Cara felt sick as she watched Cooper struggling with the officers who were trying to subdue him. He looked enraged. Like an animal. The camera had zoomed in on Cooper's face by this point, but suddenly Cooper's face seemed to change as if he had just snapped out of a trance. His look of anger turned to sheer horror and panic as if he was saying, "What have I done?"

As the video came to a close, Cara noticed other videos of the debacle on the page. Some had Rocky music, slow motion, and other effects. There was also a press conference video, and she clicked on that one next.

As the video opened, Cooper Madison stood in front of a Cubs backdrop and behind a podium with an array of microphones from every major television station. He looked down, then slowly up. He took a deep breath, and began:

I would like to start by saying I am sorry... I'm sorry to Vance Hightower, whom I have always had a ton of respect for... I'm sorry to my manager, Skip Parsons, who has always been there for me... I'm sorry to the entire Chicago Cubs organization, Major League Baseball, and the fans... I fully accept my 10 game suspension and $100,000 fine... In addition, I will be making a donation to the Chicago Public School System for an additional $100,000 and will also pay for all of Vance Hightower's medical bills and then some... I am thankful that Mr. Hightower did not press charges, although I would not have blamed him if he did, as my attack on him was inexcusable... Lastly, at this time I would like to announce my retirement from baseball, effective immediately following the 10 game suspension... Thank you...

22

Gasps, questions, and whispers immediately filled the press conference room. Cooper Madison had just dropped his retirement bombshell and walked away from the podium, and apparently, the game.

He was only 27 years old and entering the prime of what was almost certainly going to be a Hall of Fame career.

The only people that knew he had decided to retire were Cooper, Skip, Louis Isaacs, and the Cubs management. They worked out a deal forfeiting the remainder of his contract, with the only stipulation being that if he chose to return to baseball that the Cubs would have his rights. They tried to talk him out of it, even offering to let him take an extended leave of absence, but Coop was adamant that he had made his mind up.

Even though he was forfeiting about $38 million, Coop was set for life in regards to money. He had always been careful with his money and knew he was in a position to direct his focus on where his heart was long before he ever threw a pitch in the majors.

As he walked out of the press room, Coop saw Skip Parsons waiting for him, along with the entire Cubs team. He gave Skip a tearful hug and continued down the line with each of his teammates. There was a car waiting for him right outside the stadium, and it whisked him away before the reporters desperate for answers could get to him.

Behind the wheel of the black SUV was Cubs clubhouse attendant Louis Isaacs, per Coop's request.

"Well, you certainly know how to make an exit, Coop..." Louis deadpanned as Cooper entered the SUV, "It's all over the radio already."

Coop chuckled, "Well, Mr. Isaacs, at least I'm good for something these days..."

"I have your luggage in the back, and the rest will be sent down via truck, courtesy of the team," Louis said as they pulled out onto Waveland Avenue.

"I appreciate that Louis, and for helping me get all the stuff at my condo packed up."

"Well, I wish I didn't have to do it in the first place, but I am honored you chose me to help," Louis answered, knowing not to say too much at a time like this.

"Well, it's important to me to only be surrounded by people I can trust right now, Louis, and you are at the top of that list. Always have been..."

"That's just about the nicest compliment I could ever receive, Coop..." Louis answered, his voice and eyes starting to show emotion for the first time since Cooper Madison came to him last week for help.

"Well, it's the truth... now don't start crying on me or I might take the keys back..."

"Take what keys back? This is my SUV!" Louis laughed.

"Not those keys... these keys," Coop said as he handed Louis the keys to his condo, "You should know the layout of the place pretty well by now after helping me pack, right? It's yours now. I paid it off, and the Cubs are going to give you a couple days off to move your stuff in. I want you and your family to live there, Louis. You're going to need the space as those three little ones grow up..."

"Coop... I... I can't accept that. It's..." Louis protested.

"Nonsense... you already did, well sorta... I knew you'd say no, so I put it in your kids' names, with you and your wife as the custodians. I know you want to send them to good schools, but also be close to the stadium for work, and this is the best solution for all of you. You've been a great friend ever since I joined the club, and I appreciate how you always treated me like a normal guy... even if your jokes sucked…" replied Coop.

"I don't know what to say, Coop…" Louis managed to respond.

"You don't need to say anything, Louis," Coop continued, "Just make sure that those three kids have the *best* possible life that they can… oh, and, let your wife decorate the place any way she wants. That's all I ask."

"How can I ever repay you?" Louis asked.

"You already have. You're one of the best fathers I know," Coop responded.

The SUV pulled onto I-90 westbound, towards Chicago O'Hare International Airport.

Cooper Madison had a private jet to catch and it was headed for Gulfport, Mississippi.

23

Cara had just finished watching the press conference video when her alarm went off again. She turned it off but decided she had to know more about Cooper Madison before she took a shower and got ready for the day.

On the suggested videos list, there was one entitled, "Cooper Madison Cleans Up Nicely". She clicked the play button, and it was from a local news affiliate near Pass Christian, Mississippi.

In the video, Cooper Madison is shown working alongside other volunteers, helping rebuild their hometown. While Cooper himself declined to comment, other people certainly spoke for him. Everyone said he was just a regular guy who lost a loved one like so many others, and they all commended him for walking away from millions to be back home. They spoke of his donations to the safety forces, food pantries, and schools in the area. Over a million dollars, some guessed.

The next video that caught Cara's attention was one entitled, "Madison Flies the Coop?". Despite the corny title, Cara clicked play. In this video, there were some outtakes of Cooper Madison from the first video she watched, showing him cleaning up flood debris and handing out water. However, those were followed up by townspeople saying that they had no idea where he went after spending the past two months there. One day he was just gone. Most of those interviewed said that they didn't blame him for leaving. He was just trying to help his hometown, but people wouldn't leave him alone - especially reporters and paparazzi photographers.

Cara looked at her clock, she only had 15 minutes to get ready and get to class. She logged off her computer and began her day as she had two AM classes, followed by a shift at Stucky's.

24

Across town, Cooper Madison had just finished his morning walk and was enjoying a cup of coffee and a granola bar on his private balcony as he watched the sunrise over Lake Erie. A seagull landed on the corner of the balcony, and Coop locked eyes with it. The seagull didn't budge as Coop raised his coffee mug to his lips, slowly. Coop had learned that Lake Erie seagulls were fearless scavengers - always daring to push the limits of human contact in hopes to get a morsel of food.

Just as Coop was about to toss a bite of his granola bar to the bird his cell phone rang, and the startled gull took flight.

The caller ID had the name "Todd Taylor" on it. Todd, or "T-Squared", had been Coop's agent since he came into the league in 1996. Todd was a Mississippi native who had starred in baseball in the late 80's at Ole Miss prior to suffering a career-ending shoulder injury as a junior. Luckily for Todd, he had a fallback plan. He graduated Magna Cum Laude from Ole Miss and then was top five in his class from Duke Law School. While attending Duke, he managed to snag a summer internship after his second year with IMG's baseball division via a former Ole Miss teammate who happened to be a client.

IMG's main office was in Cleveland, Ohio, as the founder Mark McCormack was an Ohio native. Todd Taylor had been called "T-Squared" since his days at Ole Miss, and IMG was no different. T-Squared quickly earned a reputation at IMG similar to the one he had as an infielder at Ole Miss: tenacious, tough, intelligent, and personable.

He made such a great impression at IMG during those 2 short months in the summer of 1990, that he was offered a permanent position as a junior agent in the baseball division upon graduation from Duke in 1991. Within 2 years T-Squared was taking on his own clients, and his reputation amongst MLB players landed him plenty of players.

Fair or not, professional athletes tend to trust agents who played their sport at a high level more than a bookworm who couldn't hit water if he fell out of a boat. The fact that a lot of his clients actually played with or against him in college only expanded their comfort level with him. They knew that he could've been a pro himself, had it not been for the injury.

He had their respect. He was one of them.

His biggest client came in the form of another southern boy in 1996 when Cooper Madison contacted him at IMG in the months leading up to the draft. Coop remembered watching T-Squared play in college at Ole Miss, and even though Coop pulled for Mississippi State, he was a fan of good baseball players first and foremost. When Coop started researching agents, he was pleasantly surprised to see that one of the best young agents in baseball was Todd "T-Squared" Taylor. It didn't hurt that they were both from Mississippi, either.

During his playing days, especially early on, Coop loved getting phone calls from T-Squared. When Coop was an 18 year old on his own in the minors, his agent would check on him three times a day, just to make sure he was okay. They became fast friends off the field, as well. Coop was a groomsman in his wedding, and T-Squared even set Coop up with the former Miss Mississippi.

On this morning in 2006, Coop let the call go to voicemail. Out of all the people, Coop felt he let down by retiring early, the two that stood out above the rest were Skip Parsons and Todd "T-Squared" Taylor. The latter of which still called him about once a week, just to check up on him. Lately, though, Coop stopped answering because he knew what his agent wanted to know: was he ready to play again.

The Cubs were heading into the final part of an awful season and had no chance at a Wild Card spot. Since they still owned the rights to Cooper Madison, the Cubs were in a position to add a late-season arm - even if it hadn't thrown a pitch in over a year. T-Squared told Coop when they last spoke that the Cubs wanted just that.

The offer on the table was for Coop to return to the organization upon the completion of a physical, make a few appearances in the minors to get back in shape, and then activate him to the MLB roster in time for a couple starts. From the Cubs perspective, it was a win-win. Even if Coop failed, they'd have a lot of tickets sold to witness it.

Coop knew it was juvenile to ignore his agent, who also happened to be one of his best friends, but he also knew that if anyone could talk him back into baseball it was Todd Taylor.

He also knew that he was not physically or mentally ready for that, at least not at this time. While he missed being in the clubhouse with his teammates, the adrenaline of being on the mound in front of a sold-out crowd, and to an extent the enormous paycheck that came with those things, he knew that he was right where he should be.

He didn't need to figure out who Cooper Madison was, he needed to figure out who Cooper Madison would become.

25

Cara hopped on her Vespa scooter after her second class of the day and headed towards Stucky's Place for her lunch shift delivering food to the hungry masses of Cleveland.

Friday lunch shift meant one thing: chaos.

Even workers who brown bag it all week tend to celebrate by purchasing lunch on a Friday. That, along with staff parties, and Stucky's "Free Friday" promotion made for a busy shift, but also typically a lot of tips.

A few years ago, Stucky noticed that even though his usual Friday sales were solid, he wanted to give them a boost. Never afraid to take a gamble to increase sales, Stucky began to offer a free large one-topping pizza to any delivery order over $25. The gamble paid off in a big way, as most of his lunch orders leading up to his promotion were under $25. It was genius, as the average per order increase in sales alone covered the cost of the free pizza, which was actually one of the cheapest menu items to make.

In the three years since "Free Friday" at Stucky's Place began, he saw his Friday profits triple. While it was a chaotic way to end each week, Cara always enjoyed the extra money in her pocket.

"Hey Stuck!" Cara said as she entered a very busy Stucky's Place just before her 11-3 shift was to begin.

"Carebear!" Stucky replied, "How was class?"

"Eh… I'm ready to be done. I have a major case of senioritis."

"Senioritis? It's only September!" Stucky boomed.

"Don't remind me…" Cara said as she started loading the delivery bags for the first trip of the day.

Like everything else in her life, Cara had a system in place for bagging the orders and determining the best routes to take. Cara was one of three delivery drivers on Friday, but she was in charge of who took which order where. Even Stucky deferred to Cara, often jokingly calling her "Boss".

After she sent the other two drivers on their way, she grabbed the next ticket on the line and began bagging the order. She felt her stomach drop as she noticed the customer name: Madison - Westcott Hotel Suite 1100.

After bagging the order, Cara started making her way out the back door to her Vespa but stopped to ask Stucky if he knew who his most famous client was.

"The pitcher?!?!" Stucky exasperated, with a mixture of statement and question.

"That's the one… Apparently, I'm the only person in the world who didn't know who he was until recently," Cara answered.

"He was the best! What a shame, though. He really lost it. Gave up millions. You know his father died in Katrina, right?"

"I do now, thanks to the wonders of the internet," Cara replied.

"Cooper Madison… Ordering from my restaurant!" Stucky seemed to think aloud, before adding, "Hey, what's he like? Did he tip well?"

"I'd tell you if I actually saw him in person, but he definitely knows how to leave a tip," Cara said.

"Here, give him one of my VIP cards," Stucky said, reaching for the small stack of gold-embossed business cards that he always carried with him in the event he ran into a local celebrity or athlete.

The cards, each with an individual number on them, entitled the owner to priority service during busy times, and also a free appetizer with each order. Even though Stucky rarely gave them out, he was always excited to grant one to those he felt worthy.

The card he gave Cara to give to Cooper Madison was numbered 0014, and the first 13 who received one were nowhere near the caliber of the former pitcher.

"No problem, Stuck," Cara chuckled as she took the card and exited the back door. She imagined Cooper Madison wouldn't be near as excited as the person who bestowed the honor upon him.

26

Cooper Madison was looking forward to a big lunch. After letting his agent Todd “T-Squared” Taylor’s call that morning go to voicemail he decided to get a long workout in.

Coop had not used his sprawling home gym in weeks, and aside from the occasional morning walk, he was as out of shape as he had ever been. After thirty minutes on the treadmill and another hour of lifting weights, he called Stucky’s Place.

As good as the chicken parmesan was the first time he ordered, he opted to try something different and ordered a large pizza with bacon. Coop loved bacon and he often joked that it should be its own food group. He added a large dinner salad for good measure.

During his time as a professional athlete, he only allowed himself to enjoy pizza after a good outing on the mound. Luckily for him, that was more often than not. The rest of his meals were strictly prepared by his personal chef per his nutritionist's orders. Those consisted of lean proteins, complex carbohydrates, and massive amounts of fruits and vegetables. Sometimes Coop felt that he pitched better knowing that a big greasy pizza was his reward.

Since his abrupt retirement from baseball, Coop abandoned everything else that went with it - including his strict diet. In the first few weeks after his announcement, Coop inhaled everything he had prohibited himself from enjoying for the better part of a decade: Chinese food, Buffalo wings, ice cream, burritos, and of course, pizza.

He realized very quickly why he had abstained from most of those delicacies, as he put almost 20 pounds on in that first month. He also felt lethargic all the time and knew that while he would never forsake those things again, he had to take it in moderation going forward. From that point on if he was going to eat pizza, he had to work out first.

After phoning in his order to Stucky's Place, Coop decided to call T-Squared back because he felt guilty for ignoring his call earlier.

"Well, I'll be damned… am I being, pranked? Or is this the real Cuppah Madison…" Todd Taylor quipped on the other end of the line.

"Very funny, T…" Coop replied.

"I'm starting to get a complex, brotha…"

"We've been through this before, T, you will always be my favorite person to ignore calls from…"

"Well I got that going for me I guess…"

"That and the millions of dollars I made for you over the years…" Coop jabbed.

"About that… Coop…" T-Squared replied, never missing a chance for a clean segue, "How's the arm feeling?"

"Wouldn't know… unless you're asking how good I am at lifting a can of beer…" Coop answered, knowing that his agent wouldn't leave it at that.

"So you're saying you are well-rested… that's great news!"

"Oh, I got that on lockdown, T…"

"Skip wants to know what the chances are you'll make the whole city of Chicago go nuts later this month, Coop," Tim continued, "He said he will ease you in with a couple rehab appearances in the minors and will only use you as a reliever during the your time with the big club."

"I'm done, T, and even if I wasn't it's too late in the game. I wouldn't help anyone at this point," Coop answered.

"You'd help ticket sales just by being in a uniform…"

"Yeah, and I'd also be taking someone's spot on the roster who actually wants to be there. Tell Skip I appreciate the offer, but no thanks. This is why I don't want to answer the phone."

Coop clicked “End” on his phone, abruptly ending the call.

T-Squared immediately called back, but Coop let it go to voicemail. He didn’t feel as guilty this time as he made his way to the bathroom to take a shower.

27

Cooper Madison replayed the phone call from his friend and agent in his head as the hot water from the showerhead rained down on the back of his neck. He knew why the Cubs wanted him back, and he didn't blame Skip for trying, but he also knew that he was not ready for that.

His thoughts were interrupted by the sound of his doorbell ringing, and it took a few seconds for it to register.

"Shit! The pizza!" Coop yelled to nobody in particular. He had totally forgotten about the delivery from Stucky's after his phone call with T-Squared.

Coop jumped out of the shower and grabbed a towel as he ran to the nearest intercom. Luckily for him, it was right outside the bathroom door. He pressed the talk button and said, "Uh, give me a minute… I'll be right there..."

On the other end of the intercom stood Cara Knox, holding her pizza delivery bag with his salad on top in a separate bag. She was startled when she heard his voice through the intercom, especially since she had been preparing herself for another closed-door meeting with the mysterious occupant.

"Umm… okay?" Cara replied into the small speaker next to the door. She wasn't even sure if he could hear her on the other end.

When Coop heard the delivery girl's voice through the intercom as he frantically dried off, he knew he better put more than a towel on. Still somewhat wet, he grabbed a pair of athletic shorts from his bedroom drawer and threw them on before running down the hallway towards the entry door.

Cara could hear what sounded like footsteps running towards the door before a scream and a loud thud shook the door from the inside, making her jump back.

"Jee-zuss Christ…" said a voice from the other side of the door. "Way to be an athlete, Coop…"

A very puzzled Cara stared at the door as it slowly opened, revealing a very tall, very wet, very shirtless, and very embarrassed looking Cooper Madison.

"I… uh… slipped…" Coop managed to say as he stood in front of the Stucky's delivery girl, who was even prettier in person as opposed to through the lens of a peephole.

"Umm… are you okay?" Cara replied, trying to make sense of everything that was unfolding in front of her.

"Oh yeah… I uh… I'm fine," said Coop, trying not to show that his left elbow, which he had smacked on the floor, wasn't hurting as much as it was.

"Well, that's good… I...umm...have your food…" Cara said, gesturing to the bag in her hand with her eyes. When she looked back up, she tried not to stare too much at his shirtless stomach and chest. While Coop felt he had really let himself go, he still was in better shape than 99% of the population, and Cara had never seen anything quite like this up close and personal.

"Uh...yes...yes you do… Shit… I mean shoot… I'm sorry… I need to get your money… Please, come in…" Coop stammered as he stepped aside and let Cara in.

He was so flustered from his wipeout in the hallway that he didn't even seem to think twice about letting someone inside.

"Wait here, I'll be right back… you can set the food on the counter..." Coop said as he raced down the hallway to get his wallet.

"Try not to fall again…" Cara joked, immediately regretting saying something so lame.

What the hell was that, Cara…

Coop chuckled as he heard her joke. Even though it was kind of lame, he liked the fact that she wasn't afraid to say something at his expense like so many people were at this point in his life.

As Coop emerged from the hallway, Cara was both disappointed and relieved that he had put a shirt on.

At least I won't stare as much...

"This should cover it," Coop said as he handed her a $100 bill.

"Umm.... the order was only $21.50… do you have anything smaller, by chance?" Cara continued, "I don't carry enough change for that."

"Keep it…" Coop insisted.

"I can't… that's ridiculous…" Cara replied.

"Seriously… I uh… I don't have anything smaller than that," Cooper said, almost embarrassed that he was telling the truth. "Besides, I am really embarrassed right now and I figure if I give you a big tip you might totally forget that I slid into my front door…"

This response made Cara laugh out loud, which then made her snort in a way that she tends to when she is really laughing hard. She was laughing so hard that she didn't even have a chance to feel embarrassed by it.

The unexpected snort, coupled with the ridiculousness of the events of the last few minutes, caused Coop to do the same and soon they were both doubled over laughing.

It was one of those moments where only the participants would ever find that much humor in it, but neither of them seemed to care as they laughed hysterically.

Once the laughter wore off a bit, they each tried to find the right words to say next.

"I… umm… have to get back to work," Cara said, wiping tears of laughter from her eyes. "Thank you for the generous bribe… err tip… I already forgot that you wiped out into your front door…"

"See… it worked!" Cooper replied, playing along. "Please let me walk you to the door… it can be dangerous there…"

"And they say chivalry is dead…" Cara replied, chuckling.

"Not where I'm from ma'am…" Coop responded, emphasizing his southern accent for effect.

"Oh crap! I almost forgot to give you your VIP card!" Cara said as she produced the gold-embossed business card and handed it to Coop. "My boss wanted you to have this… he is a big fan."

"Oh… uh… thanks," Coop said, the realization that she obviously knew who he was sinking in.

Sensing this, Cara tried to lighten things up, "Listen, your secret is safe with me. I won't tell anyone that a half-naked Cooper Madison slipped and fell today…"

"It sounds so much worse when you describe it," Coop laughed. He appreciated the fact that she knew what he was thinking.

"It's all good… unless CMZ offers me more than your generous tip…" Cara said playfully, referring to the celebrity gossip website as she slowly exited the door.

"I'll match whatever they offer!" Coop replied, feigning anxiety.

"I'll hold you to that!" Cara played along.

"Wait… between all my athletic exploits I never got your name."

"Oh… I'm sorry… It's Cara… Cara Knox…"

"Well, Miss Cara Knox, it has been my pleasure to make your acquaintance," Coop said with his best southern boy charm.

"Well thank you, Mr. Cooper Madison," Cara replied in her best "Gone with the Wind" accent.

As they said goodbye, Cooper Madison watched his new favorite delivery girl walk towards the elevator and press the call button. It had been a long time since he had let his guard down, let alone with a young lady, and as the elevator doors began to open she turned and smiled at him. As he smiled and gave a wave, he slowly closed the door and returned to the sanctity of his apartment.

28

As Cara stepped into the vintage elevator, she was still smiling and replaying the past few minutes in her head. This did not go unnoticed by Manny, the elevator operator who had wished her good luck on her first delivery.

"Are you smiling because you just broke the record for being the longest delivery ever made to his apartment?" Manny asked wryly.

"Oh...no... just thought of something funny," Cara replied, keeping her promise to Coop. Manny wasn't buying it.

"Riiiight...okay," he chided, but knew well enough to leave it at that.

Manny and Cara exchanged pleasantries as the elevator doors opened to the spacious lobby of the Westcott Hotel, and Cara waved to Henry as she hopped on her scooter and sped off back to Stucky's Place.

The "Free Friday" rush was heavier than usual and made the time pass quickly. Before Cara knew it she only had a half hour to go in her shift. There were no deliveries to be made, so Cara helped with the side work as usual - folding pizza boxes, chopping vegetables, and cleaning any areas that needed it.

Cara was in the middle of folding a pizza box when Stucky yelled for her, "Cara! Line 1!"

It wasn't uncommon for Cara to get phone calls at work, especially from her family, but when she heard Cooper Madison's southern drawl on the other end of the line when she answered the call it startled her.

"Uh...yes, is this Miss Knox?" Coop asked.

"Oh....umm.... yes this is her... I mean this is Cara... this is she," Cara replied awkwardly, planting the palm of her hand against her forehead in embarrassment.

"Listen...I'm sorry for bothering you at work, and all, but would you be interested in... uh... coming over to watch a movie?" Coop inquired, still in disbelief that he was doing this. He had to, though. After she left he almost called and placed another food order just to get her back over again.

He wasn't sure what it was about her that he liked so much, but he knew that he wanted nothing more than to figure out just that.

Coop had given up on dating not long after his father passed, despite the efforts of his friends to set him up. He went on a few dates, but he could never get past the part that every girl seemed to already know everything about him before they met him. He was pretty sure that some even studied like they would for a test.

He sensed something different with the cute delivery girl, so he summoned up the nerve to ask her over.

"Umm, do you mean go see a movie? Like at a theater?" Cara asked.

Coop's heart sank. The thought of going out in public to a movie theater with a girl and what any media outlets would make of it terrified him.

Before he could answer, Cara rescued him, almost as if she could read his mind.

"Listen, I would love to go see a movie. I can't even remember the last time I was in a movie theater, but I have a rule. No movie theater dates with a guy until he invites me over to his house and cooks for me first. If he does a good job, then we can discuss a movie."

As the words rolled off Cara's tongue she couldn't believe that everything came out so smoothly, let alone when talking to a famous athlete.

She wasn't sure what it was about him that enabled her to feel so comfortable, but she knew that she wanted nothing more than to figure out just that.

"Oh… cook, huh? I've never had to audition for a date before," Coop answered, relieved but also caught off guard. After all, professional athletes don't usually have to work too hard to get a date.

"Well, I love food too much to date a guy who can't cook," Cara said, even more shocked than before at her newly found brashness.

"Well then, do you like shrimp?" Coop asked, praying she'd say yes.

"Oh, I love shrimp!"

"Do you like your shrimp to have a kick?"

"Let's just say that I have a shirt from Wild Wings Cafe that says I like my food spicy," Cara responded, referring to the time her friends dared her to take the 9-1-1 hot wings challenge.

"I'll take that as a warning. How does tonight at 7 o'clock sound?"

"See you then…" Cara responded coolly, and then hung up. Her palm returned to her forehead again. Who was this person saying all these things?

Then it hit her.

Holy crap... what am I getting myself into? He probably has a girl in every city! He dated Miss Freaking Mississippi!

Then she looked at the clock, which read 3:02 pm.

What am I going to wear? Should I tell someone? Who would even believe me? No... I'm not telling anyone... Am I supposed to bring something? What am I DOING??

These thoughts continued as she rode back to Viking Hall on her Vespa. She had a couple of hours to get herself together still, and she even started to think about backing out but quickly erased that as an option because she had a feeling that Cooper Madison wasn't the type of guy who would give up that easily.

She had to go through with it.

29

Cooper Madison heard the phone click on the other end before he could respond, and he wasn't sure what had just happened. What he did know was that he had to get some groceries, and fast.

Going out to the grocery store at this time of day in the city wasn't an option, so he called one of the only other people that he had formed a relationship with since moving to Cleveland: the Wescott's concierge, Simon.

Simon's sole duty was to make sure that the guests at the Wescott are happy, even if it means arranging for a specific grocery list to be purchased and delivered on a Friday afternoon. Especially if that guest is Cooper Madison.

Coop gave him a list of ingredients to make his father's famous shrimp boil, which included gulf shrimp, corn on the cob, Andouille sausage, onions, and redskin potatoes. He already had plenty of Old Bay Seasoning, beer, and Tony Chachere's Creole Seasoning, all of which were a must for any proper boil.

As usual, Simon came through and the goods were delivered to Coop's door within 90 minutes, which gave him enough time to clean the place up a little and start prepping the meal.

Coop inspected the four pounds of gulf shrimp first to check for quality. He always lamented the fact that he had to pay $14 a pound for shrimp that were likely frozen and from China when he could get fresh gulf shrimp off the boats in Pass Christian for $2 a pound. Nonetheless, these would have to work.

Once the pot was filled with all of the delicious ingredients that reminded him of home, he turned up the heat and got dressed for his guest.

As he picked out a pair of jeans and a form fitting t-shirt, he still couldn't quite wrap his head around what it was that led him to call the delivery girl up and invite her over. He had made a complete fool out of himself in front of her. Maybe it was the way she handled that whole situation? It had been a long time since he felt that comfortable that quickly with another person. Let alone an attractive young woman.

Across town, Cara had opted for the RTA bus as opposed to her scooter. She had actually styled her hair in something other than a ponytail for the first time in weeks and didn't want to mess it up. She decided to dress casually in khaki shorts and a tank top, both of which showed off her tanned and toned body in a way that made the bus driver do a double take when she boarded.

As the bus made its way towards the Wescott Hotel, Cara started to feel the nervous pit in her stomach worsen. She also began to devise an escape plan if the evening wasn't going well, or if she felt that all he wanted was sex. As attracted to him as she was, she wasn't going to be added to the list of "Cleat Chasers" - girls who only try to hook up with professional athletes.

Once at her stop, Cara hopped off the bus and as it pulled away she stared up at the Wescott Hotel. She always loved delivering food there. It was elegant and beautiful and had an amazing view of Lake Erie. She never imagined that she would ever be visiting under these circumstances.

30

Simon Craig reassured the voice on the other end of the phone that he would personally see to it that the caller's guest would be warmly greeted upon her arrival.

"Yes, Mr. Madison. Of course, sir. Is there anything else I can assist you with? Very well, sir. Please do not hesitate to let me know otherwise, Mr. Madison."

As Simon hung up the phone, he took a deep breath and replayed the past few hours in his head. Sure, Cooper Madison had asked him to get some groceries before, and occasionally other small requests, but nothing like this.

Most guests at the Westcott had Simon perform such tasks on a daily basis. Having a full-time concierge was one of the perks of staying at the Westcott, after all, and Simon loved his job. He was a fixer by nature, and he took great satisfaction in solving problems for the wealthy residents of the Westcott Hotel.

Simon was entering his mid-20's and had graduated with a degree in Hospitality Management from Bowling Green State University prior to working at the Westcott. While most little boys his age dreamed of becoming professional athletes, firemen, or astronauts, young Simon Craig used to dream of being Alfred - butler to Bruce Wayne, also known as Batman.

It was very rare that Cooper Madison asked him for anything, let alone something urgent.

I wonder who the girl is? Probably a pageant winner. At the very least a local news girl.

When the evening doorman held the door open for Cara Knox to enter the Westcott Hotel, Simon did a double take. Then it hit him.

Oh. My. God... Cara??

"Hello, Simon…" Cara said as she approached the usually unflappable concierge, who was anything but in this moment.

Simon quickly composed himself, and responded as professionally as possible, "Miss Knox, how are you this evening? Mr. Madison is expecting you."

"Please… you don't have to talk to me like that. It's creeping me out," Cara jokingly admonished.

Simon grinned, and as he led Cara towards the elevator, he whispered, "You must have made quite an impression on a delivery…"

"Very funny, Simon," Cara responded.

"Well, you are a *lucky* girl. He is *gorgeous*... and that accent? Kill me now!" Simon chided.

"Wait… you're not straight, Simon?" Cara deadpanned.

"Oh, now look who has the jokes!" Simon replied, feigning sincerity.

"I kid… I kid…" Cara continued, "You know you're my favorite concierge in Cleveland."

"And you know that you're my favorite delivery driver, with the exception of Alonzo from UPS."

Simon's tone then changed to serious, "Seriously, though, Cara. Cooper Madison has never had a girl up here, let alone anyone for that matter. Trust me, I would know. You must have made some kind of impression on him."

The gate to the elevator opened and interrupted Simon, and in essence, brought him back to the reality of his job.

"Thomas, please see to it that Miss Knox makes it to the 11th floor. Mr. Madison is expecting her," Simon said to the evening elevator operator, Thomas, quickly switching back to his best professional speaking voice.

"Of course, step on in Miss Knox," Thomas responded, as Cara entered the elevator.

Simon gave Cara a wink as the gate to the elevator closed, straightened his tie, and returned to his concierge desk while replaying the exchange that he had not seen coming.

31

The phone rang in Suite 1100 as Cooper Madison tasted one of the pieces of Andouille sausage from his steaming shrimp pot.

"Mr. Madison," Simon began on the other end, "Miss Cara Knox is on her way up. Will there be anything else I can help you with?"

"Thank you kindly, Simon," Coop replied, "I think I'm all set."

"Very well, Mr. Madison. Enjoy your evening."

"You too."

It's game time... Why am I so nervous? Get it together, Coop...

Coop could hear the gate of the 1908 Otis "Birdcage" elevator open from inside his suite. The elevator, which had been meticulously maintained in all of its original glory by the owners of the Westcott Hotel, was one of Coop's favorite amenities at his new residence. It reminded him of so many similar elevators still in operation in and around the French Quarter in New Orleans.

Coop could see Cara Knox exit the elevator through the peephole on his front door, and he found himself verbalizing the first thought that came to mind.

"Whoa..."

He was happy that she had not dressed up for the occasion, as his relationship with the former Miss Mississippi had soured his view on women who always had to be dressed to the nines, even if they weren't leaving the house.

As he gazed upon Cara as she approached the front door to Suite 1100, he felt a strong appreciation for the designer of her tank top and khaki shorts combination.

Before Cara could knock, he opened the door.

"Miss Knox…" greeted Cooper, summoning his best southern hospitality.

"Well hello, " Cara responded, obviously startled that he was waiting for her. "I was kinda hoping for those last few seconds to collect myself before I knocked…"

Thanks a lot, Simon...

"Would you like me to close the door so we can have a do-over?" Cooper mused.

Cara laughed, "No, I'm good…"

"Please… come on into my humble abode…" offered Cooper as he stepped back and gestured with an open arm to the suite behind him, which was anything but humble.

Cara smiled and entered, immediately noticing the enticing smell coming from the kitchen.

"Something sure smells wonderful. Did you actually cook it yourself, or do you have a butler slaving away back there?"

"I will have you know, Miss Knox, that I pride myself on my ability to cook many meals. As long as those meals involve a shrimp pot, that is…"

"Okay the whole 'Miss Knox' thing is creeping me out now," Cara chided. "While I truly appreciate the southern charm, please just call me Cara."

Cooper held his hands up, feigning surrender.

"No problem, Cara. My apologies…"

"No… I'm sorry," Cara replied, immediately feeling guilty. "You see, I suffer from a serious affliction. I have an inability to think before I speak at times, and I'm pretty sure that they forgot to install the filter when they made me…"

"Don't…" Coop countered.

"Don't what?" Cara asked, puzzled.

"Don't ever apologize for that," Coop replied. "I find it completely refreshing. I've spent the better part of my life surrounded by people who *always* had a filter on around me."

Cara was taken aback, and before she could respond Coop continued.

"Like earlier today. When I went to get your money, you made the joke about me not fall-"

"Oh my God, that was such a *lame* joke," Cara interrupted.

"Well, I won't argue with that," Coop laughed. "It was pretty lame, BUT… you weren't afraid to say it. Do you know if I had done that in front of Simon he would've pretended that it never happened? Or he would have blamed the maintenance crew for waxing the floor too much!"

"Well, it's never been an issue for me. Unfortunately, not everyone is as accepting of my audacity as you."

"Well then, I guess that's their loss, isn't it?" Coop countered, his steely eyes locking in on Cara as she glanced up.

"Thank you…" Cara managed to reply, almost forgetting what she was trying to say.

His eyes give him an unfair advantage…

"I have enough people in my life who I have known for years and I am pretty sure that I have never seen most of them let their guard down around me," Coop explained. "That's probably what I miss most about playing. My teammates were always genuine because they didn't have any other reason not to be. We were all in the same boat."

As they stood just feet from the kitchen, they held each other's gaze for a few seconds.

Then Cara broke the silence, "Coop…"

"Yes…" Coop replied.

"That was the most pathetic thing I have heard in a long time!" Cara said as she busted out laughing, "Oh my God… *poor me… people only want to kiss my ass…*"

Coop, staring in utter disbelief, could only manage to say, "Well, yeah, when you put it *that* way it sounds pathetic…"

By this point, Cara was almost crying from laughter, and Coop was certain that while he was on the receiving end of the joke there was also no place else he wanted to be in that moment.

Her wit gives her an unfair advantage…

"Hey, you asked for it!" Cara managed to calm down enough to remind Coop of his earlier request. "You told me you never wanted me to change."

"Yeah… about that…" Coop replied, with no intention of finishing the thought.

"Listen, I know what you mean," Cara said. "I just couldn't help myself. I warned you… no filter..."

"Like I said, don't ever apologize either," Coop reminded her. "I deserved that."

"Well, on another note, I'm freaking *starving*," Cara changed the subject. "And whatever you got going on in that kitchen smells amazing."

"Well then," Coop said, "Let's get after it. *Mizz-ippy* style. Follow me..."

Coop led Cara into the large kitchen area, and instead of plates and silverware on the kitchen table, there was beige colored newsprint-like paper spread out like a tablecloth.

"Don't worry," Coop said, noticing Cara's odd expression as she saw the makeshift tablecloth. "It'll all make sense in a minute. Have a seat."

As Cara sat down, she noticed two plastic bibs like one would typically wear while dining on lobster at a seafood restaurant.

"You are going to want to wear one of those," Coop said as he poured the contents of the pot into a large metal strainer.

"Fancy!" Cara joked.

"Only the best!" Coop replied as he carried the large metal basket to the table and proceeded to dump the contents right in the middle, directly on top of the paper.

Cara stared at the steaming pile of food before her. There was enough shrimp, corn, sausage, and potatoes to feed 10 people.

"Are there more people coming over?" Cara asked, wide-eyed.

"This is just the appetizer," Coop deadpanned.

"Very funny… It smells and looks delicious," Cara said. "I'm impressed."

"Much obliged, Cara. I can't make many dishes, but I can surely boil the hell out of some shrimp. Now dig in, girl!" Coop encouraged as he sat down and tied his bib on. "Just throw the shells off to the side."

"Do you have any cocktail sauce?" Cara asked.

"Cocktail sauce? You mean that stuff you *Yanks* put on seafood that hasn't been cooked properly?" Coop retorted. "Take a bite and tell me if you still want some."

"Look at you with all the rules," Cara laughed as she bit into a jumbo gulf shrimp that she had just peeled.

Coop eyed her as she slowly chewed the slow-cooked crustacean, waiting for a reaction.

"Who said anything about cocktail sauce," Cara said sarcastically. "Shrimp this good should never be ruined with that gunk."

"There's help for you, yet, Cara Knox," Coop replied.

"Wow… this is delicious! It's like each shell contains its own set of spices," Cara raved. "I've never had anything like it up here in Cleveland."

"Well, I do aim to please," Coop said, as he also took a big bite of shrimp. "My parents used to have a boil every Sunday when I was a kid. We'd go down to the docks and buy 20 pounds of shrimp fresh off the boat from the Vietnamese fishermen."

"That must have cost a fortune!" Cara implied. "Shrimp is like 10 bucks a pound."

"No ma'am, not in Pass Christian, it's not," Coop corrected her. "We typically paid between 2 to 3 dollars a pound at the docks. Shrimping is a big industry on the gulf coast… or at least it was..."

"Are you freaking kidding me?" Cara exclaimed. "I would eat shrimp every single day for that price!"

"Sometimes we'd throw crawdads in there, along with some blue crab if we felt like it. If we went fishing off the coast we usually had a bunch of Black-Tip Shark fillets in the freezer that we would throw on the grill, too," Coop explained.

"Crawdads?" Cara asked, puzzled.

"You mean you've never sucked dat head and pinched dat tail?" Coop asked, referring to the technique used for eating a crawfish, knowing that his audience would have no idea what he was referring to.

"*Excuse* me?" Cara asked, eying him sideways.

"Crawfish? Mudbugs? Mountain lobsters? Up here, I believe they call them *crayfish*," Coop said, mockingly emphasizing the latter's northern pronunciation.

"You eat *crayfish*?" Cara asked, incredulously. "We used to catch those in the creek by my house. *Ewww…*"

"Don't knock it til you try it," Coop said. "They're really good. If you like lobster, you'll probably love crawdads."

"If you say so…" Cara replied, still not able to shake the thought of eating one of the little critters she used to try and catch with her brothers in the many creeks of the Cleveland Metroparks.

"I almost forgot!" Coop announced abruptly, standing up. "I forgot to get us some drinks. What can I offer you? I have beer, wine, Barq's, soda, bottled water, and a lifetime supply of Gatorade - thanks to my last endorsement deal."

"I'll have what you're having," Cara replied. "Any of those sound good."

"Barq's it is, then!" Coop said as he grabbed two clear glass bottles of Barq's Famous Olde Tyme Root Beer from his refrigerator and two frosted mugs from his freezer, before rejoining Cara at the table.

"Wow, frosted mugs and everything," Cara stated, "I must say that I'm impressed. Just one question, though. Why did you refer to it specifically as Barq's instead of just saying root beer?"

"Well, where I'm from, there is no other root beer worthy of drinking," Coop replied. "You see, Barq's was invented in Biloxi, Mississippi, which isn't far from my hometown. The owner was actually from Nawlins, so they like to claim that it's from there, but we all know the truth. Most restaurants and sandwich shops along the Gulf Coast won't even carry another brand of root beer."

"Wow, I never knew... great food *and* a history lesson. I must say, I am impressed!" Cara responded.

"I'm full of useless information. Lots of time on airplanes and in the clubhouse between starts," Coop replied. "How's the corn?"

"It's amazing! Everything is. The only problem is that I think you've ruined Red Lobster for me. There's no way that I can ever go back there after this," Cara said.

Coop took a long swig of Barq's and smiled as he watched Cara eat. He loved that she was getting her fingers dirty and never once asked for a fork.

Cara, realizing that she was being watched, decided to change the subject as she raised the frosty mug to her lips.

32

"Aren't you going to ask me the typical questions?" Cara asked, taking a sip.

"And what would those be?" Coop replied.

"You know, like where am I from? Do I go to school? I feel guilty because I feel like I know so much about you thanks to the magic of the internet."

"Are you saying you *stalked* me?" Coop interrupted, playfully.

"Stalked is a strong word. I prefer *researched*," Cara replied.

"Well, I guess this is the best way I could put it. I *want* to know everything there is to know about you. I don't just want to know where you grew up and where you went to school, or why you deliver food. To be honest, I didn't ask because I just got caught up."

"Caught up?" Cara asked.

"In you…" Coop continued, "I have been caught up in you since earlier today when I opened the door. I can't really explain exactly what that means, but I do know that whatever it is has led me to invite a complete stranger over to my place and cook dinner for her and worry if I was wearing the right shirt and if she would even show up and…"

"Stop…" Cara interjected.

"I'm sorry, that probably wasn't the answer you were looking for," said Coop.

"No… no, it certainly wasn't," Cara replied. "But I honestly don't think you could've answered it any better than you did."

"Really?" Coop asked.

"Really," Cara responded. "As my dad used to say it was *perfectly imperfect*."

"I'm sorry, when did he pass?" Coop asked.

"Oh, he's still alive," Cara quickly replied, realizing that her wording would've led him to believe otherwise. "I just haven't heard him say it for a long time…"

"Oh, gotcha," Coop answered, sounding relieved.

"I'm glad you said what you did because I am having a lot of the same feelings," Cara said.

"Yeah… if you would've told me this morning that we'd be sitting here, I would've said you're crazy as an outhouse rat," Coop replied.

"An outhouse rat? That must be a Southern expression," Cara said, laughing.

"Don't even get me started on Yankee expressions!" Coop countered. "Like, why do y'all call soda, *pop*?"

"*Touche*, you got me there," Cara admitted, taking an exaggerated sip of her frosty root beer.

"Have you had your fill?" Coop asked, gesturing towards the table, which despite their efforts was still half-filled with shrimp, corn, sausage, and potatoes.

"I can't eat another bite," Cara said, raising her hands in surrender.

"I'm full as a tick, too," Coop said with a hint of pride before continuing. "Would you like to go out on the balcony?"

"Sure, but only after you show me where the bathroom is so I can wash up," Cara replied, referring to her hands.

"Oh, of course. It's the first door on the left," Coop said, pointing towards the hallway off of the kitchen.

As Cara excused herself and made her way to the restroom, Coop put the leftover food into a large plastic container. One of his favorite parts of a shrimp boil was using the leftovers the next day to make his mom's jambalaya recipe.

After putting the container in the refrigerator, Coop picked up the corners of the makeshift paper tablecloth and brought them together in the middle which enabled him to pick up all of the shells at once and discard them into the garbage can.

As Coop was washing his hands at the kitchen sink, Cara emerged from the hallway.

"Wow, you clean up fast," Cara said as she gestured towards the now-clean table.

"That's the beauty of the paper," Coop said, drying his hands.

"I think I might start putting paper down at every meal," Cara laughed. "No more dishes!"

"Makes cleaning up faster than a knife fight in a phone booth," Coop mused as he motioned for Cara to follow him towards the door to the balcony. "Follow me, I'll show you my favorite place to chill."

33

"Lake Erie looks amazing from up here," Cara Knox said as she gazed out over Cleveland's Great Lake from the balcony of Suite 1100 at the Westcott Hotel.

The sun was setting over the western horizon as the Cooper Madison leaned against the stone balcony next to Cara.

"I try to catch every sunrise and sunset out here. It reminds me of home. I used to love watching the sun set over the Gulf."

"I don't blame you," Cara replied. "It's breathtaking."

"And peaceful…"

"Seeing it from up here reminds me of something my dad used to say," Cara laughed. "Lake Erie is like a pitching wedge - good from about 150 yards out."

"That's funny," Coop chuckled. "It definitely is not as pretty up close. The last time I was on the shore over at Edgewater Beach I almost stepped on a syringe and about a dozen used condoms."

"That sounds about right," Cara responded.

"Can I ask you something? That's the second time you referred to your father as if he was no longer with us. Why?"

"Sorry, I guess it's a force of habit," Cara replied, "My dad is alive but in a lot of ways, the man he used to be died about 5 years ago."

"How do you mean?"

"He was in a bad accident on the job at the Ford plant. He ended up in a wheelchair and hasn't been the same since. It's like he's just given up in a lot of ways."

"Dear Lord, I'm so sorry to hear that," Coop replied.

"That's why I work at Stucky's, I'm in my senior year at CSU and money has been tight since the accident, so I work for Stucky to help out. He used to work with my dad at Ford long before the accident."

"Do you like college?" Coop asked.

"Yeah, but I'm ready for it to be over."

"Sometimes I wish I would've gone to college. Even just for a year," Coop said as he looked out over the lake.

"Well, I think you made the right choice," Cara laughed.

"Yeah, I know I did," Coop relented. "But, I do feel like I missed out on a lot of stuff."

"Well, as someone who didn't miss out on those things, I can assure you that they weren't as great as you might have imagined. But, I do get where you're coming from."

"What's your major?" Coop asked.

"Business, but I have no idea what I'm going to do."

"You fixin' to take over corporate America?"

"Right now I'm just *fixin'* to land an internship this winter and finish my degree," Cara laughed, mocking Coop's choice of progressive verb.

"I can't help the fact you don't know the proper way to talk," Coop joked.

"What do you say if you're planning on fixing something?" Cara mused.

"Well, I suppose I'd be fixin to fix it…" Coop laughed.

"I give up…"

"Please don't…" Coop deadpanned, his words immediately signaling a shift in tone, before cracking a wry smile at Cara.

"Same…" Cara replied, smiling back.

"Well, at least we can agree on that…" Coop said as he gazed towards the sunset.

"Nothing…" Cara replied.

"Come again?" Coop asked.

"Nothing…" Cara repeated, "I say it when I agree with something, but I know that no matter what words come out of my mouth that they won't do it justice. So, I just say 'nothing' and that's my way of saying that whatever the other person said was perfect."

"Nothing…" Coop said, "I like that."

"Nothing…" Cara agreed.

34

Simon Craig's phone sprang to life at his concierge desk approximately 10 minutes before he was scheduled to clock out for the evening.

The concierge service at the Westcott Hotel ran in two shifts, and Simon worked the second shift from 3-11 Monday through Saturday because that's where the action was. The first shift, which ran 7am-3pm, was too boring as it was basically playing secretary for the business guests.

"Yes, Mr. Madison… No sir, it's not too late, sir… I will handle everything," Simon said as he hung up the phone.

Well, that's a first. Cooper Madison ordering a late night car service? Especially ordering it with no firm destination... Cara, girl, what did you do to that boy...

Simon called Burning River Livery, a local Town Car and limousine company whose moniker referred to the fact that the Cuyahoga River had once famously caught fire.

Typically, when Simon called Burning River late in the evening it was to discreetly shuttle his business class guests to and from a local gentlemen's club in style. Therefore, when he called on this particular evening he had to explain that he was in need of their best available driver for an unspecified amount of time and no specific destination. Also, the driver would need to be someone who could be trusted to be discreet. In exchange, the driver would be paid handsomely, as money was not an object for this client.

Burning River Livery said that would not be a problem and that they would have a Lincoln Town Car there in 15 minutes.

Even though it would mean that he had to stay late, Simon had a rule that he would never leave work until he was certain that all of his obligations were fulfilled.

When he was a college intern, Simon once saw a concierge book a limousine for a guest prior to clocking out and leaving for the day. The limousine never showed up, and subsequently there was no concierge on staff to help the very angry guest. Needless to say, that concierge was not back the next day, or any day after that. Simon decided to use that as a reminder to always finish the job, regardless of how long it required.

Besides... I need to know what is going on...

35

"Good evening, Mr. Madison. I am calling to inform you that your Town Car has arrived, as requested, Sir," Simon Craig informed the famous tenant of Suite 1100.

"Good deal, thank you, Simon," Coop replied. "We are on our way down."

Minutes later the doors to the elevator opened and Coop emerged with Cara Knox in tow. Simon made sure to meet them as they stepped out of the elevator so he could personally escort them to the waiting luxury car.

As he approached the couple, Simon tried his best to get a read on Cara and the two caught each other's stare for a brief moment. Cara gave Simon a quick wide-eyed expression as if to say she wasn't really sure what was going on either. She also knew Simon well enough to know that he was dying to know.

Sorry, Simon, that's all you get for now...

A lanky man, who appeared to be of Indian descent, welcomed the trio outside. The driver, dressed in a black suit, opened the back door to the shiny black Lincoln Town Car for his new clients.

"Have a wonderful evening Mr. Madison," Simon said as the driver closed the door.

"Thanks again, Simon," Coop answered, discreetly slipping the concierge a hundred dollar bill. "For everything..."

"My pleasure, sir," Simon replied.

"Bye, Simon!" Cara said as she rolled down the window from the backseat.

"Goodbye, Miss Knox," Simon said with a smile and a subtle nod, before turning around and heading back to the Westcott Hotel.

She better give me a play-by-play...

"Where shall I take you, Sir?" the driver asked after entering the car.

"Actually, that's a question for her," Coop replied, gesturing towards Cara.

"We're heading to Brook Park," Cara said. "Take the Snow Road exit off I-71, please, and I'll tell you from there."

"Absolutely, Miss. My name is Rahul. Please do not hesitate to ask for anything," the driver said, with a hint of an accent.

"Thanks, Rahul. My name is Cara and this is Cooper," she replied.

"Welcome, welcome," Rahul answered as he merged onto Interstate 71 South towards Brook Park.

Earlier that evening, while out on the balcony, Coop asked Cara to tell him more about where she was from.

"I'd rather show you," Cara had answered. "Do you have a car here?"

"Not at the moment, actually," Coop replied. "But, I can get us one."

When Coop went back inside and used the phone, Cara assumed he was calling a taxi. She didn't realize he had rented a Town Car until she walked outside.

"So, why don't you own a car?" Cara asked as the Town Car made its way southbound.

"Oh, I own a few cars," Coop said matter-of-factly. "I just don't have any that I can drive here in Cleveland right now. I have a couple in storage in Chicago, and the other has been in a shop on the east side for the past month."

"What's wrong with it?" Cara asked.

"Well if you ask the guy that I'm paying to fix it, every single thing you can think of," Coop laughed. "I swear I could buy the same truck three times over for how much it has cost me to refurbish this one."

"Refurbish? Is it an antique?" Cara asked.

"No, it's not that old, but it suffered a lot of damage and has sentimental value," Coop replied. "It was the truck I bought for my daddy after I made the majors…"

"Oh…" Cara said, regretting that she kept asking questions, "I can see why you'd want to fix it up."

"So," Coop said, wanting to change the subject, "How much further until we get there?"

"Well, our first stop is just a mile or so from the exit. You'll get the honor of seeing where I grew up."

"And the second stop?"

"Stop number two is Berea High School, where I went. And after that, the third stop will be my favorite place to go when I need to clear my head."

"Well, I cannot wait to see all of them," Coop responded earnestly.

As the car approached the Snow Road exit, Cara instructed the driver to follow it to the light and then take three consecutive left-hand turns, which led them to Gilmere Drive, one of the many streets in Brook Park that was lined with early 1970's split level homes.

"That's my house, on the right."

Cara pointed out a light green split level home with a long driveway that led to a detached garage that had an old basketball hoop hanging over the door. In addition, Coop noticed that there was a wooden wheelchair ramp that led up to the front door.

"Shall I pull into the driveway?" Rahul asked.

"Oh my god NO!" Cara implored. "Just slow down please."

"Don't you want to go in and say hello?" Coop chided, knowing the answer before he asked.

"Yeah… No…" Cara said. "This night has already been dizzying enough."

"Well, it looks like a fine home," Coop declared.

"It is, though it was a little crowded. Thankfully, I had my own room since I was the only girl."

"I'm sure that made your brothers jealous as all get out," Coop laughed.

"Amongst many other things."

"Where to next, Miss Cara?" Rahul asked as the Town Car slowly pulled further away from her house.

"Berea High School, please," Cara informed the driver. "It's on the corner of Bagley and Eastland."

"As you wish. I know exactly where it is," Rahul responded. "When I first came to this country from India I took citizenship classes there at night."

"Are you a US citizen now?" Coop asked.

"Yessir, next month will make 5 years!" Rahul answered, obviously very proud of that fact.

"Congratulations, Rahul," Coop replied. "Do you have a family here, too?"

"Yessir, my wife and five children are all US citizens now," Rahul explained. "We live in Lakewood."

"That's awesome!" Cara said. "Do you ever miss India?"

"I miss my family members who live there still," Rahul answered. "But, we love America very, very much. Many opportunities."

"Are you a baseball fan, Rahul?" Cara asked, looking over at Coop, who shot her a look.

"I am more of a cricket fan, but I have been to an Indians game. I just do not understand the game very well. Why do you ask?" Rahul asked.

"I noticed the Chief Wahoo air freshener hanging from the rearview mirror," Cara replied, thankful that she had an alibi prior to asking the question.

"Oh, of course," Rahul said. "My boss is a big Indians fan and he has them in all of our vehicles."

Coop gave Cara a wry smile, and she responded with a subtle wink.

This girl is sharp as a tack...

"Which entrance shall I use?" Rahul asked as the car approached Berea High School, a large building that was erected in 1929 and had a mix of both gothic and post-modern architectural features thanks to multiple additions over the years.

"Turn in here at the front and follow the bus lane," Cara instructed.

"That's a *big* school," Coop announced as he leaned over in front of Cara to peek out the window on her side of the car.

Good God he smells wonderful...

"It used to be one of the biggest schools in the area, but our student population has really dropped over the past decade. It's a great town to live in so most people never leave. Now, there's too many people without kids," Cara explained.

"You smell good..." Coop whispered in Cara's ear as he settled back in his side of the car.

"So do you..." Cara answered, blushing.

"Is it open?" Coop asked, nodding towards the school.

"I doubt it, especially this late on a Friday," Cara answered. "Besides, I want to take you to stop number 3."

"Ah, yes, the mystery spot," Coop recalled.

"Rahul, do you know where the Coe Lake Gazebo is?" Cara asked.

"Is that the one by the public library?" Rahul answered.

"That's the one!" Cara replied.

"As you wish, Miss Cara," Rahul said with a smile.

36

Coe Lake Park was a short drive from Berea High School and had gone under major renovations over the past decade, which included a beautiful gazebo and a geyser-like fountain. It was also a local favorite for fishing, kayaking, and walking.

For brave local teens, it was also considered a rite of passage to go cliff diving off of one of the bluffs that overlook the lake.

Rahul pulled the Lincoln Town Car up to the sidewalk that led to the large wooden gazebo, which was painted white and an ode to colonial America. The gazebo was the first phase of a project that would later include a boardwalk pier and an amphitheater.

"We are going to get out for a bit," Cara informed Rahul.

"Absolutely. I will be right here waiting for you to return. Please, take your time," Rahul replied.

"I can see why you like to come here," Coop stated as the two walked along the sidewalk that leads to the gazebo.

"It's too dark to really do it justice… you should see it at sunset," Cara answered.

"I bet there's some big ol' catfish under this thing," Coop announced as he walked onto the gazebo, which had a platform that extended over the lake.

"Biggest one I ever caught was at this lake," Cara said.

"Wait just one second… you fish, girl?" Cooper asked, stopping dead in his tracks for effect.

"Since I was old enough to bait my own hook," Cara proudly replied, "My dad used to take me fishing in the Metroparks all the time growing up. The funny thing is, none of my brothers liked going with him, but I loved every minute of it. I miss it, I haven't been in years..."

"Well, that's something we are going to have to remedy right quick, Miss Cara Knox!" Coop exclaimed, obviously excited to hear about this latest development.

"I'd like that," Cara replied.

"Me too," Coop agreed.

"Sometimes in the summer they have bands and orchestras who put on free concerts at this gazebo," Cara informed. "I've even seen some weddings here."

"It reminds me of where I grew up," Coop answered. "We have one just like it in War Memorial Park. It overlooks the Gulf and every year at Christmas the town would put on a big celebration there. Now, it's just another thing that needs to be rebuilt..."

"I'm so sorry…" Cara said as she took a step closer to Coop, who had made his way to the center of the gazebo. "I wish I could-"

"Nothing…" Coop cut her off, invoking their newfound password from earlier in the evening.

"Nothing…" Cara replied.

Coop took a step closer to Cara, who was now directly in front of his hulking frame. Her hair had been blown around in the breeze and was now covering her right eye.

With a gentle touch of his large left hand, Coop brushed her hair to the side completely revealing a face that looked full of both anticipation and nerves.

Instead of going in for a kiss, Coop pulled her in close and whispered in her ear, "You still smell good…"

"So do you…" Cara answered, feeling her heart start to race. The tension that had been building up between the two all night was at an all-time high.

Cara felt the left side of Coop's stubbly cheek against the side of her face and she wondered how something so rough could feel so perfect.

I can't believe this is happening...

At the same time, Coop wondered how the months and months of voluntarily being alone seemed like the biggest mistake of his life knowing that this girl was out there.

Thank God I slipped today...

Coop slowly moved the left side of his cheek away from hers, but close enough that it grazed the tip of her nose, soon after followed by his.

His eyes were closed as Cara's locked in on them, anticipating the steely gaze that she had first noticed while searching his name on the internet. When he finally did slowly open his eyes Cara could feel her heart through her chest.

His eyes still give him an unfair advantage...

Coop leaned in and pressed his lips against hers in a way that was both gentle and firm.

Cara felt herself melt in his arms, which were now wrapped around her hips, but also securely over her arms.

Coop let that first kiss linger before pulling her face close to his chest and resting his chin on top of her hair. He could not remember the last time he held anyone so close, let alone a beautiful young woman.

After a few minutes in that embrace, Cara pulled away enough so that she was facing him.

"Coop..." Cara began in a way that a question was sure to follow.

"Yes..." Coop replied, not sure what was coming next.

"Will you take me fishing tomorrow?" Cara asked in a way that, out of context, could never have held the same sincerity that she had in her voice.

The question seemed to have caught Coop off guard, but the tone of her voice made it easy for him to recover. This was about more than casting a line in the water. Cara was asking him to do something that she obviously had been yearning to do for quite some time. Something that was very important to her, it just happened to be fishing.

"I thought you'd never ask..." Coop responded.

This time it was Cara who initiated the kiss, and with it, she felt some of the sadness that had been wrapped around her heart dissolve.

37

Rahul Ansari noticed the young couple emerge from the Coe Lake Park Gazebo as they made their way down the path towards the waiting car. Unlike when he dropped them off almost thirty minutes earlier, this time they were holding hands.

Young love…

Rahul opened the back door to the Lincoln Town Car and as the two entered he asked where he would be taking them next.

"Viking Hall at Cleveland State, please," Cara replied.

"Of course. I believe I also know where that is," Rahul responded before closing the door and making his way back to the driver's seat.

"So what time are you picking me up to go fishing?" Cara asked Coop, his right hand intertwined with her left.

"Typically, I like to have my first line in by sunrise…" Coop deadpanned.

"*Sunrise*?" Cara said incredulously.

"The way I see it," Coop continued, "You got at least 4 hours to sleep before I pick you up…"

"Well, I like you, but not that much…" Cara called his bluff.

Coop laughed and raised his hands in surrender.

"How does 9:00 sound?" Coop asked.

"Sounds a hell of a lot better than 5:00!" Cara laughed.

"Then it's a date," Coop said.

"No, it's a second date," Cara corrected him.

Coop stared into Cara's eyes and smiled.

"Nothing…" Coop said.

"Nothing…" Cara agreed as she laid her head on his chest for the remainder of the car ride back to Viking Hall.

Once there, Coop walked her to the door and gave her a gentle kiss accompanied by a firm and lingering hug.

"See you before ya know it," Coop reminded Cara.

"Can't wait!" Cara said as she closed the door behind her.

Rahul held the rear door of the Town Car open for Coop as he made his way back from the entrance to Viking Hall.

"We have one more stop, Rahul," Coop informed the driver.

"Of course, sir. Where shall I take you?" Rahul asked.

"There's a 24-hour storage facility not far from my place," Coop replied. "I have to grab my fishing gear before you take me back to the Westcott."

"Absolutely, sir," Rahul confirmed. "Shall I arrange for another car to pick you up tomorrow, as well?"

"Actually, I think I'm going to rent a car myself and drive. It's been too long," Coop answered.

"It is a freedom that we often take for granted, I suppose," Rahul stated as the Town Car pulled away. "I find that the longer I have lived in America the more I seem to take for granted the simple freedoms that I once longed for in India. My children even more so…"

"That seems to be what we do best in our country, sometimes…" Coop agreed.

The two continued in silence as they made their way towards CLE 24/7 Storage Incorporated, an around the clock self-service storage facility located in a former underground parking garage near the Westcott Hotel.

What used to be a parking garage was now a series of storage lockers located where the parking spots once were. The access drives enabled the customers to drive right up to their unit and access it 24 hours a day via an electronic keypad where the parking attendant used to sit.

Once inside, Coop directed Rahul to his unit, which was a 10'x12' locker on the second level. Coop used this to store the majority of the items he was able to salvage from his father's house in Pass Christian after Katrina.

Most of the items housed inside the locker were damaged to some degree from the storm: Family pictures in water damaged frames, his late mother's favorite blanket that kept her warm as she battled the cancer that eventually killed her, and many other items that Coop was able to gather from what was left of his childhood home.

Perhaps the least damaged items that Coop was able to rescue after the storm were he and his father's fishing gear, which had been in a tall plastic storage locker in the garage when Katrina wreaked its havoc.

Jeffrey had taught Cooper how to fish at an early age and he loved to tell people that his son had landed his first bass while he was still in diapers. The two would often sneak off to various fishing spots in and around Pass Christian, both freshwater and out on the Gulf of Mexico.

While Coop loved going after Black Tip shark in the Gulf, his favorite spots to fish with his dad were the small inland channels and lakes where they would go after largemouth bass and catfish. While landing a big one was always the goal, they both seemed to find the most joy in just spending time together.

Coop selected the two fishing rods that were in the best shape and also his father's tackle box, which was his father's before him. It was an old "Firestone Deluxe" metal tackle box that was greenish in color and had two trays inside it. Firestone, who had long been a giant in the automotive tire industry, made a brief foray into the world of fishing in the 1940's.

Inside the old box was an array of lures, hooks, weights, bobbers, and everything Coop would need to catch a fish with Cara. Some of the rigs were likely older than Coop and probably even his late father.

It's like a time capsule...

Coop took a deep whiff of the contents of the box before closing it.

Smells like home...

Coop flicked the switch to the storage locker light and rolled the door back down in place.

"It looks like you are ready to catch the fish!" Rahul said as Coop locked the storage unit door.

"Just don't let the fish know…" Coop laughed as he and Rahul placed the fishing gear into the trunk.

"I will take you home now?" Rahul asked.

"Yessir, I suppose I should sleep for a couple hours before I pick her up."

38

It was just after three in the morning as Cooper Madison made his way back towards the Westcott Hotel, yet Charlie Knox was still wide awake as usual less than 15 miles away at his home in Brook Park.

A full uninterrupted night of sleep was no longer an option since the accident thanks to the combination of pain and the drugs that were supposed to make the former go away.

Charlie used a morphine pump every night to help him fall asleep, but as strong as the narcotic pain reliever was it only lasted about 4 to 6 hours. This meant that Charlie would get about 5 hours of drug-induced sleep each night only to wake up no later than 3 AM feeling as if he should be ready to go for the day.

A common misconception is that paraplegics would not feel any pain below the waist. In reality, paralysis is caused by damage to the body's upper motor neurons that control the muscles that are no longer in use.

This pain, along with a lack of daily exercise required to fall into a deep sleep cycle tends to keep him up from the hours of 3 to 6 most nights, his only relief coming when he can activate his pain pump again and repeat the process.

Joanne Knox had tried to get her husband to understand that if he became more active he would sleep better. Last year, she had hired a personal trainer her son Johnny recommended to give Charlie extra exercise on top of his regular physical therapy sessions, only to watch Charlie refuse to participate. After three sessions of paying for modified exercise services that weren't even being attempted, she canceled.

Charlie's paralysis affected more than just his legs. His condition meant that Joanne's role at home changed from spouse to caregiver, and any resemblance of a romantic relationship seemed to have been left in that emergency room at the hospital. They had not slept in the same room since the accident, let alone the same bed, as Charlie needed to sleep in a hospital bed each night.

Eighteen months after the accident Joanne decided to surprise Charlie in his bedroom for their anniversary. Wearing lingerie that she had purchased from Victoria's Secret, she climbed into his bed and straddled him. For a moment all the pain disappeared as they kissed with a passion that had been absent for far too long.

Joanne, knowing that Charlie's condition would not let them consummate their anniversary in the traditional sense, seductively whispered in his ear what she wanted him to do to her instead.

This set Charlie off and the next thing Joanne knew was that she had been thrown off the bed and onto the hardwood floor.

"I GET IT… I'M HALF A MAN, GODDAMNIT!!" Charlie screamed. "ARE YOU HAPPY??"

"That wasn't what I meant, Charlie!" Joanne shrieked back through tears. "How do you think I FEEL? Do you think that you were the only victim of the accident Charlie? You won't even look at me anymore…"

"Get...the...hell...*out*…" Charlie said, his voice low yet emphatic.

Joanne, now standing, shook her head and slowly walked out of the room.

I will never try again. Ever…

The day after the rebuffed attempt at romance, Joanne hired a full-time nurse to sit with Charlie as she left for Las Vegas for three days. Alone. She had to get away, and she didn't even tell her children where she was, just that she needed a break.

For those three days, Joanne Knox did her best to check off Vegas from her bucket list. She barely gambled aside from a few penny slots, but she took in the sights, slept in each day, got drunk, danced at a club, and saw some amazing shows.

She even was hit on a few times by younger men, as Joanne had always appeared to be much younger than she was. She didn't accept any of their offers but relished in the fact that she was still desirable.

As so often is the case, Charlie reverted back to having an almost childlike affect towards his wife upon her return. He began to view her more and more as a nagging maternal figure and less as his wife. He would fight her every step of the way when it came to menial tasks like brushing his teeth, getting dressed, and even talking to his children on the phone.

As hard as it was for Joanne to see her husband retreat from their relationship, it was even harder on his children. Charlie had always been a source of strength and stability for his family. He worked hard to provide for them and was an affectionate and loving father.

While Joanne was more prone to mood swings as a parent, Charlie was steadfast - never too high, never too low. He rarely ever yelled at his kids, but when he did the world stopped.

Charlie's relationship with Cara was affected the most. Not to say that Jason, Christopher, and Johnny's relationships with their father weren't affected, but Charlie had always had a special bond with his "Tomboy Princess". He was her protector and wanted to remain in that role until the day he died. In Charlie's mind, the accident stripped him of that.

39

"So, tell me about your family," Coop asked Cara as he threw a cast in the glass-like water of Ranger Lake, a small pond located near the former Metro Parks Ranger Station in Strongsville.

When he asked the owner of the bait shop he stopped at earlier that morning for a good spot to catch some bass, this was one of a few ponds that the owner pointed out.

"What do you want to know?" Cara replied as she reeled her line back in for another cast.

"Everything…" Coop answered with a smirk.

"Well, I have 3 older brothers. Jason is the oldest. He's even older than *you...*" Cara joked.

"Really? That is old…"

"He was 16 when I was born. He's a homicide detective for the Cleveland Police Department. He has a wife, Erica, and a daughter named Gabrielle who is turning 6 on Monday. She calls me Auntie Carebear."

"Carebear?"

"It's what most of the people in my life have always called me, including my brothers."

"That's adorable… Carebear..."

"Eww, I will draw the line at you calling me the same thing that my dad does!"

"Okay… sorry, Carebear…"

"STOP!"

"No promises… what about the others?"

"I have two more older brothers."

"So you're the baby… Carebear?"

"You better watch it, Madison!"

"Okay… okay… What are their names?"

"Christopher is about the same age as you and is in the Navy. He just got back from a tour on an aircraft carrier in the Middle East. He's on leave until his next deployment."

"What does he do?"

"He works with computers or something… I'm not really sure what he does, but I do know that he's not allowed to talk about it much."

"Is he married?"

"Christopher?" Cara laughed. "No way. That would require him settling down. Let's just say he really enjoys his bachelorhood."

"What about your third brother?"

"His name is Johnny. We're 'Irish Twins'... he is a personal trainer and competes in drug-free bodybuilding competitions. He's a health nut to the point that it's annoying, but ever since my dad's accident it's like he is trying to prevent anything bad happening to him."

"What's your daddy's name?"

"My *daddy*? Yet, you make fun of my nickname?"

"Sorry, it's a Southern thing. What is your *dad's* name?"

"Charlie…"

"I'm sure that being in a wheelchair has been very hard on him," Coop said as he reeled his line in a bit.

"It's been hard on all of us, especially my mom, Joanne. She has pretty much become his main caregiver."

"Does she work?"

"She cleans part-time at the Ford Plant, but only three days a week on the nights that one of us can help out with Dad. I typically go on Mondays," Cara said as she threw her line out again.

"Does he need a lot of help?"

"Not so much anymore, but my mom likes someone to be at home with him just in case. My dad on the other hand… let's just say he hates having 'babysitters' as he calls us…"

"I'm sure that's tough for a man…"

"It is… some days are better than others, though. Especially when his granddaughter visits him."

"Gabrielle?"

"Yes, but she only lets us call her Gabby," Cara laughed. "Except for my dad. He always calls her Gabrielle and she never says a word. It's like it's their special bond or something. It's really sweet… it reminds me of how he used to be with me…"

"I'm sure he misses that just as much…"

"I'm not so sure about - HOLY CRAP I GOT A BITE!!" Cara screamed as she realized that her bobber had just disappeared under the surface of the water.

"Set the hook, girl!" Coop yelled as he quickly reeled in his line so he could help her if needed.

"Oh, it's set! He's a big one…" Cara grunted as she reeled faster, the bobber now appearing closer to the shore. About a foot behind the bobber a flash of silver appeared momentarily as the fish tried to shake the hook.

"You ain't kidding, girl! Look at that! Yeah, buddy!" Coop encouraged with the fervor of a father who wanted nothing more than for his child to just catch one fish and make the trip a memorable one.

"Come on fishy… come to mama!" Cara coaxed as she reeled the fish in close enough to shore so that Cooper was able to grab the line near the top of her now completely bent rod to prevent it from breaking.

"Look at that bad boy!" Coop exclaimed as he grabbed the largemouth bass by putting his giant thumb inside its lower lip and held it up for Cara to see. Even compared to his large hands, this fish was huge.

"Holy crap!" Cara yelled. "That's the biggest bass I've ever caught!"

"I'm guessing he's at least 6 pounds and almost a foot long. You go girl!"

"Bring it here! I want to hold it… I wish I brought a camera..."

"I have one on my cell phone. It's not the best but it'll do the trick."

Coop handed Cara the bass and pulled out his cell phone, which was a Motorola Razr Vc3 flip phone that featured a pretty good digital camera for 2006.

"Say cheese…" Coop said as Cara beamed next to her catch.

"Hold on, I have to kiss him now," Cara informed Coop.

"Kiss him?"

"When I was little my dad used to always make me give the fish I caught a kiss before throwing them back in the water so that I wouldn't be afraid of them."

"Well then, *don't get no ideas Mr. Bass...she's with me…*" Coop said as he mockingly shook a finger at the fish before Cara released the beast back into the wild.

"I didn't peg you for the jealous type…" Cara said as she playfully approached Coop.

"Did you see his lips? How can I compete with that?"

"Oh, forget about him, he's already gone…"

"Typical man…"

Cara planted a long kiss on Coop.

"Thank you," Cara whispered as she pulled away.

"No, thank *you...*" Coop chuckled.

"Seriously, though. Thank you for taking me fishing. I really missed it."

"You're more than welcome, especially if you thank me like that every time."

"Deal…"

"Just when I thought I couldn't love fishin' anymore..."

"Nothing…"

"Nothing…"

40

The sound of a camera shutter clicking repeatedly in the distance interrupted Cooper and Cara. Coop swung his body towards the area that he believed it to be coming from. As he did he caught sight of a man near the bushes that separated the pond from the turnpike.

As soon as the man realized he had been spotted he began to run towards the parking lot which was about a hundred yards away from both he and his subjects. He was a balding middle-aged man who was short and stocky.

"You have got to be kidding me…" Coop said as he started to run towards the photographer.

Goddamn paparazzi…

Cara stood frozen in place, unsure of what to make of the situation as she watched Coop sprint towards what appeared to a guy with a camera running for his life. She could see that the man's face was a strange mixture of terror and elation.

Before Coop could reach him, the man jumped into a small sedan and peeled out, kicking up gravel as he sped off.

"Asshole!" Coop screamed as he flipped the bird in the direction of the fleeing car.

Coop spun around and looked at Cara, his face red with anger and eyes to match. Cara remained in place, still unsure as to what had just transpired. Realizing that Cara was startled, Coop made his way back to her.

"I'm sorry… it's just this damn guy has been hounding me since I played in Chicago…"

"Is he paparazzi?"

"Unfortunately…"

"Who does he work for?"

"He's a freelance guy… his name is Gary Boardman, but I prefer to refer to him as 'Asshole'... He sells his pictures to the highest bidder…"

"Why would he want pictures of us fishing?" Cara asked, puzzled.

"Because the public can't stand not knowing what's going on in the lives of people who would rather they not, and I've done as good a job as anyone avoiding it since I moved to Cleveland."

"Oh…"

Coop was now face to face with Cara, and he gently grasped her elbows with his strong hands.

"Listen… I hate to say it but those pictures are probably going to end up online."

"Just because we are fishing together?"

"Fishing… getting coffee… running in the park… it doesn't matter to them. They're vultures and you're going to be the 'Mystery Girl' because they love that crap."

Cara's face displayed that this was all starting to sink in, and Coop decided to give her a way out.

"I will totally understand if you don't want this in your life. I can have my agent make a statement that we're just friends and if you never want to see me again it'll blow over soon and…"

"Is that what you want?" Cara interrupted.

"Absolutely *not*, but I also don't want to ruin your life."

"I think I can handle it…"

"I don't think you understand… There will be even more cameras now. They'll follow you around campus and at work… They'll start asking everybody that knows you questions, and some people will sell you out. They'll lie, Cara."

"You really know how to woo a girl, Cooper Madison…" Cara laughed, which made Coop pause.

"I just don't want to see you get hurt…" Coop replied.

Cara put her finger to his lips as if to silence him.

"Nothing…" she whispered.

He tried to speak again.

"Nothing…" she repeated.

Coop slowly moved her hand away from his face as he leaned in and kissed her gently on the lips. As he pulled her close to him, Cara put her cheek on his chest. She could feel his heartbeat through his shirt.

"You know, this is all your fault…" Coop whispered.

Cara took the bait.

"And how is that?"

"For the first time in months, I actually wanted to leave my apartment. If you weren't so damn cute we wouldn't be here right now."

"The feeling is mutual…" Cara smiled, her cheek feeling at home on his chest.

"Nothing..." Coop replied.

"Nothing…"

41

Coop threw the fishing gear in the back of the pickup truck that he was able to borrow that from Henry Wilson, the football player-turned-doorman at the Westcott Hotel.

Before Cara could open the passenger door, Coop opened it for her.

"Well, thank you, kind sir…"

Coop smiled as he thought of his conversation earlier that morning.

"What do you need my truck for?" Henry asked, curious as to why the reclusive Cooper Madison suddenly wanted to experience the freedom of the open road.

"I'm just fixin' to go fishin'…" Coop replied, coyly.

"Mmmmmhmmmm…"

"Yessir..."

"What's her name?" Henry asked, knowing that whenever a man has an abrupt shift in attitude that it was usually the result of a girl.

"Can't a guy borrow a truck and go fishing up North without all the questions? Down South, nobody would think twice about lending their truck to a guy who wants to fish!"

"Well too bad we ain't down South… here, just have her back before I get off work at three," Henry said as he handed Coop his keys.

"Thank you kindly, Henry. I'll be sure to fill it up with gas, too."

Coop gave Henry a pat on the shoulder and walked away before Henry added one more thought.

"And Coop… make sure you open the door for the lady. They like that…"

"What lady?" Coop winked and walked away.

"So, what else do you have planned for me today?" Cara asked as Coop climbed into the truck.

"Late lunch?" Coop countered.

"I was hoping you'd say that… I'm starving!"

"Do you mind if we pick something up and head back to my place? I have to get the truck back soon."

"Is this whole truck story just your way of getting me alone in your apartment again?"

"No, ma'am… but, now that you brought it up…"

"Typical guy…" Cara laughed.

"Only since I was born…"

"Well, don't get your hopes up… I have to be at my parent's house by five for dinner. We are having Gabby's birthday party."

"Sounds like fun… I bet she will be excited. What did you get her?"

"A Baby Alive doll. She's a doll that eats food and even soils her diaper…"

"Good Lord… they've thought of everything..."

"I can't wait to see her face when she opens it!"

"I'm sure she will love it, *Auntie Carebear…*"

"Stop!"

"I think it's adorable!"

"I just can't have you calling me Carebear… it's too weird…"

"Well, then I'm fixin' to come up with a new nickname for you."

"How about Bass Master?"

"I think Kevin Van Dam might take issue with that…"

"Is that Jean Claude's brother?"

"Very funny… he's like the Derek Jeter of bass fishing."

"Oh *that* Kevin VanDam… of course! Everybody knows him…"

"Nice recovery…" Coop said as he smiled at Cara, who was grinning proudly in the passenger seat. The windows of the truck were partially down, allowing just enough wind into the car to gently tussle the few locks of hair that had made their way out of Cara's ponytail.

Somehow, the rogue strands of hair made her even more attractive to Coop, especially since she didn't seem to notice or care that her hair wasn't perfect at all times. This was a true departure from the women Coop typically dated.

The pair stopped at a drive-thru just outside downtown Cleveland and picked up some fast food goodness. Coop was elated when Cara ordered a burger and fries, thankful that she did not balk at the idea of getting fast food.

She's so real…

It was just after two o'clock as they pulled into the parking garage at the Westcott Hotel.

"I should probably leave the windows cracked so his truck doesn't smell like fast food," Coop said as he parked in the employee section of the garage.

"Whose truck did you borrow, anyway?" Cara asked.

"From the doorman—"

"*Henry*?" Cara interrupted, "I love Henry! He's my favorite doorman in the city!"

The realization that Cara would obviously know the doorman since she delivered food to the hotel on a daily basis finally occurred to Coop.

"He's a good man…" Coop said.

"I never have to worry about locking my scooter up when Henry's out front, that's for sure. C'mon, let's go give him the keys back!"

Before Coop could protest, Cara snatched the keys from his hand and exited the truck. It was obvious to Coop that keeping his new lady friend a mystery around the Wescott Hotel was simply not going to happen.

Maybe I don't want to, anyway…

42

Cooper Madison chuckled to himself as he washed his hands after eating the greasy burger and fries lunch with Cara. The look on Henry's face when Cara gave him his keys back was priceless.

Never to be caught off guard for long, Henry quickly recovered and asked Cara if Coop had opened the door for her. He then shot Coop a look of approval.

At least I think it was approval...

"What's so funny?" Cara asked as she saddled up next to Coop at the sink.

Before he could answer, Coop's phone began to ring. It was his agent, Todd "T-Squared" Taylor.

This can't be good...

"Hello?" Coop said as he motioned to Cara that he would be quick. The last thing he wanted to do was talk shop with his agent when his time with Cara was limited.

"Who's the girl, Coop?"

"Come again?"

"Who's the girl that you're making out with next to a pond? And why am I finding out about her from the internet? I'm hurt, bro..."

That asshole already sold his pictures?

"Now's not a good time, T-Squared. I have company over," Coop did his best to let Todd know he couldn't have this conversation right now.

"Well, if it's the girl in the pictures make sure she knows that she's all over CMZ. They're calling it 'Coop's Catch' - pretty funny, actually…"

"Bye, Todd," Coop said as he abruptly ended the call. He thought he would've at least had a day before the pictures hit the internet.

"Is everything okay?" Cara asked as she dried her hands off next to the kitchen sink.

"It depends how you take the news that the pictures of us at the pond are already making the rounds on the internet…" Coop replied.

"Oh… that was fast…"

"Yeah…" Coop said as he studied Cara to see how she would react.

"What website are they on?" she asked.

"CMZ…"

"I want to see them…"

"Are you sure?"

Cara's look answered his question.

"I'll get my laptop," Coop said as he left the kitchen.

He made his way over to the kitchen table where Cara was now seated and handed her his laptop computer.

Cara immediately went to CMZ's website just as she had done thousands of times before. She loved reading up on celebrity gossip, but now she was about to see how it felt to be on the other end of things.

The lead story on the front page of the website jumped out at her.

"Coop's Catch"

Cooper Madison, former big league all-star turned recluse was spotted near a small fishing pond outside of Cleveland today with a mystery woman. Madison has rarely been seen in public since his abrupt retirement from baseball following the tragic death of his father during Hurricane Katrina.

An eyewitness commented that the two seemed very cozy with one another as is evident in the pictures in the gallery below. If anyone has any information on who this new mystery woman is, contact us at tips@CMZone.com.

Cara clicked on the picture of them kissing that accompanied the story on the front page of the website. It redirected her to a gallery of 11 more pictures of Cooper and her in various stages of their kiss and embrace. The last picture was of an angry Coop pointing toward the photographer.

Even though she had sunglasses on she knew that it was only a matter of time before somebody recognized her and submitted it to CMZ. She imagined her ex-boyfriend Kenny taking great pride in sending that email and offering to sell his story to the highest bidder.

If he does, I'll kill him... Oh my God, I'm feeling sick...

Just then she felt Coop's strong hand on her shoulder. She placed her hand over his and looked up behind her at the strapping southern gentleman.

You better be worth it, Cooper Madison...

"I should probably call my family and let them know what to expect… what *should* they expect, anyway?"

"It depends… to be honest. Once the gossip columnists find out who you are they will probably just try to call them and get some dirt. I'm not that big of a celebrity in the grand scheme of things, which is a good thing. If you were seen kissing Brad Pitt your family would have to move out of the country…"

The joke made Cara laugh, albeit nervously. She imagined reporters hiding in her parent's shrubs.

Then it hit her.

"Oh my god, Gabby's party… They're not going to show up tonight at my parent's house are they?" Cara asked as she abruptly stood up.

"I highly doubt it, but I don't want to lie and say I know for sure…"

"I'm sorry," Cara said as she put her head on Coop's chest. "I hope I'm not being a pain in your ass…"

"Please, if anyone should apologize it's me. I wish there was something I could do to help."

After a brief pause, Cara squeezed Coop tight and asked him to do the one thing that she could think of that would make any of this easier.

"Come with me tonight… to my parent's house."

Cara realized that her question had completely caught Coop off guard. She could tell that he was trying to find the right response.

Why did I ask that? Who invites a guy to meet her family after 24 hours?

Before he could answer, Cara rescued him.

"I'm sorry… I didn't mean to ask that. It's just when you said that you wished there was something you could do to help it was what popped into my head. I didn't mean it… I mean I would love for you to come over, but it would probably just make things more complicated… not to mention you probably think I'm a psycho now since I asked you to meet my parents so soo-"

"Whoa...whoa...whoa…" Coop interrupted. "Slow your roll, girl… Give me a little more credit than that! I don't think you're a psycho and I would love to meet your family. It's just that going out at all today was a huge step for me. I haven't been out of the apartment with anyone else, let alone on a date of any kind, since I've lived in Cleveland. I just don't know if I'm ready for tha—"

This time it was Cara's turn to interrupt as she placed her index finger over his lips.

"Nothing..." she said.

Coop acquiesced, realizing that she was letting him off the hook without any further explanation on his part.

"Nothing…" he replied.

"Listen… I'm going to head back to my dorm. My brother Jason is going to pick me up there before the party."

"Okay… I understand. Let me at least call down to the lobby and arrange a ride for you?"

Cara's first instinct was to reject his offer of a ride. She could just as easily hop on the RTA bus, after all. However, she could tell that he felt bad and wanted to help.

"That would be nice of you."

"It's the least I can do. Hold on - I'll call down."

He phoned the front desk and had Simon arrange for a cab to pick Cara up. They said it would be waiting for her in a few minutes.

Coop walked Cara to the elevator and pressed the button to call it to his floor.

"I want you to know that I had a really fun time today," Cara said as the elevator made its way up.

"Despite everything?" Coop asked.

"Yes…"

"I did too… I hope you have fun tonight," Coop said as he leaned in and kissed Cara softly on the lips.

The familiar sound of the Otis Birdcage elevator reaching its destination brought the kiss to an abrupt end.

"Call me later tonight?" Cara asked.

"Absolutely…"

43

As she waited for her oldest brother Jason to pick her up, Cara held the wrapped Baby Alive doll that she could not wait to give her niece Gabriella as she stood in the lobby of Viking Hall. It was all Gabby wanted for her birthday and Cara made it *very* clear to everyone else that they better not buy it for her.

In addition to the feeling of anticipation, Cara also could not shake the uneasy feeling she had ever since seeing the CMZ story. In an instant, the world that she had always felt she could blend in to changed.

I wonder if anyone is hiding in the bushes waiting to snap more photos?

Cara had already logged on to CMZ at least a dozen times in the short time she was back at Viking Hall. Apparently, her identity was still a mystery.

Maybe nobody I know even saw it?

Just then she saw her brother's car pull up to the front of the building where she was waiting. She put her head down and felt herself walking a little faster than she normally would to his car. It did not go unnoticed.

"You must really want to get to the party," he mused as she got in the car and gave him a hug.

"You have no idea…"

Jason gave her a quizzical look.

"Everything okay, Carebear?"

"Just one of those days I guess..."

Jason knew his baby sister well enough to know that she was lying through her teeth, but he also knew her well enough not to push the issue.

"I wish I could say that my day was anything other than boring. I swear I'm living the real-life version of that movie 'Groundhog Day' ever since I started working on this goddamn Edgewater case. Every day is a repeat of the day before..."

The Edgewater Park Murders had captivated the public's attention ever since the first body was found on the beach of the public park on Lake Erie in 2005. In the year since, two additional bodies have been found at Edgewater, and Jason had been assigned as lead detective on the case.

All three of the victims were young women who likely had illegally immigrated, and all had been strangled to death. The last two victims also appeared to have been mutilated by a knife or some other sharp object. Jason was concerned that the killer, known as the Edgewater Park Killer or EPK, was starting to become even more violent in his tactics.

"I've been reading a lot about that case. I'm not going to lie, it's cool to see my big bro's name in the newspaper. That's some scary stuff. What was that girl's name? Stoya something?"

"Fedorov. Stoya Fedorov. Ironically, her name means 'Gift from God', but this case certainly hasn't felt like that," Jason replied.

Only one of the victims, the first one, was ever positively identified. Stoya Fedorov had only recently immigrated, albeit illegally, to the United States prior to her demise. The only reason she had been identified was because she needed an emergency appendectomy and was rushed to MetroHealth for the surgery.

The autopsy showed that the victim recently had an appendectomy, and Jason had a hunch to see if MetroHealth had any record of his Jane Doe. Since Metro was a county hospital, and likely would've been the only local hospital that would've performed her surgery, it was worth a shot. County hospitals, like Metro, are publicly funded and will not turn patients away - even if they do not have insurance. Had she not had that operation and been entered into the system, there would've been no record of Stoya Fedorov on US soil.

"You'll solve it. I know you will," Cara said.

"I wish the public had as much faith in me as my little sister does…" Jason chuckled.

"Jason, I have to tell you something…" Cara suddenly stated.

"I *knew* something was up, Carebear. Talk to me…" Jason replied.

For the remainder of the drive, Cara proceeded to fill her eldest brother in on the events of the past few days. She told him everything.

After Jason got past the initial shock that his sister was dating arguably the past decade's best pitcher in baseball, he turned his attention to the matter of the paparazzi.

"What's this photographers name?" Jason asked, already imagining different ways he would like to arrest him for harassing his baby sister.

"His name is Gary Boardman," Cara responded. "Maybe we can get a restraining order against him?"

"That won't happen, unfortunately," Jason responded. "He didn't break any laws by being at the lake where you were fishing. Unless he crosses the line, there's nothing you can really do from a legal standpoint."

"Well that's just shitty," Cara said.

"What I *can* do is run a background check on him and see if he has any outstanding warrants or even unpaid parking tickets. If he does, it'll give me a reason to have him picked up and we can lean on him a little bit. Make sure he knows to tread lightly. Unfortunately, there are so many of them out there. Even if he gets thrown in jail, there'll be more to take his place. These guys are like cockroaches," Jason added.

"Well, it's still shitty…" Cara reiterated.

"I hope this Cooper guy is worth it. Not gonna lie, I'm concerned. I dealt with a lot of professional athletes over the years when I was a patrolman and most of them are assholes."

"He is… worth it I mean. I can't explain it, but I just know deep down that he is."

Jason looked at his baby sister and nodded.

He better be...

"Listen, do you want me to go in first and kind of fill everyone in on all of this so you don't have to?" Jason asked as he pulled into the driveway of their childhood home.

"Do you think that's necessary?" Cara replied.

"You *did* grow up with our family, right? Do you really want to have to explain what's going on to everyone and answer questions all night?" Jason asked with a chuckle.

"Touché," Cara responded, thankful that her big brother was willing to act as her pseudo public relations agent. Besides, this was Gabby's night.

"Okay, give me a few minutes. Everyone else should be here by now. I'll fill them in and threaten to arrest anyone who asks you questions about it."

"*Arrest* them? You're such a dork, Jason, but thanks. It means a lot," Cara said sincerely.

"Guilty as charged… I'll come and get you when the coast is clear."

44

Jason must have done a really good job explaining Cara's situation to everyone at the party because the only people who remotely brought it up were her brothers Christopher and Johnny. They both wanted to make sure that she knew they'd kill Cooper Madison if he ever mistreated her.

Gabriella absolutely loved her Baby Alive doll, and made sure everybody at the party witnessed it "pooping". What really made her day was seeing her father smile when Gabby hopped up on his lap when it was time to blow out the candles on her cake. She had not seen him smile like that in months.

Just as Cara's mom Joanne was wrapping up pieces of leftover birthday cake for the guests to take with them came a knock at the front door.

"I'll get it!" Gabby said as she bounded across the room.

Nobody paid much attention to it until they heard her rapid-fire questioning the visitor like only a six-year-old can.

"Who are *you*? It's my birthday. Do you want cake? Is that for *me*? Thanks!"

Gabby came bounding back into the kitchen holding what appeared to be a very large and professionally wrapped present.

"Cara someone is here to see you and he gave me a *big* present!"

Cara made her way to the front door and locked eyes with Cooper Madison as he stood just inside.

"I hope y'all don't mind me showing up unannounced, and all, but I should've said yes when you asked me. I wanted to say yes, and I don't know why I didn't. I apologize."

"You don't have to apologize for anything, I shouldn't have even asked you. It wasn't fair of me."

"Well, I sure am glad that you did."

"Me too..."

"Come on inside. We have plenty of cake and ice cream."

"Did you tell them?" Coop asked.

"Jason took care of that for me, thank God. How'd you get here, anyway?"

"I called for a car. Rahul's outside."

"Awe, we should invite him inside."

"He will just decline. Company policy won't let him leave the car unattended. Besides, I think he likes the peace and quiet. The guy *does* have five kids at home…"

"I can't even imagine…"

Gabby's shrieks of joy interrupted the conversation.

Cara immediately looked at Coop.

"What on earth did you get her?"

"Well, I can't take all the credit. Simon actually went and picked it up for me."

"That explains the perfect wrapping paper."

"That obvious, huh?"

Gabby ran up to the couple and screamed, "Thank you so much! This is the best birthday ever!"

Cara shot Coop a look.

"I just had Simon pick out a few things for her new Baby Alive doll."

Cara glanced down at the box that Gabby had just dragged into the family room. Inside was what appeared to be every Baby Alive accessory ever made.

"A few things, huh?" Cara laughed.

"I mean, what's the point of having the doll if you don't have the right accessories, right?"

"Well, you didn't have to do that. But, I'm impressed… and I'm pretty sure that you've at least won Gabby over."

"What about you? Have I won you over yet?"

"So far…"

"Mission accomplished, then..."

"Come on in and meet everyone. I will warn you that all three of my brothers will likely threaten your life if you hurt me. Just play along, although Jason does carry a gun…"

"How comforting…"

Cara led Coop into the kitchen and dining room area, where most of the guests had congregated.

All eyes were on them as Cara introduced her guest.

"Everybody, this is Cooper. Be gentle with him. I kinda like this one…"

Coop wasn't sure if she was joking or being serious.

"Hope y'all don't mind me crashing Miss Gabby's party."

"Nonsense… welcome to our home," Joanne replied, "Would you like some cake and ice cream?"

"Yes, ma'am… that'd be great."

"Well aren't you a true southern gentleman," Joanne countered as she handed him a plate of cake and vanilla ice cream.

"Is that a Mississippi accent I detect?" boomed the voice of Ed Delaney as he approached Coop and shook his hand. Ed had always attended Knox family functions, especially since the accident.

"Yessir… sure is…"

"I knew it! I was teetering between Alabama and Mississippi. I've been to both states quite a bit over the years for work and recognized that dialect. I wish everyone up here was as polite as you folks are down there."

"I do miss southern hospitality at times, but y'all are doing a great job so far tonight."

Everyone chuckled at that, and Cara went around the room and introduced him to everyone else in attendance.

"This is my oldest brother Jason and his wife Erica, my next oldest brother Christopher, my Irish twin Johnny, and last, but not least, my dad, Charlie."

"It's very nice to meet y'all," Coop said as he went around and shook hands with everyone.

When he got to Charlie, he made sure to look him in the eyes when he shook his hand.

"It's a pleasure to meet you, Mr. Knox."

Charlie looked up at Coop from his wheelchair and squeezed his hand firmly.

"Please, just call me Charlie. I'm not much for formalities."

"Yessir..."

"Give me a hand, Cooper. I'd like you to help me outside. Need some fresh air. There's a ramp right through the patio door," Charlie said as he gestured towards the back patio door that was attached to the kitchen.

"Sure thing, Mist... I mean Charlie."

Cara knew full well what was going on. Not only did her father not need anyone's help to go outside, he typically abhorred it. She also knew that her dad needed to do this, more for his sake than hers.

As Coop pushed Charlie down the three-tiered ramp towards the detached garage, he noticed the old basketball hoop that was hanging over the garage door and driveway. It was one of the old white and orange crescent-shaped hoops that were popular in the 80's when Charlie installed it for Jason. It no longer had a net on it, but you could tell that it had been used quite often during its time perched above the garage. There was also the faint remnants of what was once a painted free throw line.

"Listen, Cooper. I know that when you look at me you probably see a weak and feeble man, because, well, I am. But, I'm also Cara's father, and like any father, I want to protect my baby."

"Yessir, absolutely-"

"Let me finish, son..."

"Yessir, I'm sorry, go on..."

"Even if I wasn't in this goddamned wheelchair, I know that it wouldn't make much of a difference. You're a damn giant, so I'm not going to threaten you with physical harm if you hurt her. Instead, I'm just going to ask you what the hell you're doing with her in the first place?"

"I would never hurt your daughter, Charlie. As far as what I'm doing with her, well, I sure hope that you would know that by now sir... If you don't mind me saying."

"Come again, son?"

"Well sir, I've only known your daughter for a couple days and I already know what an amazing young woman she is. She isn't afraid to challenge me, and she's the first girl I've met since I was a kid who didn't seem to give a damn that I used to be a pro baseball player. She didn't even know who the hell I was when she met me. I've never met anyone quite like her. I haven't had much of a social life for months. Hell, I rarely even leave my apartment. Then comes along this delivery girl who seems to make me *want* to be outside those walls if it means I get to see her. So, I guess to answer your question, I'll just say that I can't possibly tell you anything that you don't already know..."

Charlie looked up at the young man standing in front of him, and kind of chuckled. That chuckle soon turned into a full out belly laugh.

Cara, watching from inside the patio door, couldn't believe her eyes. She had not seen her father laugh like that in ages.

What the hell did he say to Dad?

"I have to give it to you, Cooper. That was *some* answer, young man. You sure talk a lot for a guy that has been living like a recluse, you know," Charlie laughed.

"I wouldn't call myself a recluse. I just needed to hit the pause button on life for a bit, I suppose."

"I can empathize, but I'm not gonna lie, Cooper – I have some reservations about your intentions with my daughter. From the sound of it, she's going to be the one making the major adjustments, not you. You're used to that life… She's used to blending in, and to be honest, I've always found some comfort in that. Life is complicated enough as it is…"

"Likewise, I'm not going to lie and tell you that I know exactly where any of this is going, either. What I can tell you is that I can't think of anything I want to do other than find out just that."

"Fair enough… Just make me one promise."

"Yessir?"

"Even though she likes to present herself as this tough and independent young woman, it's just a front. At the end of the day, she's as vulnerable as any of us. Don't ever forget that…"

"I won't…"

"Then you have my blessing… for now."

45

"So, are you going to tell me what the hell it was that you said to my dad to make him laugh like that?" Cara asked as Rahul drove the couple away from her house.

"Were you spying on me, Cara Knox?" Coop replied, incredulously.

"Um, yeah, of course I was spying on you!"

"I honestly just answered his questions… nothing more."

"How did you do that?"

"Do what?"

"Disarm him so quickly. I've never seen my father let his guard down that fast."

"I guess it was my southern charm…"

"You're not going to tell me are you?"

"Nope…"

"Well then… you suck…"

"Wow… is this our first fight? How cute!"

"Very funny, Cooper Madison…"

"Listen, sometimes it's best to take what was a wonderful moment and leave it that way."

"Ugh… did you get that off of a fortune cookie?"

"You are a feisty one tonight, aren't you?"

Cara feigned an angry face at Coop, but when she looked into his eyes she couldn't help but give in to the facial muscles that she was fighting to keep from smiling.

"Thank you…" she said.

"For what?"

"For coming tonight, it means a lot, even if you won't tell me what you said to my father..."

"You're welcome… I'm just sorry that I didn't take you up on it when you asked."

"Well, you certainly made up for it."

The two leaned in towards each other and passionately kissed each other as if the world around them no longer existed.

Rahul, who saw the embrace occur in his rearview mirror, waited until there was a break in the action to ask where it was he should take them.

"Mr. Madison, shall I drop you off at the Wescott?"

"Yes, both of us, and it will be the final stop of the night," Cara answered before Coop could.

"Of course, Miss Knox," Rahul confirmed.

"Are you sure?" Coop asked Cara.

"Positive."

"I just don't want you to think-"

Cara pressed her index finger against his lips.

"Nothing…"

Coop smiled and relented.

"Nothing..."

46

"Good morning… or should I say afternoon?" Cooper Madison asked as the athletic form of Cara Knox entered the kitchen where he was making a late breakfast. She was wearing one of his old heather gray "Property of Chicago Cubs" t-shirts, which was so big on her frame that it easily covered the fact that was just about all that she was wearing.

"What time is it?" she asked as he handed her a mug of coffee.

"Just past noon, perfect time for Sunday brunch…"

Coop set down two plates of scrambled eggs and toast on the kitchen table and pulled out a chair for Cara.

"Look at you... coffee, breakfast, *and* you pulled the chair out for me? I must've done something right last night..."

"I'd say so…" Coop replied as he leaned in and gave her a soft kiss on her cheek as she was seated.

"You weren't so bad yourself, you know…" Cara responded before taking a sip of her coffee.

"Thanks… I think?" Coop chuckled as he sat down at the table.

"I'm sorry, I'm not good at this part…"

"It's okay, I was just 'gettin your goat'…"

"I'm assuming that means teasing?"

"Yes, ma'am…"

"I'm going to need a translator, I think…"

"Don't worry, you'll catch on."

Cara stared at Coop for a moment as she struggled to find the right words.

"Listen, there are so many things I want to tell you about how amazing last night was… I'm just not very good at expressing my feelings like that."

Coop smiled and nodded.

"You don't have to say anything, Cara."

"I know… it's just that I'm still processing all of this. Everything's happening so quickly…"

"I feel the same way, trust me. In the past few days, I've gone from barely leaving my apartment to a family birthday party for a girl I just met."

Cara looked down at her plate, slowly moving the scrambled eggs around with her fork. Coop reached across the table and firmly grasped her hand.

"I just want to you to know, Cara Knox, that if given the option I would do it all over again. I just hope you feel the same way."

Cara looked up, revealing a single teardrop making its way down the right side of her face.

"I do…" she managed to reply.

Coop wiped away the tear from her cheek with the back of his long and thick fingers, which still showed signs of wear and tear from his pitching days.

Before Cara could respond, Coop's cell phone sprang to life from its place on the kitchen counter. Coop hopped up to answer it and made a face of annoyance when he saw the caller ID.

"T-Squared… to what do I owe the pleasure on this fine Sunday…"

"Have you seen CMZ?" the voice of Todd "T-Squared" Taylor barked on the other end.

"No sir, not since yesterday…" Coop replied as he signaled to Cara that he was going to step outside the kitchen to continue the call. He went out onto the balcony and closed the door behind him.

"They found out who she is. Turns out her ex-boyfriend is a fan of CMZ and he has already sold his story."

"How bad is it?" Coop asked, already knowing the answer.

"Well, I don't think that Miss Knox is going to like the way her ex has portrayed her. Of course, I don't think any of my exes would paint a pretty picture of me, either…"

"What did he say?"

"Standard ex-boyfriend stuff, but he also eluded to some unflattering accusations about her sex life, without actually saying anything…"

"She doesn't deserve this…"

"Nobody deserves this type of crap, Coop, but it is what it is. If you really like this girl, you better start getting ahead of these things. Do an interview with-"

"An interview? We just started dating!" Coop interrupted.

"No shit, Coop, but the longer you wait, the more chances everybody else in her life has to write the narrative."

"She's going to hate me…"

"She'll get over it. Just show her those big beautiful eyes…"

"Screw you, T…" Coop managed to laugh. Todd always had a way of getting him to relax.

"Listen, I'm going to set you up with one of my clients at ESPN, Shane Aspen. He's been dying to do a piece on Cooper Madison. Everybody has. We will give him an exclusive and he can work Cara into the piece. He's on our side, so it won't be a hatchet job and I'll get a final say before they broadcast it."

"So, what, they're gonna come here? This is exactly why I came here to begin with, T…"

"Well, if you really care about this girl it's the best way to handle your side of things, and also you can let people know that you're still alive…"

"Let me holler back at you after I talk to Cara."

"I'll be waiting…"

Coop pressed "END" on the phone and walked back into the apartment. As he approached the kitchen table he could see Cara staring at his laptop.

Oh, boy…

As he made his way around and sat down next to her, he could see that her tanned face was red with anger and humiliation.

"He is such a lying scumbag… how could he do this to me?" Cara said, shaking. Tears were welling up in her eyes.

"Cara...I..."

"I knew when you walked out that something obviously happened. I had to see for myself…" she interrupted. Coop took the cue and just let her go. He'd been there before, many times, and it never gets any easier to see someone write things about you that aren't true.

"He basically called me a slut…" Cara said as she stood up abruptly and pointed at the computer screen.

Coop tried to grab her hand, but she pulled back and started yelling at him instead of the screen.

"I am *not* a SLUT! In fact, I'm the furthest thing from a slut! I've had sex with *two* people in my life. TWO! Then he said that I'm just after your money!"

Cara wasn't finished.

"I am going to *kill* him. I am going to go over to his place and I am going to beat the freaking crap out of him..."

Coop stood up and wrapped his arms around her in a bear hug, and Cara began to weep. He felt her body start to go limp and he eased both of their bodies to the kitchen floor and held her as she cried.

"How could he…" she said over and over as she wept.

"It's going to be okay…" Coop whispered as he held her.

"How can you even say that?"

"Unfortunately, I've had a lot of experience…"

"Everyone is going to think I'm a gold-digging whore…"

"Not everyone, but some will, and that's just the way it is. What matters is how those who really know you feel about you, and I think you already know the answer to that."

"Oh my god… my family is going to read this… if they already haven't…"

"They probably have, and they certainly will. People will make sure they do. It's human nature."

"What should I do? Should I call them?"

"Only if you think it will make *you* feel better. If not, then don't. You need to focus on what's going to make *you* feel best at this moment."

"Slashing Kenny's tires would be a start…"

"That would just add fuel to the fire."

"I know, but it would feel great…"

"My agent thinks that I should do an interview with ESPN."

"ESPN? About *me*?"

"Not exactly… they've been after me to do an exclusive interview for months. A lot of people have questions for me since I left Mizz-ippy…"

"Why *did* you leave?"

"A lot of reasons, I suppose. Mostly, I just felt like my life there washed away with the storm. Even though we were doing good things and making progress, I couldn't escape the empty feeling knowing that what I lost could never be salvaged or rebuilt."

"It didn't help that the press wouldn't leave you alone, I'm sure."

"No, it certainly did not. I felt like they were trying to take this tragedy and turn it into a hero piece about me. That was the last thing I wanted. I just wanted to blend in."

"I can relate…"

"Just another thing we have in common, I suppose…" Coop chuckled.

"Do you want to do the interview?"

"No, but it's the best way to set people straight about you, and me, and a lot of things. It'll give *us* a chance to tell the story."

"Then let's do it," Cara said.

"You sure?"

"Positive. But, it has to be today."

"Today?"

"Yes, today. If they want it bad enough they'll make it happen."

"Why today?"

"Because if I don't get to say what I want to say, today, then I'll lose my mind."

"Well then, I'll call Todd…"

47

"So, I understand that there's a new woman in your life. Can we meet her?" Shane Aspen asked as the camera panned away revealing Cara Knox seated next to Coop on the couch, holding his hand.

In a matter of five hours, Todd "T-Squared" Taylor arranged for his young ESPN anchor client to arrive in Cleveland with a camera crew for *the* exclusive interview of his young career.

The first few minutes of the interview revolved strictly around Coop, his move to Cleveland, and whether or not he would return to baseball for the last stretch of the season with the Cubs. Coop ruled the latter out, for now.

Shane Aspen had been with the Worldwide Leader in Sports for almost five years, mostly as a reporter and fill-in anchor. The network wanted to send one of their veteran reporters out for the story, but Todd Taylor was calling the shots today, and *his* guy was about to get his big break.

"Yes, I certainly do, Shane. This is Cara Knox, and she's a native Clevelander," Coop said, just as he had rehearsed in his head multiple times.

"Cara, it's a pleasure to meet you. I understand that you and Coop met in an unusual way. Would you like to share?" Shane prompted.

"Uh… yeah, you can say that it was definitely not how I ever anticipated meeting a guy…" Cara responded.

"Not to mention a famous athlete," Shane interjected.

"Well, in reality, I had no idea who he was. I'm not a big baseball fan and I actually had to look him up on the internet," Cara laughed, looking at Coop.

"It was a bit of a blow to the old ego, Shane," Coop chuckled.

"Are you serious? No clue?" Shane said incredulously.

"None. Zero. If I didn't know his name from the order slip, I wouldn't have even known what name to look up."

"Okay, let's backtrack here a second. What order slip?" Shane led Cara, just as they had discussed he would.

"Well, in addition to attending Cleveland State University I also work for a restaurant called Stucky's Place as a delivery driver. Earlier last week this guy ordered some food and I delivered it to him."

"And you really had *no* idea who he was?"

"Nope. I just thought he was some kind of an eccentric rich guy living in a penthouse."

"Why did you think that?"

"Well, because he never opened the door for me to see him…"

"Coop, is this true?"

"Sadly, yes… since I've moved to Cleveland, I've really tried to keep a low profile. I've had a rough year, to be honest, and I was really just trying to escape, well everything… you know, to regroup I guess."

"So, Cara, if he never opened the door, how'd you two meet?"

"Well, he ordered from Stucky's again on Friday," Cara answered.

"The food must be really good at Stucky's, Coop!"

"It really is, Shane. You need to stop there whenever you're in town," Coop replied, making good on his promise to Cara that he'd throw Stucky a bone.

"So did you open the door for her this time, Coop?" Shane asked.

Coop replayed the scene from Friday where he slipped and fell while running to get the door when Cara arrived with his order. Cara interjected her point of view and Shane made sure to throw in little quips and questions to help tie the whole thing together.

The couple then relayed their versions of Friday night and Saturday: Coop's seafood boil, the car ride around town, the ill-fated fishing trip on Saturday, and even Gabby's party.

"So, in reality, this relationship is only a few days old, but it certainly sounds like it has been a whirlwind few days at that," Shane continued, "I say that only because of what happened after the CMZ story originally broke."

Next, Shane referenced the original CMZ story and subsequent follow-up article that her ex-boyfriend Kenny had peddled. Shane did his best to discredit Kenny as a jealous ex looking for his fifteen minutes of fame and even provided Cara with a chance to speak about the betrayal she felt from him.

"I really feel bad for Kenny, despite the fact he did this," Cara said. "He's obviously struggling with the reality that he's been in college longer than most doctors, failed as a college basketball player, and has let partying get the best of him. That's why I broke up with him a long, long time ago. I worry about his health and safety, Shane. He has a lot of issues, and I find it sad and pathetic that he decided to take those issues out on me."

"It certainly seems to be that way, and I can only imagine that it's taken a toll on you," Shane agreed.

"I feel something awful about it, to be honest," Coop said.

"How so?" Shane asked.

"Well, because, she didn't ask for any of this attention, and since she met me she's had her entire life opened up for examination. It's new for me in a way, too. I've always seemed to date other people who were either already in the public eye, or at least desperately trying to be. I've never had to worry about protecting someone from it, and I feel like I failed her right from the start."

"For the record, I do *not* feel that way," Cara said, looking straight at Coop.

"I don't know how you don't," Coop replied, looking into her eyes. The two seemed to forget that they were being interviewed. Shane, sensing this, wisely nodded to his crew to keep rolling.

"Because I'm the one who insisted on you leaving your comfort zone, and for whatever reason you did. Because, I wanted to go fishing… A girl you just met. You threw away months of carefully planned solitude and privacy just to take me *fishing…*"

Cara's last sentence was barely audible as her eyes began to well up.

"The only thing you made me do was realize I *wanted* to take you anywhere you wanted to go. I didn't feel like I was throwing anything away," Coop responded.

"I just feel like I've complicated what was a blissfully uncomplicated existence for you," Cara replied as a tear made its way down her cheek.

"I don't think you realize yet just how much I want to know you, all of you, even if it's complicated…"

The two kissed, their lips slowly pressed together as Coop's hand gently lifted Cara's chin up.

Shane Aspen waited a few seconds and then signaled for the crew to cut and that snapped the couple out of their trance.

"Oh my God, I'm sorry…" Cara immediately turned red and felt embarrassed.

"Please, don't be," Shane responded. "You two have no idea how amazing that was. If I hadn't already gone over the entire interview with you beforehand I would've assumed you had scripted that last part. But, you can't script that stuff. That was raw emotion. I have a feeling that I just interviewed America's newest sweethearts. Listen, we have some exterior shots to get and then we will send Todd the final edit by tomorrow morning for approval. The network is planning on airing this tomorrow night in a primetime special during SportsCenter."

"America's *newest sweethearts*?" Cara asked, sounding like the words were poison in her mouth.

"Yeah… that's not what we were going for, Shane…" Coop agreed.

"Listen, even if we cut that last part out, America is going to eat you two up. You guys are like a living, breathing Julia Roberts movie. Unfortunately, while it might not be what you *want*, it's what you're gonna *get*. Might as well embrace it. Life could be worse," Shane replied.

48

"I love you, too, Sweetie. Thanks for letting us know. Make sure you get some sleep and I'll see you tomorrow night. Bye…"

Joanne Knox hung up after her rare, albeit long, phone conversation with her daughter. Cara told her all about Kenny's CMZ article, the ESPN interview, and that she was staying at Cooper Madison's place that night because she didn't feel comfortable being at Viking Hall.

Cara had also made one request of her mother.

"The ESPN interview is going to air tomorrow night at six. I know you're supposed to work and it's my night with dad, but I really was hoping you might be able to switch shifts with Clarice and stay home. I'll bring dinner and maybe we can all watch together?" Cara had asked.

"I'm sure I can get Clarice to trade me shifts, and even if she can't I will make sure I'm there to watch with you."

"Thanks, Mom..."

It had been a long time since Joanne's independent and stubborn daughter had made her feel needed. While it wasn't under the best circumstances, she still found herself cherishing the moment.

"Will Cooper be joining you?"

"As long as you guys are okay with it..."

"Of course we are. He seems like a really sweet guy, not to mention he's *gorgeous*, Cara. And that southern charm…"

"Mom, staahhpp," Cara urged.

"I'm just telling you that as far as I'm concerned, he seems like he'd be worth the trouble…"

"Okay, you're grossing me out now, Mom…"

"Oh Cara, you're too easy to rile up…"

"He is, though… at least I think he is…"

"Worth it?"

"Yeah… I can't explain it…"

"Then *don't*, Cara. Just take it for what it is and enjoy the fact that you seem to have found something that's inexplicable. One thing I've learned in this life is that everything doesn't have to make sense to be good."

"Perfectly imperfect, right?" Cara said, referring to her father's favorite quote.

Joanne glanced over at her husband as Cara said the words that he had uttered so many times before. He was sitting in his wheelchair watching a rerun of Bonanza. She would give anything to hear him say those words again.

"Should I invite your brothers over?"

"I'd rather not… this will be uncomfortable enough as it is."

Charlie's voice brought Joanne's replay of the conversation to an abrupt end.

"Are you going to tell me what my daughter said, or just stand there with that dumb look on your face?"

Joanne's eyes narrowed.

"She called to ask why her father is such an asshole to her mother…"

"BS… she already knows the answer to that."

"She wanted to let us know that she's going to be on TV tomorrow night and asked if I'd switch shifts with Clarice and watch it with her. She and Cooper are going to bring dinner."

"TV? What for?" Charlie asked, dropping the sarcastic tone for once.

Joanne told him about Kenny's interview with CMZ and how ESPN wanted to do an exclusive interview with Cooper.

"*Kenny* did that?"

"Apparently he got paid a lot of money, too."

"I'll kill him… I never liked that kid."

"I think that Cara can handle herself, Charlie. If I know our daughter, Kenny is going to wish he never said a word."

"Maybe we did something right, I suppose."

"We did a lot of things right, Charlie. You just don't seem to want to remember them."

Charlie didn't respond, instead, he wheeled himself into his bedroom, effectively ending the conversation.

Joanne followed, but not to continue the talk. Instead, she would help him get into his bed, with the assistance of the hydraulic lift that was part of his bedroom set-up. It kind of resembled a hammock and would lift Charlie onto his bed. Joanne just had to help him get into the hammock from his wheelchair.

If anyone ever wondered if Joanne still loved Charlie, they would only need to see this nightly ritual to know the answer. She did it without fail or complaint, no matter what had transpired throughout the day leading up to it. There were times that Charlie was so awful to her throughout the day that she had to summon all of her good intentions to complete the task.

But, as was this case on this night, she always did.

49

Tonight on SportsCenter at six o'clock, Cooper Madison sits down with ESPN's Shane Aspen in his first televised interview since abruptly leaving baseball last year. Make sure to tune in and hear about where he's been since dropping out of the public eye and if he is planning on making a comeback this season.

The sound of the television echoed through into the kitchen where Cooper Madison and Cara Knox were enjoying a Monday morning cup of coffee together. Cara studied Coop as he seemed un-phased by what was on the television.

"Do you ever get used to hearing your name on national TV?" Cara asked.

Coop smirked and silently chuckled before responding.

"I suppose it's like anything else in life. The more it happens the less of an impact it has on you."

"I don't think I would ever get used to it…"

"You'd be surprised. I'm sure there are things about your life that used to be a big deal to you and now they're not."

"I suppose… but none of those things are broadcast to millions of people, either."

Coop relented, but then brought up the subject of the interview.

"Are you nervous about tonight?"

"It's all I can think about," Cara admitted.

"Whenever I'm nervous about something I can't really control I think about something my daddy used to say…"

"Which was?" Cara asked.

"It's never as good as you think it's gonna be, but it's also never as bad, either."

"Those are some wise words…"

"He was a wise man…"

Cara let his words hang for a moment before changing the subject.

"I told my parents that we'd be there around five and that we'd bring dinner."

"Sounds like a plan. I'll arrange for a car to take us. Where do you want to get food from?"

"I was thinking we could get Chinese? My parents love Chinese food. Do you like it?"

"I love it… especially that General guy's chicken."

"You mean General Tso?" Cara asked, referring to the popular deep-fried chicken dish named after a Hunan general, who ironically had nothing to do with its origin.

"Yeah, he's my favorite Chinese general…" Coop deadpanned assertively, seeming very proud of himself before continuing on in a very authoritative voice.

"I believe he conquered the Moo Goo Gai Pan River Valley and later on defeated the enemy at the Battle of Lo Mein…"

"Wow," Cara said in fake awe. " You are such a wealth of knowledge. Have you ever considered going on Jeopardy?"

"I actually was a few years ago… it was 'Dumb Jock Week'. All of the questions were True or False, and they gave us crayons to write our 'Final Jeopardy' answers. I came in fourth place…"

"Aren't there only three contestants?" Cara took the bait.

"Yeah, but I was so bad that they gave me fourth..."

Cara laughed and stood up out of her chair at the kitchen table. She had on another one of Coop's old t-shirts and a pair of his mesh shorts which were rolled at the waist numerous times so that they'd fit.

She pulled Coop's chair away from the table and swung his legs towards where she was standing and straddled him.

"Well, they must not have had the right categories for you to answer," Cara said as she leaned closer to his face.

"And what categories would those have been?" Coop said, playing along.

"Well, I'd say that last night you swept the board in anatomy..." Cara whispered, referring to the previous night's activities. Her lips gently making contact with his ears as she spoke.

Just then Cara's cell phone, which had been charging on the kitchen counter, sprang to life. The ringtone was sound clip of Eric Cartman saying, "God I hate you, Kenny," from the television show *South Park.*

Coop gave Cara a quizzical look as she hopped up and ran over to the phone and pressed ignore on her phone.

"You have *got* to be kidding me!"

"Why didn't you answer it?" Coop asked.

"Because I don't *ever* want to talk to that asshole again," Cara replied in an irritated tone.

"So, I'm assuming the ringtone wasn't a coincidence and that was Kenny?"

"Yeah... I'm sorry, I should've changed it a long time ago. I really should just block his number."

"You have nothing to apologize for. Besides, I love *South Park.*"

"I used to... but now just hearing the name Kenny makes me sick."

"I can relate. I can't watch the Miss America pageant anymore for the same reason..."

Cara gave him a look that said, "*No you didn't...*"

"Okay, bad analogy... I'm sorry. I'll just shut up now," Coop declared, his hands up in surrender.

"Why *did* you break off your engagement with the beauty queen?" Cara asked.

"I didn't... *she* did, not long after she moved out to LA hoping to make it as an actress. I guess she didn't need me to boost her public image anymore. To be honest, I was glad. She was so high maintenance, but I didn't realize just how much until we were done."

"Oh... well, it was her loss."

A notification buzzed on Cara's phone indicating that she had a new voicemail. She sighed as she pressed play and raised her phone to her ear.

"*Cara... it's Kenny... I know you're probably ignoring my call on purpose, but, uh, I was hoping we could talk. Give me a call...bye.*"

Cara shook her head in disgust as she put the phone back on the counter.

"What'd he want?" Coop asked.

"He wants me to call him. He knows I'm mad and I'm sure he's worried what I might say about him. I wish I could see the stupid look on his face when the interview airs tonight."

"Are you going to call him back?"

"Hell. No."

"Do you want me to call him for you?"

"Definitely not. He's not worth our cell phone minutes. Besides, I can handle Kenny, and the best thing to do is ignore him because he hates that the most."

Coop nodded in agreement before adding, "Well, I'll respect your wishes this time, but I can't promise I'll be able to if he keeps calling."

Cara made her way back over to Coop's lap.

"I have a feeling Kenny won't be an issue after tonight, but even if he is, he's *my* issue to deal with. Not yours…" she said as her face came within inches of his.

"I just want to protect you…" Coop replied.

"And they say chivalry is dead…"

"Not where I come from..."

In one motion Coop stood up and lifted Cara, as well, and carried her down the hall towards his bedroom.

50

"I'm worried about you, Cara. This is so much happening at once and there's no way that you could possibly prepare for everything that is coming your way," Joanne Knox told her only daughter as they packed up the leftover Chinese food in the kitchen. Coop was with Charlie, who fell asleep shortly after the interview was over, in the family room.

The ESPN special featuring Cooper Madison and his new mystery woman had just aired an hour earlier and the brevity of the situation was starting to scare Joanne. Seeing her daughter on TV made Joanne regret her words from the day before when she had encouraged Cara to throw caution to the wind and embrace her new relationship.

"Well, I guess it's a good thing that it's *my* decision to make, right?" Cara responded, as if she had anticipated this conversation.

"That may be true, but it's also *my* job as your mother to look out for your best interests - no matter how old you are."

"Is that what you're doing, Mom? Because I feel like maybe there's another motive."

"Oh for Chrissakes, Cara, not this again…" Joanne threw her hands up and walked a few steps across the kitchen.

"Oh, yes, *Mother*, this again…" Cara said as she walked towards Joanne and maneuvered herself so she was face to face with her mom.

"Cara, you're being ridiculous."

"You just cannot *stand* to see me happy, can you? Just because your life didn't go the way you'd hoped. Well, guess what? Neither did mine. We all lost the man that Dad used to be, but I will be goddamned if I live my life in fear of being hurt..."

"This isn't about your father, Cara! This is about *you*!" Joanne screamed, shaking.

In the other room, Cooper Madison immediately looked over at Charlie Knox who appeared to still be sleeping in his wheelchair across the room.

Thank God he's asleep... he didn't need to hear that.

In the kitchen, both Cara and Joanne came to the realization that they had probably just crossed multiple lines with each other, not to mention the fact that Cooper and Charlie probably heard them yelling.

"I'm sorry, Carebear…" Joanne said as she began to cry.

"No, I'm sorry, Mom. I didn't mean what I said."

"Yes you did, and that's okay Cara... Not to mention, it's probably true to an extent..."

The two embraced as each shed tears.

"Do you think your father heard what I said?" Joanne whispered.

"I'm sure Coop did, but hopefully Dad is still asleep."

"Just promise me one thing, Cara."

"What's that?"

"You'll finish college. On time. We've all sacrificed a lot for this, and it would destroy your father if you didn't."

"I will. On time…"

The two hugged once more and decided to start assessing the amount of damage control that would be needed in the family room. Both were relieved to see Charlie still asleep in his wheelchair, but Coop was nowhere to be seen. Cara immediately felt her stomach drop.

Oh God, he ran away...

Just then Coop came through the front door.

"Sorry, y'all… I had a phone call and I didn't want to wake Mr. Knox. Is everything alright?" Coop seized the opportunity to escape what could've been an awkward situation when his phone rang. Even though he had heard Joanne, he didn't want to add to her stress by getting involved. This way, he could pretend that he was outside the whole time.

Joanne and Cara looked at each other.

"No, everything is great," Joanne said. "We just didn't hear you leave and were worried."

"Sorry, ma'am… Actually, it was your son, Jason, who called. He wants me to join him, Christopher, and Johnny for golf tomorrow since it's his day off…"

"Do you golf?" Cara asked. "Because my brothers will say that they're good, but they actually are just good at drinking beers and smoking cigars while they play."

"Well then, I'll fit right in… we are meeting tomorrow morning."

"Won't that be nice, and you can go while Cara goes to class," Joanne said as she glanced over at Cara.

Coop picked up on the intent of Joanne's comment and did his best to quell her fears about Cara.

"She better go to class! She's so close to that degree, after all."

Joanne smiled and nodded in approval.

"Well, thanks for the pep talk, you two. I was planning on going to class. Believe it or not, I want to graduate," Cara said as she gathered her things, signaling to Coop that it was time to leave.

"Thanks again for the hospitality, Miz Knox, and please let Mr. Knox know the same."

"Bye…" Cara said as she walked out the door, Coop following. A Town Car awaited outside.

"Anytime, kids… Be safe!" Joanne yelled after them.

A few feet away from her Charlie Knox pretended to wake up as the door closed. He had heard everything, and like Coop, decided to avoid the awkwardness of addressing the situation.

I like this kid…

51

Cara Knox closed the door to her dorm room at Viking Hall and exhaled. She never thought that she'd view this place as a sanctuary, but recent events have deemed it to become one of the few places that still seem "normal" to her.

Coop's driver had just dropped her off from his Town Car at the rear entrance to the building. Earlier, Cara explained to Coop that she needed some normalcy and wanted to stay in her dorm room and go to class the next day like a regular student.

"Besides, you have a big day tomorrow on the golf course. You better rest up," Cara had said after breaking the news that he'd be alone tonight.

"You're right. To be honest, I'm kinda sick of you anyways," Coop chided.

Cara chuckled as she thought of the exchange, and how even though she wanted normalcy for the evening she already felt herself missing him.

A sudden knock on the door interrupted her train of thought. It had been a long time since anyone had knocked at her door.

Maybe it's Coop?

Cara opened the door and immediately recognized the smiling face outside her door. Unfortunately, it wasn't Cooper Madison's. It was a sophomore from her Statistics class named Brittany, whose last name had escaped Cara.

What does she want?

"Hi… Brittany, right?" Cara asked.

"Hi, Cara!" Brittany replied as if she didn't even hear Cara's question.

I'll take that as a yes...

"What's up? Do you need help with stats?" Cara asked.

"Oh, no, I was just seeing if you wanted to hang out?"

"Oh… umm… to be honest I am really tired and was planning on getting to bed early. It's been a long day…"

"Okay! Well, maybe tomorrow?" Brittany replied.

"Maybe…" Cara said as she closed the door, hoping that Brittany would take the hint.

Well, that was weird...

It didn't take Cara long to come to the realization that Brittany's visit was no coincidence. After all, Cara had barely spoken to the spunky sophomore in class.

She obviously watched the interview...

A moment later another knock came at the door. Cara, assuming that it was Brittany again, swung the door open without checking first.

As soon as she opened the door a bright flash momentarily blinded her. Once she could see clearly again, Cara noticed a college-aged female running down the hall and out the nearest exit door. She didn't recognize the girl. Regardless, she hoped that it was just a curious college kid and not a professional who snuck in to get a shot of Cara in her dorm room.

I'm going to have to be more careful opening the door...

Cara decided to hang a makeshift "Do Not Disturb" sign on her door and after that got ready for bed. She was emotionally and physically drained, and it didn't take long for her to fall asleep.

That sleep, however, was interrupted by the ringing of her dormitory phone just before midnight.

Who the hell is calling me now?

"Hello?" Cara answered.

"Is this Cara?"

The female voice on the other end seemed distant as if it was on a speakerphone. Cara could hear giggling in the background, as well.

"Who is this?" Cara asked firmly.

"Does Cooper Madison have any rich friends?"

The voices on the other end of the line erupted in laughter.

"Grow up…" Cara said as she hung the phone up. She decided to pull the plug on her dorm phone and if anyone wanted to reach her they would have to call her cell.

The rest of the night was pretty quiet, with the exception of a few random knocks, followed by footsteps running away. Cara barely slept. She had a class in the morning followed by a shift at Stucky's in the afternoon.

Tomorrow is going to be a long day…

52

Thank God I have my own bathroom...

One of the other benefits of being one of the only seniors to reside on campus at Viking Hall was the fact that the single occupancy rooms for upperclassmen on the 5th floor also had their own bathrooms. In light of recent events, Cara was very thankful to be able to shower in the privacy of her own room.

After getting ready, Cara sent her old roommate Mallory Perriman a text asking if she'd walk with her to her morning class. Mallory also had a class in the same building at that time, and Cara had not talked to her since the night of the fire alarm.

Cara was confident that she could trust Mallory. They each had a lot of blackmail stories from their freshman year of college, and Mallory had always been a good friend. In fact, she was one of Cara's best friends.

Cara didn't have a big circle of friends in college, which she preferred. Mallory was second only to Cara's best friend from high school, Lucy Eckert, who was just returning from a year abroad in Spain.

Mallory responded that she would meet her at her door in a few minutes. Cara instantly felt better about going to class. She needed someone with her that she could trust.

"Good morning Sunshine! You look like shit..." Mallory said a few minutes later when Cara opened the door.

Cara could always count on Mallory to be brutally honest, and she loved that about her.

"Thanks, Mal, I slept like shit, too…"

As they began their walk to class Cara told her about the late night visitors and phone call.

"I didn't even realize that you were at the dorm. I figured you were shacking up with Mr. Baseball. You should've slept in my room. We could've snuck you up there," Mallory responded.

"Hindsight is 20/20… sorry I didn't tell you before about the interview," Cara said.

"Girl, you don't need to apologize to me. If I was in your shoes I would've already dropped out and moved into his place like a squatter!"

"You're crazy, Mal! Besides, I promised my parents that I would graduate on time. It hasn't even been a week for crying out loud! Why is everyone so worried that I'm going to throw my life away for a guy I just started dating?"

"Because he's FAMOUS! And RICH! Not to mention, HOT! Most girls would marry him TO-DAY without even knowing him on that alone."

"Well, not this girl…"

"Yeah, but you're totally in love already. I can tell…"

"I think it's too early to use the word 'love', don't you?"

"I don't, actually. I think that you can fall in love with someone the moment you get to know them. But, maybe that's just all the Renee Zellweger movies talking…"

"The ESPN guy said that we are like a real-life Julia Roberts movie…"

"See! I know what I'm talking about!"

As the two coeds made their way towards the math building for class, they were startled by the sounds of a camera shutter coming from behind the tall bushes outside the building. He came out from behind the bushes and kept snapping away as he approached the girls.

"What the hell?" Mallory said as she saw a bald, heavy-set man approaching her with a camera.

It was Gary Boardman, but this time Coop wasn't there to chase him away.

"Who's your friend, Cara? What's your name honey? You're about to be famous, might as well give me your name."

"Leave us alone!" Cara said as she grabbed Mallory by the elbow and began running towards the math building.

Apparently, Gary got what he needed because he didn't follow them any further and took off in the other direction.

"Who the *hell* was *that*?" Mallory asked Cara once they were inside.

"He's the paparazzi photographer who took the pictures of us at the lake. His name is Gary Boardman, and he's a freaking scumbag."

"Wait, so we are going to be on CMZ now?"

"Probably… I'm sorry, Mal."

"Don't be… I just wish I would've actually washed my hair…" Mallory said as she chuckled.

"I'll understand if you don't want to walk back with me after your class."

"Are you kidding me? This is the most excitement I've had in college since that toga party we got kicked out of our freshman year!"

"You're the best, Mal. Thank you…"

Cara gave Mallory a hug and they each went their separate ways to their respective classrooms.

Cara entered her Statistics class, which was located in a small lecture-style classroom and had about 40 students in it, most of whom were already in their seats and talking. There was definitely a noticeable buzz in the room. Typically, most college students were barely awake this early, and *never* this talkative.

As soon as the other students realized Cara had entered the room a hush came over the class. She felt all of them staring at her, and for many of them, it was likely the first time they even knew who she was.

This is really going to be a long day...

Cara smiled and took her usual seat towards the front of the room. She always liked to be in the front of the class, mostly so she could get out of the room quickly.

"Go Cubs!"

A voice from the back of the classroom yelled out. Cara decided not to even acknowledge it, but wasn't sure if that was a good idea or not.

Might make things worse...

Whatever talking that was still going on came to a stop as Cara's professor entered the room.

Dr. Howard Curry was straight out of central casting for what a collegiate math professor should look like. He was in his late 50's, balding, wore glasses, and had a long beard that showed more grey than his natural auburn colored hair.

Dr. Curry was also the head of the math department, was known to be very strict, and also one of the few professors who employed an unforgiving attendance policy. If you missed more than three classes, for any reason, you failed. There were rumors that he even made a student who already had three absences attend class before he could go to his own mother's funeral.

Dr. Curry greeted the class as usual and announced that he had finished grading their last exam as he began passing them out to the students.

When Cara received her exam, she noticed that below her grade of a 96% A was a handwritten note saying, "*See me after class...*"

What else could go wrong today...

The minutes ticked by like hours until her class came to an end. Cara stayed in her seat a few extra minutes as her classmates exited before she stood up and approached her professor.

"Dr. Curry... you wanted to see me?"

"Ah yes, Miss Knox... listen, I just want you to know that I saw your interview last night on ESPN. You see, I'm originally from Chicago and I am a *huge* Cubs fan. So, I just had to tune in and see what Cooper Madison was up to. Then I saw my very own student sitting next to him. I almost spit my evening cocktail out!"

He let his words hang for a moment. Cara, unsure of whether or not he was expecting a response decided just to nod and smile.

Silence can't be misconstrued...

"I just want you to know that I'm *not* a monster. I know the stories that are passed down about me each year. My favorite might be the one about making the kid miss his mom's funeral or something like that. In fact, the reason that I don't put them to rest is that it does keep the attendance rate very high in my class..."

Dr. Curry paused before continuing.

"I guess what I am trying to convey is that I know that your life is probably very hectic right now, and if you need to miss class from time to time I promise that it won't affect your grade. You are an excellent student and have always been very punctual and polite. Therefore, if you do feel overwhelmed and need a break, I will fully understand."

"Oh, okay, well... thank you very much, Dr. Curry. I really appreciate that, but hopefully it won't be needed," Cara politely replied.

"He was the best, you know..." Dr. Curry replied. "Such a shame what happened to his father, not to mention to him."

"I agree..." Cara wasn't sure what else to say.

"Well, I won't keep you any longer. Good day, Miss Knox."

"See you tomorrow, Dr. Curry."

53

"What's up Pretty Woman?" Mallory asked as she greeted Cara outside of her classroom.

"Pretty Woman? Very funny, Mal, but not even a Julia Roberts movie could possibly have some of the weirdness I just had."

"I saw you talking to Dr. Death after class. What was that all about?"

"Apparently Dr. Curry is a huge Cubs fan…"

"Really? I can't even picture him enjoying anything other than leather-bound books and math problems. So I'm assuming he saw the interview?"

"Bingo…"

"Does he want an autograph or something?"

"No, it was really odd, though. He told me that I don't have to worry about his attendance policy if I need a break."

"You're joking, right? Didn't he make a kid miss his own mother's funeral before?"

"Actually, he just told me that never happened…"

"What?!"

"He said that he's not a monster and that he knows all about the rumors."

"Okay, you're right. This is beyond a Julia movie. I might have to start calling you M. Night Shyamalan because you are blowing my mind…"

Cara's cell phone began to ring as she and Mallory were about to leave the math building and head back to Viking Hall.

"Hold on, Mal, it's Stucky. Let me take this before we try to leave."

"Okay…"

"Hey Stuck, what's up?" Cara asked her boss.

"Cara! I'm glad I got ahold of you. We are absolutely slammed here. I think every person that saw the ESPN interview is ordering from our restaurant today! We can't keep up!"

"Do you need me to come in early? I'm just heading back from class."

"That's actually why I'm calling. I don't want you to come in, actually. I already covered your shifts."

"I don't understand? I really don't mind and kind of need the money."

"Don't worry about the money. Consider it a paid vacation. Don't worry about us, we will be fine here."

"Stuck… while I appreciate it, is there a reason you don't want me to come in?"

"Well, to be honest, Cara, most of the people calling in are specifically requesting that *you* deliver their food. I'm not going to lie, it's kind of creeping me out. There's a lot of nuts out there and I don't want to put you in that position."

"Oh… I see…"

Cara felt her stomach sink. She hadn't even thought about how all of this was going to affect her job at Stucky's.

"Listen, I want you to take the rest of this week off until things die down a bit. Give me a call on Sunday and we will figure out the next step. I'll have your paycheck ready to go and even include what you would typically make in tips."

"I… don't know what to say, Stuck… I appreciate it. I'm glad that you are getting something good out of all this, at least."

"Are you kidding me? This is GREAT! We've already made more money at breakfast than we typically make the entire day!"

"That's great Stuck… I'm happy for you."

"Alright, gotta run! Enjoy your paid vacation!"

"I'll try…"

Cara pressed END on her phone and looked at Mallory, who was able to make out the gist of her conversation.

"Did you just get a paid vacation?" Mallory asked.

"Apparently…"

"Well, it's official…"

"What is?"

"I'm now completely and utterly jealous of your life!"

"Oh my God… STOP!" Cara laughed as she gave Mallory a playful push.

"Do you see any creepy bald guys with cameras out there?" Mallory asked as she peeked out the glass doors.

"No, but that doesn't mean anything. They're like overweight ninjas."

"Well then, let's just go for it."

Mallory pushed the door open and confidently began to walk outside with Cara following.

Thank God for Mallory…

54

About 20 miles west of Cleveland State University, Cooper Madison was getting ready to attempt a ten-foot putt on the 18th green at Red Tail Country Club.

Once Coop received the invite to golf with the Knox brothers he called Simon and had him pull some strings to get them a tee time at the private golf club located in Avon, Ohio.

Cara's brothers were beyond grateful to be treated to such an exclusive course, as it was a far cry from the public "tracks" that they typically frequented. Jason especially was happy, as he had always dreamed of being a member there someday. He also knew that would likely never happen on a detective's salary.

"When did you say the last time you played was?" Christopher asked as Coop sank his ten-foot putt with ease.

"It's been at least a year. I had to get my clubs out of storage this morning."

"Maybe that's our problem. We just need to take a year off and maybe we will be flirting with par, too!" Johnny laughed as Coop retrieved his ball from the bottom of the cup.

"What's it like, Coop?" Jason asked.

"How do you mean?" Coop replied, puzzled.

"What is it like to be naturally good at everything you do?"

"You've never seen me try to dance…" Coop chuckled.

"Oh, I'm sure you'd probably win 'Dancing with the Stars' if you were on there," Christopher chimed in.

"No sir… two left feet on a dance floor. Besides, I declined when they asked."

"The crazy part is that I know you're not joking. Let's grab a hot dog and beers at the clubhouse. On me, fellas," Jason said as they got in their golf carts.

"Sounds like a plan," Coop agreed.

"Well, since you're buying…" Christopher replied.

"I'll even make an exception and put that garbage in the temple," Johnny added. "I haven't had any processed meats for months. That shit will kill you, ya know…"

"So will my Glock if you bring that up again and ruin my meal!" Jason admonished his youngest brother.

"Last one there has to buy the second round of beers!" Christopher said as he sped off first with Johnny.

"Sombitch…" Coop said as he hit the gas and tried to catch them with Jason riding shotgun next to him.

"He's obviously the cheapskate of our family," Jason said to Coop.

"It's all good. That's a life skill…"

"It certainly is..."

"Y'all are lucky, you know that?" Coop said to Jason.

"Lucky? *Us*? How so?"

"You have two brothers and a sister. I was an only child, and I always wished that I had a brother to get in trouble with."

"It's nice now that they're all grown up, that's for sure. There was such an age gap when Christopher was born that I never really felt like I had any partners in crime as a kid."

"Which one of y'all was Cara closest to growing up?"

"Early on I'd say it was me, for sure. I was so much older than her that it wasn't your typical sibling relationship. Besides, she was like a chick magnet for me when she was a baby."

"That's awesome! Was she close with the other two?"

"Not really, she and Johnny were too close in age and Christopher was never really keen on having a little sister. That's probably why Cara has always kept such a small circle of friends."

"Makes sense, I suppose," Coop agreed as they pulled their cart in just behind Christopher and Johnny at the clubhouse.

"Second place is first loser!" Johnny said as they got out of the cart.

"Good thing you guys are buying, I don't think I could afford tap water at this place!" Christopher added as the foursome made their way into the clubhouse.

55

"Did you have a good time golfing today?" Cara asked as she spoke to Coop on the phone.

"Sure did. We had a blast!" Coop replied from the back of his Town Car as it made its way towards the Westcott Hotel from Avon.

"Did you win?"

"We were all winners today, Cara…"

"Jesus, you're not one of those douchebags, are you?"

"Ouch… I'm just playing with you. I played a little better than your brothers, but that's not saying much. Kind of like beating a one-legged man in an ass-kicking contest…"

"I warned you!"

"To make things better, your brother Johnny offered to be my personal trainer should I want to get back to baseball. I didn't have the heart to tell him that the ball club employs those guys already."

"Awe, you're a softie…"

"I really like your brother Jason, by the way. And he loves you to death. I shared a cart with him."

"I'm glad to hear that. At least one of us is having a good day…"

"Uh-oh… what happened?"

Cara told Coop about her evening of interruptions, the weird experience at class, her paid vacation, and also how Gary Boardman jumped out at her and Mallory.

"Well then, I guess that would make for an eventful day. I'm sorry, Cara."

"I've just been hiding out in my dorm room all day. Thankfully, the walk back to the dorm was uneventful."

"Why don't you come stay with me for a bit? At least until things die down."

"Do you really think that they'll ever die down?"

"Yes ma'am, I do. They always do. They'll find a new target to harass soon enough."

"I guess I could pack a bag for a couple nights…"

"Make it quick, I'm five minutes away from you. We can pick you up out back."

"Oh, wow… okay… let me get my stuff together."

"Hey, Cara…"

"Yes, Coop?"

"I really missed you."

"I missed you, too. A lot..."

"See you in a few…"

"Bye…"

Cara pressed END on her cell phone and took a deep breath. She only had a few minutes to pack up her things and meet Coop outside. She was surprised as to how excited she felt as she packed her bag. She certainly had never felt this way about seeing Kenny.

Cara gave her bag the once-over and made sure that she had everything she needed for the next few days and exited her dorm room. She couldn't wait to see Coop and feel the safety of his apartment at the Westcott.

56

While Cara was climbing into the back of Cooper Madison's Town Car at Cleveland State University, her oldest brother found himself sitting in the lobby of the Chief of Police just a few miles away at Cleveland's Police Downtown Headquarters.

Detective Jason Knox, of the 1st District division of the department on the city's west side, knew that something was up when he was summoned to the downtown headquarters. He ended up leaving straight from the golf course and headed downtown.

I hope they don't smell the beer... It is my day off, though...

"The Chief will see you now," said the Chief's secretary.

Jason nodded and made his way into the Chief's office, where he had never been before.

"Detective Knox, please have a seat. Sorry to bother you on your day off, but we have a pressing matter to discuss."

Chief Horace Johnston, affectionately called "HoJo" by family and friends, was a tall, slender man in his early 50's. He had been appointed to the highest position in the department just three months earlier, and in those three months, HoJo made sweeping changes to the department structure. Most of which had received mixed reviews. The media absolutely loved him, though, and he certainly seemed to love them back.

HoJo was always good for a quotable soundbyte, and he was one of the first people in his position to use social media as a means to promote all the great things that his department was doing.

While the media and the public loved him, his own officers were not as sure that he had their best interests at heart. Most officers seemed to think that he only cared about his public image rather than what was best for the department.

There were also rumors floating around the department that he used his position to pressure officers to drop charges against some powerful people. The charges were nothing major - mostly DUI and drug possession charges against wealthy businessmen. Apparently, one was a domestic violence charge against a local anchorman, too. If those rumors were true, however, it would not sit well with the police union.

As Jason took his seat he wondered what pressing matter the Chief was referring to. He glanced around the office and noticed that the walls were filled with pictures of Chief Johnston and local businessmen, politicians, athletes, and celebrities.

"I'll get straight to the point, Detective Knox. One of my sources inside the local media tipped me off that they have discovered you are the brother of Cooper Madison's new girlfriend."

"Okay... Is that a problem, Chief?" Jason replied, perplexed.

"Not yet, but it certainly could become one, especially since you're the lead detective on the Edgewater murders. You are going to be under an even bigger microscope, which means the department will be, too. It goes without saying that we really need you to make some progress on that case, and fast."

"With all due respect, Chief, we have been working nonstop on this case…"

"Nonstop?" Chief Johnston interrupted. "You mean like when you were golfing today?"

"It was my day *off*, sir. I've been putting in six days and over 60 hours a week."

"There are NO DAYS OFF when you are working the biggest case in Cleveland, Detective!" Chief Johnston boomed as he pounded his fist on his desk.

Jason, unsure of whether to respond, just stared back at his boss.

"I'm sorry, Detective," Chief Johnston continued in a much softer and controlled voice. "I should not have yelled at you. I just want you to understand that everything you do is going to be magnified. If the press sees you golfing instead of trying to catch a possible serial killer, you and the department are going to look bad."

Jason knew that no matter how he felt, or what he truly wanted to say in return, that there was only one response the Chief wanted.

"I understand, Chief. I will make sure to choose better going forward."

"Good, that's what I wanted to hear. I'd hate to have to take you off this case, son. This is the type of case that can make or break your career."

"I won't let you down, sir."

"Do you want some advice?"

"Always, sir."

"You need to make an arrest. Soon..."

"An arrest? We don't even have any suspects, sir."

"Then *find* one."

"You want me to *create* a suspect, sir?"

"I never said that. However, if you arrest a suspect, legitimate or not, it will show the public that we are making progress. Not to mention the press..."

"I don't think I can do that, sir. I can't just arrest some innocent guy and possibly ruin his reputation. What would I even charge him with if I don't have any evidence?"

"You leave that part to me, thanks to the Patriot Act we have all sorts of options. Just get me a suspect by the end of the week. Real or not…"

"Yessir, I will try my best."

"You better. Now get out of here, and it goes without saying that our discussion today shall remain between us."

"Absolutely, sir."

Jason felt dirty as he exited the Chief's office. The thought of arresting an innocent person just to make the department look good made him sick to his stomach.

I need to find a real suspect…

He called his wife, Erica, as he walked towards the parking garage.

"Hey babe, I'm not going to be home until later tonight. The Chief needs me to follow some new leads on the case."

Jason felt awful lying to his wife, but the less she knew the better.

"But it's your only day off this week!" Erica replied, upset that she would be giving up her one night of being a "normal" family this week.

"I know, babe, but when the Chief personally tells you to do something, you just do it..."

"I know… it just sucks…" a dejected Erica replied.

"Can you put Gabby on the phone?" Jason asked.

"I would, but she's next door playing with friends. Call back before bedtime and I'll put her on."

"Okay… love you…"

"Love you, too."

As Jason pulled out of the parking garage he couldn't stop replaying the meeting with Chief Johnston in his head.

Did he really just ask me to do that?

Jason made a decision as his car made its way towards his Edgewater Park that he would find HoJo a suspect. It was going to be a legitimate one, too, and he wouldn't stop working until he found one.

57

Cooper Madison told Cara that he needed to step outside and make a phone call on his balcony. She was curled up on his bed ready to take a nap in an effort to make up her lack of sleep from the night before.

"Okay, if I'm asleep when you get back in, don't wake me up…"

"I won't. Get some rest…"

Just a couple hours earlier, Cara had told Coop all about her day of harassment from classmates and photographers. He knew that he needed to do something to help protect her, so he decided to call the one person that he knew could help.

"Jason, it's Cuppah, sorry to bother you but I need your help with something. It's in regards to Cara."

"Cara? What's wrong?" Jason asked, startled.

"Nothing's wrong, she's fine, but I need your help to keep it that way."

"How so?"

Coop went on to explain what Cara had experienced since the interview aired, and that he wanted to hire some people to watch over her.

"Like a bodyguard?" Jason said.

"I suppose. Maybe not someone standing by her side at all times, but more like a guardian angel. Close by and watching out for her in the event she needs it."

"Well, I know a few retired cops who might want the job and also have a female officer in mind who might be a good fit. Are you talking 24-hour protection? Or just during the day?"

"I was thinking morning til evening."

"Okay, that should make it easier. We can go with two shifts. 7 to 3 and 3 to 11. The going rate for side jobs is typically $30 an hour, but it might be more for something this heavy."

"I'll pay $50 an hour. Cash. Just get me two very good and trustworthy people."

"Hey, this is my baby sister we are talking about here. I'm going to handle it."

"I know, I apologize. I just am worried about her."

"You and me both, bro. I'll let you know once I get a couple good people. One guy I know has a security firm now."

"Sounds good."

"Listen, I just pulled into Edgewater Park and I need to ask a few people some questions, so I have to let you go."

"Any luck on the case?"

"Luck? Not exactly. Hopefully, luck will find me, though."

"Understood. Talk to you soon."

Coop ended the call and walked back into the apartment. He went to check on Cara in his bedroom and she was out like a light. As he made his way back to the family room his phone rang. It was his agent, Todd "T-Squared" Taylor.

"How's my favorite agent doing today?" Coop answered.

"How great was that ESPN special? I told you that our boy Shane would do a great job! Lots of good buzz."

"He did do a good job, but why do I have a feeling that isn't the only reason you called?"

"Coop, I have some interesting news for you…"

"Go on…"

"The Cubs want to make one last run at you before making a move."

"That's your interesting news?"

"No, the interesting news is what they are planning to do if you choose not to play."

"If, and it's a big if, I ever play again it won't be in Chicago. I just can't. It would be too hard."

"That's where this whole thing becomes interesting. You see, the Cubs know that you probably will never pitch in their uniform again, but they want to get something for you while they still can since they hold the rights to your contract."

"They want to trade me? But the deadline has passed."

"Yes, the *normal* trade deadline has passed, but you can still make a trade if the players involved clear waivers."

"Who would want to trade for me? They'd have to take on my contract and not to mention the risk that I will never play for them."

"The Cubs said that they have an American League team who is very interested, and they are willing to give up two top prospects in exchange for the rights to your contract, assuming you clear waivers…"

"Which team?"

"They won't say, yet, but I'm guessing it's New York, Cleveland, or Detroit. The Yankees have the money to take the risk, and Cleveland and Detroit have the prospects and are geographically the favorites."

"Do you think I would actually clear waivers?"

"I do, because if any other team outside of the one that they want to trade with claims you, the Cubs can simply rescind the request and keep you on their roster. Happens all the time. If the team that they *want* to do business with claims you, then they have two days to work out a deal."

"Well, you learn something new every day, I suppose."

"I gotta make some calls now, I'll be in touch. Say hi to Cara for me. Seems like a sweet girl!"

Coop hung up and stared blankly at the wall across the room. He had never considered pitching again this season, but he also didn't realize that he could be traded after the July 31st deadline.

Maybe Cleveland…

58

Cara felt the late afternoon sun on her face as it peeked through the partially opened blinds that adorned Cooper Madison's penthouse apartment bedroom windows.

What time is it?

"Hey there, sleepyhead," Coop's voice came from across the room where he was sitting in a cushioned reading chair.

"Oh my God, you scared the crap out of me!"

Cara sat up in the bed, startled by the realization that Coop had been sitting there as she slept.

"How long have you been sitting there?"

"Long enough to know that you're even prettier when you sleep."

"Thanks… I'm not sure if I should be flattered or creeped out…"

"Do you feel better now that you got some rest?"

"Yeah, I do… what time is it anyway?"

"Just past six."

"Oh wow, I was out for a few hours."

"That's a good thing. You obviously needed it."

"I think you're right."

"Are you hungry? I had Simon arrange for some salads to be delivered. They're in the fridge. I need to detox. I've been eating too much garbage."

"Same here… salad sounds awesome."

"Hey, I wanted to run something by you, too…"

"What's that?" Cara asked.

"I spoke to your brother Jason, and we both felt that you need some protection, especially when you're walking to class."

"Like a bodyguard? You're joking, right?"

"Not really a bodyguard, more like a guardian angel. You won't even know they're there until you need them. Jason agrees that this is the right call and he already found two great people."

"Oh, great, so I should feel better that not only are you making decisions as to what's best for me, but my brother is too? At what point do I have a say in this?"

"Cara, don't be like that…"

"Don't be like what? Upset that other people are trying to control my life? You know I've done pretty well for myself so far in life."

Coop stood up before taking a seat on the edge of the bed.

"I know you have, Cara, but you also haven't dealt with anything like this before. I have, and maybe, just maybe I know what's best in this regard."

"If you're trying to make this any better you're failing miserably…"

"It's okay to have people help you, you know."

"It's also okay to want to make decisions for yourself, Coop."

"Trust me, I get that. Just think it over, that's all we're asking."

"*We're*? See this is the part that is bothering me. You and my brother teaming up on me," Cara asserted.

"That's not what we're doing, Cara. Listen, let's just go eat our salads and we can talk more about it after you've had some time to process it."

59

"So, who are these 'Guardian Angels' that my brother found to protect me from the big bad world? And who's paying for them, anyway?" Cara asked as she ate her salad.

"Your brother said that one guy is a retired cop and he's one of the best men he knows. He apparently owns a small security firm. The other is a younger former officer, a female, who he thinks you'll really like. She works for the other guy full-time now. He said that they'll each work an 8-hour shift starting at seven each morning. They will be nearby if needed, but most people wouldn't even know that they're there. And don't worry about the cost."

"I guess it won't hurt to give it a shot…" Cara relented as she picked at her salad, starting to warm up to the idea. Even though she still didn't like the ambush tactics Coop and Jason were using, she also didn't want to constantly worry about people harassing her.

"That's all I'm asking… Just give it a chance. It will only be during the week, too. I wrote their names down. Clarence Walters and Grace Brooks. Clarence will work the early shift and Grace will be around in the afternoons and evenings," Coop said as he slipped Cara the small piece of paper that had their names on it.

"Where is this Clarence guy going to meet me tomorrow?" Cara asked.

"He's going to be waiting for you downstairs and will drop you off by the building where your class is and pick you up in the same spot after. Clarence will blend in and be nearby if needed."

"I'm not going to lie, as weird as all this is and as angry as I got earlier, I kinda like the thought of someone looking out for me. Especially if that bald creeper Gary shows up again."

"I couldn't agree more."

"I know I didn't react the way I should have, but thank you…" Cara said.

"You reacted the way you felt, and I'd rather deal with that than you acting the way you think I want you to."

"Well, regardless, I feel bad. I don't know what else to say…"

"Nothing…" Coop said as he winked at Cara.

"Nothing…" she replied with a smile.

"How's your salad? I took a gamble on the Chicken Caesar."

"I love it. Where's it from?"

"To be honest, I have no idea. I just told Simon what I wanted and he delivered, as always."

"Simon is great at what he does, especially when he knows that the person he's helping is wealthy," Cara chuckled.

"You telling me that he doesn't do all that stuff just because I'm a good person?" Coop said incredulously.

"Hate to break it to you…"

"Next thing you're going to tell me that leprechauns aren't real…"

"Oh, no, they're definitely real. Wait until your first Saint Patty's Day parade downtown. You'll see them everywhere."

"Well, thank heavens. I couldn't take any more hard truths from you."

Cara's cell phone, which had been set to vibrate while she napped, began to buzz from its spot on the kitchen counter. She stood up and grabbed the phone. When she saw who it was her face lit up.

"Oh my God! It's my best friend from high school, Lucy! I have to take this."

"By all means…"

Cara flipped her phone open as she stood by the counter.

"Hey, girl! Please tell me this means you're back in town?"

Cara walked out of the kitchen and towards the balcony where she remained for the rest of the phone call. Coop finished off his salad and took a seat in front of the television on his couch.

"Oh my God! I'm so excited! Lucy is back in town!" Cara said as she came back into the apartment.

"Where was she?" Coop asked.

"Spain. She did a year abroad at a university in Barcelona through Oberlin College, where she normally attends."

"Where's Oberlin? Never heard of it."

"It's a small liberal arts college about 40 minutes west of here. It's really an eclectic, liberal place, which makes it perfect for Lucy."

"Is she one of those tree-hugging hippies?" Coop asked, jokingly.

"Oh, nice… I wouldn't call her a hippie, but she's definitely a free spirit. Lucy is one of those people who will go wherever the wind takes her in life. She's a writer and an amazing one at that. She writes poetry and short stories. She's had her work published multiple times, even in Reader's Digest. She's so good that she is on full scholarship at Oberlin, which costs almost as much as an Ivy League school does."

"Wow… she sounds impressive. How'd y'all become friends?"

"We actually didn't know each other until freshman year at Berea. I came to Berea from Ford Middle School, which is near my house. Lucy went to Roehm Middle School with all the other Berea kids. Unfortunately for me, most of my friends from Ford went to the other high school in the district, Midpark. So, it was kinda like I was a new kid at school. Lucy happened to sit next to me at freshman orientation and she talked my freaking ear off. I had never been asked so many questions in such a short amount of time. We just kinda clicked and the rest is history."

"Sure sounds like it. I still talk to my best friend from high school about once a week, and we meet in Vegas once a year. Well, we used to at least…"

"Why don't you anymore?"

"He and his wife had a baby girl two years ago and then everything that happened with me over the past year just kinda put a halt to those plans. Maybe we will go again someday."

"What's his name?"

"Landry Sterling, but everyone calls him by his nickname, Cash."

"Cash Sterling? Money and silver, eh?" Cara joked.

"You got it, but it's actually because his dad loves Johnny Cash."

"How'd you two meet?"

"We grew up next door to each other. He was an only child, too, so we were the closest thing to brothers either of us had. We were in the same grade and played football and baseball together. He was a great fullback in football and our catcher in baseball. He played D2 football at Delta State. He's a teacher now in Jackson."

"Mississippi?"

"Yes, ma'am. He moved there after college. He also coaches football."

"What about his parents? Are they still in Pass Christian?"

"No, his family moved out of the Pass when he graduated from high school. They live in Florida now."

"I see. Well, Lucy wants to meet me for dinner and then go dancing tomorrow night. Do you mind if I go?"

"You don't need to ask me for permission to see your best friend…"

"I know, but I just wanted to make sure."

"I'll arrange for a car. Where should I have it take you?"

"She wants to take me out to eat at a restaurant called Lola. She said she has a gift card and it's supposed to be amazing. Lucy said that the Chef, Michael Symon, is a rising star."

"Sounds like a great time. I'll make sure that your guardian angel is aware, too."

"Lovely… would you mind if we went dancing after dinner? It's kinda always been our thing," Cara asked.

"I think it's too early for me to be giving you any sort of permission to do anything. I just want you to have fun and be safe."

"I know, but I guess the last relationship I was in kinda made me nervous about doing things on my own. Kenny always got jealous. He hated when I would go out with Lucy and would usually show up where we were to spy."

"Darn…" Coop answered.

"Come again?" Cara asked, puzzled.

"That's totally what I was going to do. Damn you, Kenny!"

Cara laughed and gave Coop a playful shove.

"You're such a douche!"

"That I am, but I would prefer if you called me KOD from now on."

"KOD?" Cara asked.

"King of the Douches…" Coop deadpanned.

"Was that what your teammates called you in Chicago?"

"Only because I made them…"

60

The next morning Cara was greeted in the lobby of the Westcott Hotel by Simon Craig and a rather large but fit African-American gentleman with a completely shaved head and dressed in a black suit with a black mock turtleneck under the blazer.

"Cara, darling, I'd like to introduce you to Mr. Clarence Walters. He will be driving you to your classes today per Mr. Madison's request," Simon said in the most professional way, which was a side of him that Cara still wasn't used to witnessing.

"Miss Knox, it's a pleasure to meet you. I've known your brother Jason ever since he joined the force. I consider him one of my best friends, and a damn good detective," Clarence said as he extended his brawny hand to greet her with a firm handshake.

Clarence stood just under six feet tall, but he was built like one of the guys who compete in "strong man" competitions. His enormous arm and shoulder muscles were visible through his perfectly tailored suit, and his neck was quite possibly the biggest Cara had ever seen on a man. He wore what appeared to be an expensive gold watch on his left wrist and also had a wedding band on his left ring finger. In addition, he had an earpiece in his left ear like a secret service agent might wear. His perfectly manicured fingernails, clean-shaven head and face, tailored suit, and shined shoes projected the image that he was a meticulous human being who took pride in his appearance.

"Hello, Mr. Walters. It's very nice to meet you, too." Cara responded.

"Please, call me Clarence. Also, I want you to know that I am not here to be a hindrance to your daily life in any way. Aside from driving you wherever it is that you need to go, I will be out of your way, unless you need me. Here's my contact information. Please put my phone number in your phone so that you can reach me at any time," Clarence said as he handed Cara a black and red business card.

The business card listed the company as "CW Security Solutions, LLC" and had Clarence Walters listed as the owner along with his contact information.

"Well, Clarence, I appreciate that and I will do that as soon as we get in the car," Cara responded as she put his card in the pocket of her jeans.

"Well, then, you two have a great day and please don't hesitate to contact me if you need anything," Simon said as he nodded to each of them and walked away.

"Follow me, Miss Knox. My car is out front," Clarence said as he gestured towards the front door.

"Um...Clarence?"

"Yes, Miss Knox."

"Can you please call me Cara? I'm still not used to the whole 'Miss Knox' thing, and I can't imagine I ever will be."

"Of course, Cara. I understand. Now, we best be on our way so you're not late to class on my first day on the job," Clarence chuckled as he led Cara out the front door towards his black Cadillac Escalade, which also had tinted privacy windows.

Clarence opened the back passenger door, which caused Cara to give him a puzzled look. Clarence picked up immediately on her reaction.

"Sorry, Cara, but it's company policy that you ride in the back seat. Preferably on the passenger side. It's not only safer for you there, but also easier to extract you from the vehicle as quickly as possible when we reach our destination."

"Oh, I see…" Cara said as she climbed into the spacious leather back seat, which had a third row of seats behind it.

"You'll get used to it. I promise," Clarence reassured her.

"I'll take your word for it…" Cara said as he closed the door and made his way around the front of the car to the driver's seat.

Before pulling away, Clarence pressed a small button on his earpiece and said, "Alpha, this is Baker. Do you copy? Over…"

After a moment he spoke again.

"Affirmative, departing for CSU now, I'll advise when we reach our destination. Over…"

After another moment, Clarence nodded and pulled the Escalade out from in front of the Westcott and they were on their way.

"Who are you talking to, Clarence?" Cara asked.

"The boss…"

"The boss? I thought you were the owner of the company?" Cara asked, puzzled.

"Oh I am, but Evelynn, my dispatcher back at the office, also happens to be my wife…" Clarence laughed.

"Ah, that makes total sense. That's so cool that you work together! How long have you been married?"

"Almost 30 years. We have two daughters who are both a little older than you. Sasha is a first-grade teacher in Shaker Heights and Sadie works for my company as the evening dispatcher."

"Wow, a true family business."

"Not gonna lie, it's hard at times, but I wouldn't have it any other way."

"What about the other lady who is going to be working for you in the evenings? I think her name was Grace?"

"That would be Grace Brooks. She's not related to me, but she might as well be family. She was a young officer in my department towards the end of my career."

"Why'd she leave the force?"

"Well, there's a couple reasons. One is not my story to tell, but the other is that she's also trying to make it as an MMA fighter and she needed a set work schedule so she could stay on a strict training regime."

"Oh, wow. She sounds like a tough cookie."

"The toughest. I only hire the best," Clarence said as he glanced up at his rearview mirror and gave Cara a reassuring smile.

The two remained silent as they traveled the rest of the way towards Cleveland State's urban campus. Once they arrived near Cara's classroom building, Clarence instructed her to wait in the Escalade until he opened the door for her.

Cara watched as he put on a pair of black Oakley sunglasses and again pressed his earpiece to tell his wife back at dispatch that they had arrived at CSU before he exited the vehicle. Cara watched as he paused in front of his vehicle and unwrapped a piece of gum and placed it in his mouth. He then took a casual walk towards the front of the building and threw away the gum wrapper in the garbage can that was near the entrance.

Cara surmised that the sole reason he opened the piece of gum was to have a reason to walk the route she would soon be taking towards the front of the building. This way he'd be able to take a quick look around and see if anyone like Gary Boardman might be hanging around. Cara was quickly learning that every move has a purpose for someone like Clarence Walters.

I'm glad he's on my side…

Cara knew that while a commuter college like CSU doesn't get too many Cadillac Escalades dropping students off in front of their classroom buildings, she also knew that it was a busy enough campus that most people probably wouldn't even notice her get out of the car.

She was right.

Cara exited the vehicle when Clarence opened the door and per his instructions casually walked into her classroom building. He also instructed her that he would meet her in the same spot and to walk directly to his vehicle once he rolled down the rear passenger window. That was going to be his signal that the coast was clear.

As Cara walked to the first of her two classes for the day, she wondered if she'd ever get used to this new reality.

61

Across town, Cooper Madison was being faced with a new reality of his own. His agent, Todd Taylor, had just informed him that the Cubs had worked out a deal with the Cleveland Indians to trade his rights for two of their top minor league pitchers. In addition, the Indians would have to pick up Coop's remaining contract.

"Here's the deal in a nutshell," T-Squared informed his client. "The Cubs placed you on waivers at 12:01 a.m., which means that the other teams in the league can claim you within 48 hours. If any other team besides the Indians, who already claimed you at 12:02, tries to claim you, then two scenarios will likely unfold."

"Go on…"

"The first is that you would be awarded to the team with the worst record. If that's the Indians, then the deal goes through. The second is that another team with a worse record then the Indians claims you, and then the Cubs would simply rescind the waiver and maintain your rights. Since the Indians are currently sitting 4th in their own division, there aren't too many teams that could claim you before them anyways."

"So that means that the deal will go through," Coop stated.

"Sure looks that way. Listen, you're going to have about 36 more hours to wait anyhow, but start thinking about what you want me to tell the Indians front office."

"I thought I couldn't even pitch if a deal wasn't made after August 31st, though?"

"Actually, the rules just state that any player dealt after August 31st is not eligible to be on a *postseason* roster, which the Indians are in no danger of having this season."

"Oh… I didn't realize that. I just assumed I couldn't pitch at all this year even if I wanted to."

"That's why you pay me the big bucks, C-Mad…"

"Don't call me that, T. You know I hate that…"

Todd gave a devious chuckle on the other end, knowing that his intended reaction had been obtained.

"You're lucky you're also my friend, or I would've fired your ass the first time you called me that…" Coop chided.

"You know you love me, Coop. You're stuck with me anyways. No agent in his right mind would take you, trust me, I've tried!"

"Very funny, T…"

"Hey, how's things going with the new lady friend?" Todd switched gears.

"Great! She's actually in class right now."

"That's good to hear, at least one of you should have a degree!"

"Bye, T…"

"You know I'm kidding. Hey, think things over, and I'll be in touch. Peace."

Coop set the phone down on his kitchen counter and made his way out to the balcony. It was a mild, yet sunny morning in Cleveland, which Coop would soon discover to be an anomaly as autumn progressed.

While he had long eliminated the possibility of pitching for the Cubs in 2006, if ever, Coop never anticipated the possibility of being able to play for somebody else. Adding to this new twist of fate was the emergence of something that he had not felt in a very long time: doubt.

Would I even be able to do it? I haven't thrown a baseball in months.

Damn, I need a chew…

Coop had given up his smokeless tobacco habit shortly after arriving in Cleveland, for a multitude of reasons, but what made it stick was the fact he simply wasn't around it as much as he normally would've been in a Major League clubhouse.

Life as a pitcher, where you only get to play once every five to seven days, can be boring. Therefore, professional baseball pitchers are experts at finding ways to help pass the time. Some of Coop's fondest memories of playing ball were the relentless antics in the bullpen, clubhouse pranks, and creating games to make the monotony of sitting around until it's your turn to play more interesting.

When all else failed, Coop and about 40 percent of the other MLB players could always pass the time by throwing in a pinch of chew they often referred to by a multitude of slang names. Throwing in a dip, chewski, lipper, chaw, digger, snarl, wad, or fatty could often make the most mundane situations more enjoyable. The massive amounts of nicotine that accompanied it certainly helped, as well, especially when dealing with the stress of playing in front of thousands of people.

Coop first started using tobacco at a much later age than most of his friends in high school, as it wasn't until his first season in the minors when a teammate offered him some after a game.

A lot of men, and even some women, will only try chewing tobacco once in their lifetime. The main reason for this is that a single pinch of smokeless tobacco will contain about four times the amount of nicotine compared to that of a single cigarette. Combining that with the fact that it goes directly into the bloodstream will typically cause a first time user to get dizzy and even sick. That experience will often prevent further use.

However, some people do not experience any of those negative effects and they find that a feeling of euphoria will often accompany the buzz that the nicotine brings. Then they're hooked, despite the fact that they know it's a disgusting habit that often has them spitting into random bottles and cups which could later be spilled by accident. They become hooked even though they are intelligent enough to know it's a nasty, expensive, and possibly deadly habit.

Cooper Madison was one of those people.

As he sat on the balcony he debated whether or not to retrieve the unopened can of Skoal that he still had in his freezer, to only be used in case of emergency. He also thought about the last time he and his father argued over his tobacco habit while fishing prior to spring training in 2005.

"I really wish you wouldn't do that crap, Son," his father Jeffrey said, as he typically would every time he witnessed his son put a pinch of chew in his lip.

"I know, but do you have to say it every time?" Coop responded, annoyed, but also a little ashamed.

"It's not just about the fact it's dangerous, boy. It's also about the fact that you are obviously too mentally weak to stop."

Coop took a deep breath, held it for ten seconds, and then exhaled.

Nope, not today... I'll be strong for you, Daddy...

62

Jason Knox sat in his unmarked cruiser in a parking lot closest to the pier and yacht club as the noonday sun began to turn up the heat on what had been a pretty mild morning. The lot was mostly filled, which was typical for a weekday when the Cleveland weather was such that it allowed local boaters and beachgoers to play hooky for the day.

His car was dark navy with black wheels that lacked any sort of decorative hubcaps and had a spotlight mounted to the driver side mirror. Jason always felt it was ironic that despite his car's lack of camouflage, the people he was usually staking out never seemed to notice it.

Jason had been one of the first to park in the lot that morning, save for a few anglers who were looking to get an early start on Lake Erie's famous walleye. He purposely had positioned his car so that he had a direct line of sight on the Pier Grille and Bait Shop that was located between the parking lot and the water.

The hybrid grille and bait shop serves concessions to hungry beachgoers, including Cleveland's famous Honey Hut Ice Cream. For the anglers who dock their boats at the adjacent yacht club, the stand also has tackle and bait available for purchase.

There was an entirely different batch of clientele, as Jason had learned during his years on the force, which used the bait shop pavilion at Edgewater Park to buy and sell everything from drugs to prostitutes.

Over the years, the city of Cleveland not only acknowledged the problem at Edgewater but also took measures to clean it up. Uniformed Cleveland Metroparks rangers routinely patrolled the area, while undercover officers from the Cleveland police department conducted regular stings to help limit the flow of drugs and solicitation in and out of Edgewater Park.

As anyone in law enforcement in a situation similar to that of Edgewater's would tell you, it's a mess that's easy to temporarily clean up, but one that will always come back. Once their current business model has been exposed and eliminated, criminals will usually have a new and improved one up and running shortly after their release from jail.

On this day, Jason was watching one such criminal in action doing just that. He knew the young man, known on the street as "Tick", very well. When Jason was a uniformed officer he had locked Tick up for selling Adderall to college students outside the public library.

Timothy "Tick" Braun got his nickname from his mother at a young age for two reasons. First and foremost, he was tiny. Even as an adult he barely stood over five feet tall. The second was because he was constantly getting under her skin, and everyone else's for that matter. She had kicked him out of the house at the age of 16 after his third stint in a juvenile detention facility, and he had been surviving on his own ever since.

His latest arrest for selling drugs to an undercover officer was thrown out of court due to the fact that the court found the arresting officer guilty of using excessive force. During the arrest, Tick tried to run once he realized he was caught. In the ensuing pursuit, the undercover officer tackled him and while restraining him ended up dislocating his elbow to the point that it required emergency surgery just to save his arm.

The officer, facing disciplinary action, chose to resign from the force. Tick, on the other hand, walked out of the courthouse a free man. He actually had managed to stay out of trouble, and for the most part, completely out of sight in the months since his release.

Word on the street, according to Jason's sources in the narcotics division, was that Tick was out of the drug game altogether. Apparently, after his last arrest, Tick's supplier told him that he would no longer be needing his services. He told him that he was too careless and had too much heat on him.

While that was likely the case, it didn't explain why Tick had been hanging around Edgewater a lot in the recent weeks since Jason had been investigating the murders there. Jason figured that there must be a reason for Tick's return to his old stomping grounds, and he had spent much of the past two days watching him from a distance.

For the most part, Tick sat at one of the many picnic tables located around the bait shop. Occasionally, Tick would purchase food from the stand, light up a cigarette, or simply stand and look out towards the lake.

Occasionally, Tick would be joined by another customer at his table. The picnic tables were pretty big, and the two would barely acknowledge each other. It appeared as if they would just share the same table for a few minutes. The other person, always a man, would finish his ice cream and then leave.

What Jason had realized yesterday during his surveillance was that each man that joined him at the picnic table would leave his empty ice cream container on the edge of the table instead of throwing it away. Tick would act like he didn't see it, wait a few minutes for the breeze off the lake to knock the cup off of the table, and then jump up to keep the container from blowing away.

He did this every single time and each time he would pick the container up, look at it, and then dial someone on his cell phone before throwing the container in the nearby recycling bin. This last part made Jason laugh at the irony.

Like he gives a shit about the environment...

Each phone call Tick appeared to make would last no more than a couple minutes and then he would take another seat at his picnic table. This happened three more times yesterday afternoon as Jason watched before Tick called it a day and left just before 5 p.m.

Tick arrived on this day a little before eleven in the morning but had yet to have a visitor to the picnic table he was occupying. Jason was starting to get anxious, and the one part of the job he always detested the most was surveillance. Especially on a hot day.

The lunch rush was in full swing at the Pier Grille when Jason noticed a middle-aged man appear from the group of people waiting for service. The man, dressed in a shirt and tie, appeared as if he was taking a quick break from work to enjoy some ice cream. He took a few steps towards the picnic table area where Tick was seated, ice cream container in hand, and then paused to pull something out of his shirt pocket.

Jason pulled out his binoculars and could see that the man was writing something on the side of the Styrofoam pint with the pen that he had retrieved from his shirt pocket. He couldn't make out what the man was writing, but Jason's heart started to accelerate as he watched the man take a seat next to Tick.

Now we're getting somewhere...

The man, who was tall and heavyset, wore the same type of short-sleeved dress shirt and tie combo that Jason's high school science teacher wore every day to school.

This guy probably sells used cars or mattresses...

Tick barely acknowledged the man who had just joined him at the table as he lit up his third cigarette since arriving at Edgewater Park. A few minutes passed as Jason witnessed the man finish off the small pint of ice cream with little effort at all. The man nodded towards Tick as he stood up and left his empty Styrofoam cup near the edge of the table before walking back towards the parking lot.

Jason followed the man as he got into an early 90's sedan and pulled away. Using the binoculars, Jason tried to get a read on the license plate number as he drove away. Instead, he realized that the car had "Dealer" plates on it.

I knew it!

Jason panned back towards Tick, who had just retrieved the man's cup off the ground near his picnic table. He looked at the cup, dialed his cell phone, and talked for a minute before hanging up and throwing the cup in the recycling bin.

Bingo...

This time, instead of returning to his spot at the picnic table, Tick made his way towards the public restroom that was located in the same building as the concession stand.

Jason used this as his chance to confirm his assumption about what exactly was on that foam container. He quickly exited his cruiser and pulled the Indians cap he was wearing down on his head so that the brim was just above his sunglasses. He wasn't sure if Tick would even recognize him anymore, but he didn't want to take the chance in the event it was just a quick bathroom visit.

Jason walked as fast as he could while still trying to remain casual. There were still a lot of people waiting to get ice cream, food, and cold drinks so Jason knew he'd be able to blend in with them if need be.

As he approached the recycling bin where Tick had just discarded the pint in question, Jason picked up a smashed soda can that happened to be on the ground. With the can as his excuse to use the recycling bin, Jason took a quick look around before placing the can in the bin by reaching his arm all the way inside the makeshift hole that had been cut out on top of what was really just a blue garbage can and lid.

I need to buy more hand sanitizer for the car...

As he let go of the can, Jason became thankful that the can was almost full, so he didn't look too ridiculous with his arm submerged in a recycling bin. His fingers encountered what felt like a plastic water bottle and what he hoped was a deflated balloon before they experienced the texture of a Styrofoam cup with a gooey film coating the inside of it.

After its extraction from the depths of the blue container, Jason took a quick look at the cup and saw that a phone number had been written on the side in black pen: 555-216-7854. He wasted no time getting back to his car and was thankful that Tick didn't see him.

Jason had been a detective long enough to know that he should not get too excited about his discovery. However, he had been working so long on this case with absolutely no quality leads, that he could barely contain his joy when he placed the cup in a ziplock bag and made his way back to the station.

While Jason certainly didn't think Tick was the Edgewater Park Killer, or EPK as dubbed by the media, he was pretty sure that he was his perhaps his only chance to find out who was.

63

"Clarence, my man, how's everything going with the new gig? You keeping my sister safe, or what?" Jason Knox asked his former colleague from his cell phone as he drove towards 1st District headquarters.

Clarence couldn't help but notice that Jason's voice seemed more alive than it had in months. The EPK case was really wearing on his old protégé, and he had been worried about Jason's mental well-being. Clarence knew firsthand that a good detective could lose himself in a big case, and in some instances, never recover.

"Who is this? I want to say it's my old friend, Jason Knox, but I haven't heard him this happy in months…" Clarence responded as he waited in his Escalade for Cara's class to end.

"Damn straight it's me, and you won't believe who I've been watching the past two days."

"I'll bite," Clarence replied. "Who?"

"None other than one Timothy Braun…"

"Tick?! I thought that little shit was out the game, or better yet, dead," Clarence replied, shocked.

"He was, and might still be out of the drug game, but he's definitely up to something. I'm on my way to figure out what that is, too. Just thought you'd get a kick out of it."

"Hey, you think I should I tell Grace?" Clarence asked.

"I wouldn't, at least not yet. Actually, don't tell anyone, for that matter."

"Roger that."

"Take care of my baby sister."

"Like she was my own!"

As he ended the call, Clarence peeked at his watch. Cara's class would be letting out in ten minutes. It was time for him to pull to the front of the building and do a once-over on the scene.

Even though Clarence didn't anticipate anything worse than the occasional paparazzi or ex-boyfriend harassing Cara, he never would let that deter him from planning for the worst and hoping for the best. It was the cornerstone of his success not only as an officer but later as a detective and owner of a security firm.

He parked his SUV in the drop-off zone near the entrance of Cara's building, left the engine running, and exited the vehicle to scan the area just as he had earlier in the morning.

One of the benefits of being a former cop was knowing most of the patrolmen, and even some of the campus police, in the area. He had already contacted many of them to let them know that he'd be working a daily security detail for a high profile student at Cleveland State University. Since there weren't too many of those at CSU *not* named Cara Knox, he didn't have to explain much more than that.

After making sure the area was secured, Clarence returned to the vehicle and rolled down the rear passenger window. As he had instructed her earlier in the day, this would let Cara know that it was safe for her to exit the building.

A few minutes later, Clarence saw Cara emerge from the building where she had just completed her last class of the day. As she walked towards the SUV, Clarence had one hand on his door handle and another on his earpiece as he scanned the immediate area around her.

This way he could not only exit the vehicle in a hurry, but he could also radio dispatch if needed. He felt it was better not to stand outside the vehicle like a chauffeur, as it would draw too much attention.

There were always at least five other vehicles in the drop-off zone waiting for college students and staff members. Some of them were even more ostentatious than his Cadillac.

As Cara entered the SUV without any issues, Clarence pressed the button on his earpiece and informed his wife back at the office that they were on the move back to the Westcott.

"So… what'd you learn at school today?" Clarence jokingly asked as if he was a parent picking up a child from elementary school.

"To be honest, not much. I was too busy daydreaming. There's so much going on in my brain that I can't seem to focus on much of anything," Cara said with a sigh.

"This, too, shall pass," Clarence replied, using one of the most misattributed phrases of all time. For years, many people have uttered those words thinking that it came from the Bible. In reality, it likely derived from a fable written by a Sufi poet.

"I sure hope so. Please tell me that we are on our way back to the Westcott, Clarence. I need to chill out before I meet up with Lucy tonight."

"Yes we are, and that reminds me… what time should I have Grace meet you in the lobby?"

"Well, I'm supposed to meet Lucy at Lola at six, so I'm guessing 5:30 would be good."

"I will let her know, and if anything changes, you have my card. Grace will also have a card for you tonight with her contact info. She will make sure that you get to wherever you need to go. Just let her know if it's going to be past 11, so she can make arrangements to stay on later if necessary."

"I will, and I can't imagine I'll be awake past eleven, let alone out on the town still, so I don't think it will be an issue."

"In my experience, those are the type of evenings that always tend to last the longest…" Clarence chuckled.

64

Detective Jason Knox sat at his desk staring at the phone number he obtained from the Styrofoam ice cream container earlier that day. The cup itself had been locked away by Jason in the event he would need to submit it later as evidence.

He entered 555-216-7854 into the department database to see if the owner of the number had any prior criminal offenses. It was always easier to narrow down the list of possible crimes that might have been committed if the suspect already had a prior record. He wasn't even sure if the owner of this number was a suspect at all, but maybe he would point him in the right direction as to what Tick was up to these days.

When the number came back in the system it wasn't registered to an individual person. This number actually belonged to a local business called Rides 4 Less, Incorporated. The owner of the company was named Raymond Page.

Rides 4 Less was a discount used car dealership located on the near west side of Cleveland. Small dealerships like these had been popping up in and around the Cleveland area for decades. They usually didn't last very long and were almost always located in low-income neighborhoods.

These were predatory dealerships who offered zero down with low payment options to people with little or no credit. They would get customers desperate for a car to sign loan agreements at an incredibly high interest rate with weekly scheduled payments.

It was a win-win for the dealer. If the customer actually made the payments in full and on-time, the dealer would typically get twice what the car was worth over the life of the loan. If the customer missed just two consecutive weekly payments, regardless of the circumstances, the dealer would repossess the vehicle, void the contract, and sell the car all over again to the next victim.

The dealership relied on the fact that since the customers didn't have enough money to make their payments that they certainly didn't have enough to hire a lawyer and take them to court.

Jason saw businesses like this, selling everything from cars to furniture to cell phones all over the city. Their whole existence was to prey on the weak, and Jason hated them for it. Jason decided to give the number a call from his department telephone, which would mask the identity of the number he was calling from.

Time to go shopping for a car…

"Hello?" the voice on the other end answered.

"Hey there, is this Raymond from Rides 4 Less?"

"Well this is Rides 4 Less, but I'm Ray's brother, Ernie. Ray's the owner. What can I do for you?"

"Oh, sorry about that. I got the number from a guy at one of the bigger dealerships who said you guys might be able to help me out. You see, my old lady cleaned me out in the divorce and let's just say that my credit is not the best. When I went to the local Ford dealership they said that there was no way they could get me financed. One of the guys, can't remember his name, gave me this number and said to give a guy named Ray a call."

"Well, don't worry. Happens all the time, especially since Ray's name is on all the cards I hand out to the local dealers to give to good people like you who need our help."

"So you think you can help me out? I got a job and everything, just no money to put down at the moment," Jason said, hoping that his act was believable.

"What'd you say your name was?" Ernie asked in response.

"Oh, I'm so sorry. The name's Darrell."

"Well, Darrell, you're in luck, because ol' Ernie here specializes in helping good guys like yourself get out of a bad situation and into a great car."

"Oh, thank you, Jesus! You have no idea how happy that makes me. When can I come by and take a looksee?" Jason cringed as he heard the words coming out of his mouth.

"Well, I just got back in the office and I'll be here until we close tonight at eight."

"Alright, well I will try to get over there in the next hour or so. Thanks again, Mr. Page."

"Please, call me Ernie, and I look forward to it."

Jason hung up the phone and resisted the urge to call the chief and let him know that he was making progress on a lead. He knew, however, that he was going to have to get somewhere with Ernie and Tick if he wanted to stay on the case because there was no way that he'd appease the chief by making a bogus arrest.

65

Cara Knox plopped down on one of the two matching leather sofas in Cooper Madison's den. After Clarence dropped her off back at the Westcott Hotel, she and Coop had a late lunch as she shared the events of her day. Coop did not tell her about the possible trade to the Cleveland Indians because he wasn't sure if it would even happen.

No sense in talking about it yet...

"What are you watching?" Cara asked, her hair still wet from the shower she took after the late lunch. She would be heading out to meet Lucy soon but wanted a few more minutes with Coop before she left.

Coop, who was already seated in his leather recliner with his feet up and a Barq's root beer in his hand, sat up and took notice of the beautiful young lady with the wet hair sitting across from him.

"Well, now I'm watching you…" he said with a wry smile.

"Oh, right… me and my wet hair? Nice try 'Coopernova'," Cara responded.

"Coopernova? I kinda like that."

"You would..."

"Why do you do that?"

"Do what?"

"Every time I compliment you I feel like you try and deflect by making a joke."

"Deflect? Somebody's been watching 'Dr. Phil' while I've been gone."

"See! That's what I'm talking about," Coop said as he sat up to emphasize his point.

"I told you before, I don't do well with compliments. I never have, and to be honest, I've never been with anyone who gave them to me as much as you do. Well, at least nobody who gave them to me when they weren't drunk off their ass trying to get laid," Cara responded.

"Do you want me to stop complimenting you?" Coop asked.

"I didn't say that…"

"Good, because I wasn't gonna anyway," Coop laughed.

"I wish I could tell you that I'll get better at it, but I don't like to make promises I'm not sure I can keep."

"I just want you to be you, whatever that is, because I'm definitely not going to stop being me."

"I would never want you to do that," Cara said.

"And I would never want you to fake anything with me. I told you before I've had enough people in my life who I never could tell if they were genuine or not."

"Well, I promise I will always be genuine with you. Just don't say I didn't warn you later…" Cara responded.

"Warn me about what?" Coop asked.

"That I'm not perfect!"

"Nobody's perfect…"

"I know, but I just feel like when you say all the nice things you do that you're putting me on a pedestal that I know I will fall off of… You barely know me, and I barely know you, and what freaks me out the most is that once you realize I'm not the perfect girl that you have in your head you'll break my heart..." Cara said, her words coming out as fast as the tears that were welling up in her eyes.

"You think I don't have those same fears? You've only seen a side of me that is a HELL of a lot more normal than the guy who had been holed up here in for months. You don't know the guy who didn't leave his bedroom for days at a time because he felt like there wasn't a reason to even try. The guy who drank himself to sleep every night and numbed himself with pills all day just so he wouldn't feel the pain that was absolutely destroying him. The pain that made everyone feel so sorry for him, but the same pain that all those people also wanted him to hurry up and move past so he could go back to being the guy that THEY needed him to be!"

Coop stood up from his chair and whipped the empty can of root beer across the room before continuing his rant.

"You want to talk about not being perfect? Do you know that if my best friend Cash wouldn't have hopped on an airplane in June and showed up at this apartment I'd probably be, well, I'd rather not say..."

"No... how would I?" Cara responded, tears streaming down her cheeks.

"My point exactly, Cara... I'm not perfect either. But, you know what? You make me feel like I am, and I am trying my hardest to make you feel like you are, too."

"I... I don't know what to say..." Cara said as guilt began to set in.

Coop knelt down on the floor next to the sofa and gently placed his hands on her cheeks so she could see his eyes, which also had tears slowly streaming down the stubble on his face.

"Nothing..." he whispered.

"Nothing..." she replied.

"You better get goin... y'all gonna be late for dinner..."

"Y'all? I'm meeting Lucy there, though."

"Yes, but Grace Brooks is taking you there, remember?"

"Crap! I'm supposed to meet her downstairs at 5:30! How much time do I have?"

"About 10 minutes... best get a move on, girl!" Coop kissed her on the forehead and pulled her up off the couch and into his arms.

"Wait..." Cara said.

"What's up?" Coop asked as he held her.

"I just want you to know that I really appreciate what you said. All of it. Even the bad stuff... I want you to know that there's nothing you could tell me that'll make me like you any less."

"Back atcha, Cara Knox. I kinda like you, ya know..."

"Ditto..." Cara said as she gave him a big hug.

66

Detective Jason Knox hopped off the RTA bus at a stop near the intersection where Rides 4 Less was located. He looked nothing like a detective, though, in the faded jeans and slightly wrinkled button-down shirt he grabbed out of his locker at the precinct.

He always kept a few different outfit choices in there for when he was trying to blend in during surveillance. In addition to the disguise, he used a concealed holster to carry his firearm inside the rear waistband of his jeans. The untucked shirt was just long enough to cover up any outline that the gun might give off through his clothes. While he wasn't planning on needing it, he certainly was not going to leave without it.

Jason had parked his car a few blocks away and hopped on the RTA bus that would take him to Rides 4 Less. He knew that if he was to play the part of a guy in desperate need of a car, he certainly couldn't show up there in one, let alone an unmarked cruiser.

To call Rides 4 Less a car dealership was a stretch. It was really just a corner lot riddled with the types of cars that you could get for a few hundred dollars at a sheriff's auction and then sell for a profit. The "office" that Ernie Page had referred to earlier on the phone was actually just an old construction trailer and all of the signage was the kind you'd be able to get at a 24-hour copy shop.

As Jason approached the office he saw the man that he witnessed eating ice cream earlier come bounding out of the trailer door. Although Jason was almost certain that this was Ernie, he still had to make sure.

"Are you Darrell? Never did get your last name. Been expecting you, fella! Ernie Page, nice to meet ya!" the man talked quickly as he extended his hand towards Jason and gave him a firm handshake.

"Yessir, Darrell Dawkins, sir. Pleasure to meet ya…"

"Dawkins? Like the basketball player?" Ernie asked, referring to the former NBA star who had a penchant for shattering backboards in the 70's and 80's.

"Yessir, just spelled differently. Been hearing that most my life," Jason laughed.

"What'd they use to call him? Chocolate something?" Ernie asked.

"Thunder. Chocolate Thunder…" Jason replied.

"That's what it was. He was one big *brother*, wasn't he?"

Brother? A racist and a scumbag...

"So, you got some cars to show me, Ernie?" Jason said, changing the subject.

"Sure do, Darrell! Enough small talk, let's get you in a car!" Ernie said as he led Jason towards a maroon 1992 Oldsmobile Delta 88 Royale sedan - the same car Ernie drove to Edgewater Park. It had a sticker of $5995 on the window and Jason pretended to be taken aback by that.

"Ernie, this is a beauty of a car, but that's a little out of my price range. I only have about half that to spend. I told you before that my credit ain't gonna get me no loan…."

"Darrell, what if I told you that your credit was good here at Rides 4 Less?" Ernie said with a smile.

"Come again? The dealership said nobody would finance me... and my only chance at a car was paying cash?" Jason feigned ignorance.

"Well, that's because they have to do their financing through a bank, Darrell. Here at Rides 4 Less, all the financing is through us. As long as you can make your payments on time, we'll finance you ourselves!"

"Seriously? Well, that'd be great! Can we take her for a spin?"

"I got the keys right here! Took her for a spin earlier today myself, as a matter of fact."

Oh, I know, Ernie...

Ernie tossed Jason the keys and got in the passenger side of the vehicle. As Jason climbed into the driver's seat he was overcome by the smell of the two tree-shaped air fresheners that were hanging from the rearview mirror.

"So, where we headed?" Ernie asked Jason as they pulled away from the lot.

"I was thinking we could drive over to Edgewater, Ernie..." Jason said, as he suddenly changed his "aw shucks" tone to his normal voice.

The destination, along with Jason's change in tone, gave Ernie a puzzled look on his face.

"Uh... Edgewater? Why there, Darrell? This time of day it'll be packed. Why don't we take her for a spin on the freeway?" Ernie replied, eyeballing his customer.

"What's wrong with Edgewater Park, Ernie? You look like you just saw a ghost or something?"

"Wrong? Oh, nothing, I just don't like crowds, is all."

"But you do like ice cream, though, right Ernie?" Jason asked as he accelerated.

"Ice cream? I'm not really sure what that has to do with any-"

"Shut up, Ernie!" Jason yelled as he pulled into an empty parking lot and slammed the brakes.

"Hey, what the hell is going on here, Darrell?" Ernie said, obviously flustered by his customer's actions.

"The name's Jason. Detective Jason Knox. Cleveland Homicide."

Jason produced his badge and put it in Ernie's face.

"*Homicide*? What the hell do you want with *me*?"

"Relax, Ernie, I'm not going to arrest you. Yet..."

"Arrest me? For what?" Ernie asked, incredulously.

"Listen to me *very* carefully Ernie. I'm going to ask you a few questions. How you decide to answer those questions will determine where you sleep tonight. You understand me?"

Ernie shook his head indicating that he understood.

"Why'd you go to Edgewater Park earlier today, Ernie?" Jason asked.

Ernie looked shocked that Jason knew he had been there.

"Edgewater? Oh, yeah, uh, I took a lunch break and got some ice cream. I love that Honey Hut ice cream!" Ernie replied with a feigned laugh.

"Goddamnit, Ernie, I thought you understood that I'm not here to play games. Get out of the car, I'm going to have to take you in now…" Jason said as he started to reach for his gun.

"Wait, wait, wait! I'll talk, I'll talk. Just hold on, man..." Ernie pleaded.

"Last. Chance."

"I'm lonely, okay? I haven't been laid by my wife in years and a guy I know told me how I could solve that problem without having to worry about getting caught for soliciting."

Soliciting? So, Tick's a pimp now…

"Keep going. Tell me something that I don't already know and I might reconsider arresting your pathetic ass," Jason said, hoping Ernie wouldn't call his bluff.

"Okay… just give me a chance… the guy I know said that if I went to Edgewater's concession stand during certain hours and days that I might find a guy there. He said that the guy was tiny, maybe five feet at the most and that he'd be at a picnic table. He said if I saw the guy to order an ice cream and write my phone number on the cup. He said don't talk to the guy. I don't even know the guy's name! He said to sit at his table and leave the cup near the edge before leaving. He said that the guy would call me after I left with instructions."

"Then what? I know he called you, Ernie…"

"Listen, I'll tell you, but you gotta promise that I won't be arrested. If my wife finds out I'm going to lose everything, which let me tell ya, ain't very much."

"Here's what I'll promise you, Ernie. Even if you don't say another word I can arrest you on suspicion of solicitation, and I promise you I will if you don't tell me *everything*."

"Okay, okay... I'll talk… a few minutes after I left I got a call from the guy at the picnic table. He gave me an address and told me to go there and bring cash. I asked how much and he said minimum two hundred bucks."

"Go on…"

"So I go to this place, and it's a tiny motel over on Brookpark Road. Total roach motel. It's so small I've never even noticed the place before. Nasty…"

"Which motel?"

"It doesn't even have a name. It just says 'Motel'... I don't think anyone actually stays there overnight, well except for the girls…"

"Give me the address," Jason said as he held his hand out.

Ernie took a deep breath and pulled his wallet out before producing a small piece of paper that had a number written on it: 78212.

"And this is on Brookpark Road?" Jason confirmed.

"Yeah… over by all the strip clubs…"

"What else can you tell me?"

"Well, it's kinda crazy, actually. I was told by the guy to go into the office and ask if they had any vacancies for November 9th."

"November 9th?"

"Yeah… I guess that is their way of telling what you're there for…anyways, I ask the bald guy at the front desk about November 9th and he says if I'd like to continue with the reservation that I had to give him my driver's license and a hundred bucks cash."

"Driver's license?"

"They said that if I wanted to 'stay' at their motel, I had to do it. I know it wasn't smart, but I did it. I was so desperate. Before I know it these two big Russian guys come out of the back office. Both of them have guns on one of them shoulder holsters. They took a photocopy of my license and the hundred bucks and said to follow them. "

Russians?

"Where'd they take you?" Jason asked, hoping Ernie would keep talking.

"They took me in their office where they had a bunch of TV monitors set up. But they weren't watching 'I Love Lucy' reruns… each one was some sort of security camera in each of the motel rooms. Each room had a chick, most of them laying on a bed. They told me to pick which one I wanted and let me tell you it was a tough choice because all these chicks were skinny, young, and gorgeous. Like models…"

"Who did you choose, Ernie?"

"I've always wanted to be with a redhead, and one of the chicks had the brightest red hair I've ever seen. So, I chose her…"

"Then what?"

"Then they said, give us another hundred bucks. Let me tell you, officer, I would've paid five times that to be with this chick… anyways, I pay and then they handed me a key to the motel room she was in... Room 6… they warn me not to hurt her or they'd hurt me and that I had exactly one hour to finish up or it'd be another hundred bucks."

"So you went to the room… then what?"

"Well, I go to the room, open the door with the key and the redhead is already laying on the bed. She sits up and tells me to come over. She definitely had an accent, I think Russian… and I'm pretty sure that she was high as a kite because she seemed out of it. She just kinda laid there and let me do my thing. Didn't take long, but hey, it's been awhile…"

"Did you stay the whole hour?"

"Hell no. I took that key back and got the hell out of there. I'm not gonna lie, I felt a little ashamed, being married and all..."

Yeah, you're a real saint, Ernie…

"You know why they took your driver's license, right, Ernie?" Jason said, shaking his head.

"I'm guessing to make sure that I'm not a cop? I don't know?"

"I knew you weren't building rockets, Ernie, but you're a goddamn idiot. They took your license so they can extort you for more money."

"Extort? You mean like shake me down?"

"Nothing gets by you, does it? Yes, shake you down. They're going to show up at your house one day, probably in the near future, and threaten to tell your wife if you don't pay up."

"What if I just tell her that they're lying?"

"Ernie, remember the cameras in the rooms? The ones you used to pick your redhead? They got you on film you dumbass. Did you really think that they'd turn those off for your privacy?"

"Oh my god… I'm so screwed… what am I gonna do?" Ernie asked Jason. All the color had gone from his face and he was sweating profusely.

"You're going to help me catch these bastards…"

67

Grace Brooks stood next to the black GMC Yukon that her boss, Clarence Walters, gave her when she started working for him earlier that year. This new assignment, protecting the new girlfriend of an athlete, was her first full-time gig and she was thrilled.

All of the assignments that CW Security Solutions, or the "C-Dub" as she liked to call it, had given her since she joined were temporary gigs. One or two nights protecting a wealthy and/or famous client who happened to be visiting Cleveland on business were the standard shifts.

This new and indefinite assignment was a true Monday through Friday second-shift job, which is certainly not the norm for the private security business.

But, I'm not complaining...

She was still a little sore from her workout that morning at the Mixed Martial Arts—or MMA—center she trained at. Her 28-year-old body, which resembled that of an Olympic swimmer, felt twice its age on this late afternoon.

Despite her appearance, she could barely swim. Instead, her tall, triangular figure was the result of intense training and years of running long distance races. During her time at the police academy, she found herself really enjoying the hand-to-hand combat portion of her education.

After watching an Ultimate Fighting Championship (UFC) Pay-Per-View, she contacted a local gym and felt as if she had finally found her place in the world.

Grace Brooks had always felt like she never truly fit-in. She was biracial; the result of an African-American military father and Korean mother, and her father's career meant that she had to move often. The two years that she lived in South Korea as a teenager were the hardest.

In South Korea, where the words "skin color" and "peach" are synonymous, being biracial is often looked at as an affliction. She didn't feel accepted by the other American kids on the base, and wandering off the base often held the strong possibility of being treated rudely by the natives.

Thankfully for her, Grace's family moved back to the States prior to her last year of high school. While she hated the weather during that first winter, she loved the cultural diversity of her new high school in Cleveland, Ohio. Cleveland is also where she found her love of running and joined the cross country and track teams her senior year.

Upon graduating from high school she opted for community college and obtained an Associates Degree in Criminal Justice before joining the police academy. It was there that she found her love for MMA, and also fell in love with being a cop.

Her first assignment was in the 1st District and that's where she met her mentor, and future boss, Clarence Walters. Later on, she would also meet a new detective, Jason Knox, as well. Now, she was working for both of them.

Who would've thought...?

Cara Knox walked out the front door of the Westcott with Cooper Madison towards Grace and her SUV.

"Hello, Miz Brooks. I'm Cuppah Madison, and this is Miss Cara Knox," he said as he shook her hand.

"Hello," Grace said as she shook each of their hands. "I look forward to working with you."

"Well, I'm fixin' to head back upstairs. Y'all be safe and have a good time," Coop said as he gave Cara a kiss on the cheek before walking away.

Grace opened the rear passenger door for Cara and then followed the same procedure that Clarence had given earlier in the day before leaving.

Before pulling away, she pressed the small button on her earpiece and said, "Alpha, this is Charlie. Do you copy?"

After a brief pause, she continued.

Over…Affirmative...we are on our way to Lola...Affirmative...Over..."

"So, when did you start working for Clarence?" Cara asked, hoping to strike up casual conversation.

"About six months now, ma'am," Grace answered.

Cara felt weird to be called "ma'am", especially by someone older than her.

"Please, call me Cara… I keep saying to people that this whole situation has been weird enough," Cara chuckled.

Grace Brooks looked back at Cara in the rearview mirror and smiled. She felt a little sorry for the young lady in her back seat.

"Will do, Cara."

"So I hear you're a fighter?"

"Well, I am training to be one. Mixed Martial Arts. Have you ever seen a UFC fight?"

"Actually, yeah I have. One time my ex took me to a party where they ordered the pay-per-view. Are you going to try and fight in one of those?"

"I'd love to, but that's a long shot. First, I have to compete locally and then see how I do."

"When's your first fight?"

"Hopefully, sometime in the next few months. Unfortunately, there aren't many women in the sport, period, let alone in Ohio. Until then, I will just keep on training."

"Did you take karate or anything like that growing up?" Cara asked.

"No, I actually was a runner, which helps with the conditioning aspect of the sport. I didn't get into it until I was in my early twenties."

"It probably comes in handy in your job, too. I know that I wouldn't want to mess with you!" Cara laughed.

"Well, you won't have to worry about that," Grace replied with a laugh. This was the most that any of her clients had ever talked to her. Most of them would barely even acknowledge her existence, and to Grace, this was a welcome change.

A few minutes of comfortable silence passed before Grace maneuvered her SUV into the valet line at Lola. When the valet sprinted over Grace waived him off as she spoke to dispatch via her earpiece.

"Alpha, this is Charlie. Do you copy? Over… Affirmative… Over…" Grace said as the valet, puzzled at first, realized the situation. Lola had its fair share of high profile customers, along with their entourages and security details.

Grace opened the door for Cara and told her to call her when she was ready to be picked up as she handed over her business card.

"I'll be parked right over there if you need me. Have a great time," Grace said as she closed Cara's door.

"Can I get you something to eat?" Cara yelled back as she entered the restaurant, forgetting for a moment that Grace was there for business, not pleasure.

"No thanks, but I appreciate the offer," Grace said with a smile as she climbed into her vehicle.

68

As soon as Cara crossed the threshold of the entrance to the famous Lola Bistro, she was startled by the shriek of her best friend Lucy Eckert's voice.

"Carebear! I missed you so much!" Lucy, who had been waiting near the hostess station, exclaimed as she met Cara with a big hug.

"Lucy, oh my god I missed you, too!" Cara replied, squeezing her friend.

"Cara, I have so much to tell you, and from what I understand you do too..." Lucy smirked.

Lucy Eckert was a petite girl with strawberry blonde hair. Though she was raised by hippies and attended perhaps the most liberal college in the country, Lucy never let herself be pigeonholed. One day she would dress like she was on her way to Woodstock, the next she would rock one of the latest trends. She didn't care what anyone thought of her, and that's what Cara admired most.

"You have no idea, and I cannot wait to hear all about Spain!" Cara answered.

A female hostess approached the two friends and interrupted their mini-reunion.

"Excuse, me, Miss Knox? Your table is ready, please follow me," the lady said as she gestured towards the dining room area.

Lucy gave Cara, who was just as puzzled as she, a look. The hostess picked up on this and informed them that a Mr. Madison had arranged everything for their reservation that evening, including the bill.

"I guess I don't need to use my gift card, after all," Lucy mused.

Cara, not sure what to say, just smiled and shrugged her shoulders.

The trio passed three empty table before entering a small area near the kitchen. All six of the tables, in what was apparently a VIP section of the restaurant, had a direct view of the kitchen.

"Here you are, ladies. You will be dining tonight at one of our 'Chef's Tables' where you will have a lovely view of our extremely talented kitchen staff as they prepare your meal. Please enjoy," the lady said as she placed two menus down and signaled for a busboy to remove the extra place settings while another poured them water.

"Okay, tell me about Spain," Cara said as they were seated.

"Forget Spain, Cara. First, I need to know about this Mr. Madison. I heard you were dating some baseball guy, and for the record, I'm *so* glad you dumped that loser, Kenny."

"Well, his name is Cooper, and I'm still apparently learning that he's full of surprises," Cara said as she gestured to their VIP table.

"You must be doing something right… Did I see you get dropped off out front? I thought the president was in town before you stepped out of that monstrosity of a car."

Cara laughed and during the appetizer and salad portion of the meal went on to tell Lucy all about Cooper Madison, how they met, and what had transpired over the past week.

"Now, tell me about *Spain,*" Cara insisted as they were served their main course, which was a delicious bacon wrapped Sturgeon with creamed spinach, parsnips, and apples.

"Well, let's just say that I not only fell in love *with* Barcelona, but I also fell *in* love there, too."

"What's his name? Tell me everything."

"*Alejandro…* he was a senior in my creative writing class at Universidad de Barcelona," Lucy said, making sure to emphasize the pronunciation of her Spanish beau's name.

"Oooh, I love that name. Go on…"

"Well, despite being absolutely gorgeous, Alejandro was also an amazing writer - in both English and Spanish - and he was well-versed in the language of love, too…" Lucy said with a sly smile.

"Isn't that a prerequisite if your name is *Alejandro*?" Cara joked, emphasizing his name.

"Girl, he should teach a class… but, even more, I fell absolutely in love with him. It was unlike anything I have ever experienced, and I probably never will again," Lucy's tone changed and her eyes began to water.

"What happened?" Cara asked.

"He broke my heart just as quickly as he stole it. Before I left he told me it would never work since his life was in Spain and I had to return home. I told him I'd *stay*, Cara. I told him I'd throw *everything* away to be with him… but, it turns out, that wasn't what he wanted."

"Oh Lucy, I'm so sorry…"

"He told me that he loved me, but never had any intentions of ever being in a committed relationship. Not with me or anyone else. He told me that the love we had for each other wasn't meant to burn forever, but rather burn bright and hot before going out…"

"Whoa…" Cara said, unsure if she hated Alejandro, or if she was truly impressed by his break-up skills.

"Writers, right? He even made dumping me sound poetic. I wonder how many other American girls have heard that line from him…"

"I'm not going to lie, Lucy, I'm terrified of being hurt like that, too," Cara replied.

"Why? 'Baseball Guy' seems pretty amazing so far."

"He is, I just know that all fairy tales tend to come to an end, and I feel like I'm living in one right now."

"You know what?" Lucy asked.

"What?"

"So *what* if it doesn't work out, Cara?"

"Well, for one I'd be heartbroken…"

"Well, as someone whose heart is currently on the mend I can tell you that I would do it all over again with Alejandro. All of it..."

"You would?"

"Absolutely, Cara. I never, EVER, imagined that I'd ever fall in love with a man so quickly and with so much passion. I truly feel we're lucky if we get to fall in love like that just one time in our lives. The truly blessed get a second chance. Maybe Baseball Guy is your one time? And I know that if I *ever* find myself in that situation again, I'm not going to dwell *one second* on whether or not it will end because that'll take away from the beauty of the moment…"

"Well, when you put it that way… why can't I be so good at using words like you are?" Cara asked, smiling.

"Because, then you wouldn't be you, and that would be awful. Because you're the best," Lucy replied, her usual cheerful expression seemingly restored to its natural state.

Just then, the waiter came over and placed their dessert in front of them.

"The '6 a.m. Special', ladies, featuring a brioche French toast with maple-bacon ice cream and caramelized apples. Enjoy!"

"Well, I'm glad Baseball Guy is picking up the tab for this wonderful meal because my gift card probably wouldn't have covered much past the salads," Lucy declared with a laugh.

"Stop calling him Baseball Guy, you dork," Cara jokingly admonished.

"Okay, okay… Oh my god, this is delicious," Lucy said after she took a bite of the bountiful dessert.

"I was just going to say the same thing!"

"So, is your bodyguard *chica* going to take us to the dance club?" Lucy asked.

"That's the plan."

"Good because I don't have money for a cab. Spain was expensive," Lucy chuckled.

"I can't *wait* to go dancing. I haven't had a good 'girls night out' in since you left," Cara said with a sigh.

"Well then, *please phone our car*," Lucy said with an aristocratic tone.

69

"I'm not sure if I'm scared of that lady or if she's my new hero," Lucy said as the bartender at Club CLE handed her two drinks. Club CLE was one of the newest and trendiest dance clubs in downtown Cleveland.

"Who… Grace?" Cara yelled in response as Lucy gave her one of the two vodka and cranberry cocktails she had just purchased from the bar. The music at the club was so loud that a normal level of conversation was simply not going to suffice.

"Yes, Grace! She's kinda badass! Here's to friendship!"

The two young women raised their glasses and took a sip.

"She *is* kinda badass, isn't she?" Cara replied as she savored the sweet and tart taste of her favorite cocktail.

On the way to the club from Lola, Cara filled the void of the short drive by informing Lucy all about Grace's quest to become an MMA fighter. Grace felt both flattered and slightly embarrassed by Cara's description of her.

"Come on, let's get out there!" Lucy exclaimed as she pulled Cara toward the packed dance floor.

Club CLE, like many of the new social spots in Cleveland, was located in a former industrial office building. The once thriving manufacturing and transportation hub boasted the nation's fifth largest population by 1920 and was so important to those industries that men like John D. Rockefeller made it his home.

Those days were long gone, however, and Cleveland went from being one of the strongest cities in the country to the constant punchline in jokes by the end of the Twentieth Century.

Cleveland entrepreneurs, like in many other industrial ghost towns, began to repurpose old warehouses and office buildings into upscale apartment complexes, restaurants, and clubs.

The buildings themselves were built during a time period that focused more on quality materials and attention to detail, rather than to how fast the construction could be completed. That alone made renovating one of those old buildings far more appealing than the process of new construction to the developers.

A revitalization was underway in the city that was once famous for a burning river, and Club CLE was the latest addition to that trend. The building, located on East 4th Street, was one of five new restaurants and clubs to occupy the long-abandoned spaces on that street alone.

It took the developers almost a year to not only remodel the space into a nightclub, but also to bring the building's antiquated infrastructure up to modern day code. Since its opening, however, the owners of Club CLE would probably say that it was worth the wait. There was typically a line out the door to get in despite the twenty dollar cover charge, which was about twice the going rate for a Cleveland nightclub.

The interior of the three-story building had been completely gutted. The only remnants of the upper two levels were the eight original structural beams that ran from floor to ceiling and overlooking balconies that had been constructed around the outer walls. These were to be used as VIP sections complete with bottle service and leather seating.

It was not uncommon to see local celebrities and professional athletes looking down at the dance floor from their private perches on the second and third floors of the club. To occupy one of the VIP balconies, one had to pre-purchase a minimum of $400 worth of alcohol, which didn't last long at Club CLE. There were also rumors that a top Cleveland Browns draft pick had recently dropped over ten grand of his newfound wealth on one night in a Club CLE VIP balcony.

Cara and Lucy made the most of their reunion on the dance floor as they danced, laughed, and sang along when their favorite songs were played. Cara couldn't stop repeating the same phrase over and over in her head as she danced with her best friend.

God, I missed this...

Her ex, Kenny, never could grasp that girls sometimes just liked to go dancing with their female friends. Cara was never positive if it was more his ignorance of the female gender or his own insecurities that would always lead to an argument when she and Lucy wanted to go dancing together.

The argument would always go the same way.

"How would you like it if I went drinking and dancing at a club without *you*?" Kenny would typically ask.

"Kenny, if you and your buddies wanted to go dancing without me one night, *the way that I do when I go dancing without you*, I would say go right ahead!" Cara would reply.

"What's that supposed to mean? *Like I do*...?"

"It means that when we go dancing we are only dancing with each other, not other guys. I'm sorry, but I just can't picture you and your guy friends dancing with only each other all night long…"

"Oh right, like no dudes come up and try to dance with you. I'm not an idiot, Cara!"

"Of *course* they do, but guess what Kenny? We make it very clear that we are not interested! Besides, you HATE dancing, Kenny!"

Exchanges like this were a big reason that Coop's reaction when she told him about her plans for the evening made Cara do a double take. It had never occurred to her that a guy could ever be okay with it, and despite the fact he had a bodyguard accompanying her, Cara had a feeling that Cooper Madison was not the insecure type.

He has no reason to be...

The first few beats of "Yeah!" by Usher had just blasted through the speakers when Cara felt a set of unfamiliar hands grab her by the waist from behind, followed by the feeling of a sweaty body pressing up against her back.

Cara managed to push the unwelcomed hands away as she spun around to see who it was that felt entitled enough to invade her personal space. She soon realized that it was not a *who*, but rather a *whom*, as she looked at two unfamiliar men in their mid to late twenties.

The guy who had placed his hands on Cara wasn't phased as he moved in for another attempt to grind up on her. Cara could smell the alcohol coming out of his sweaty pores as she blocked his advance. He had on an untucked oxford blue dress shirt with a loosened tie and khaki pants.

Cara knew the type all too well, and she and Lucy even had a name for any young man who fit the description: Bud Fox. Named after Charlie Sheen's character in *Wall Street*, they were the type of guy she hated the most at clubs. They were typically fresh out of college, finally making some real money, and they thought that entitled them to whatever unclaimed girl they found on the dance floor.

"What's up, baby, you a *dyke* or something?"

"*Excuse* me?" Lucy said as she stepped between Cara and the unwanted guest.

"Oh, I'm sorry, is that your girlfriend? Can I watch?" the guy said, unfazed.

"Listen, it's just a girls night, okay? We're not interested," Cara replied, trying to keep the situation from getting out of hand. She knew where this could go, and she didn't want any more drama in her life.

"Whatever… *whores*!" the guy in the blue shirt yelled as he and his friend walked away to find their next victims.

Lucy and Cara both looked at each other, relieved that they left.

"Bud Fox!" they said in unison, laughing.

Two songs later Cara looked at her watch and realized it was getting late for a weeknight. Even though she was having a great time with Lucy, she didn't want to pay for it the next day. Besides, Lucy was back in town now, so they'd have plenty of more adventures.

"Hey, do you want to get going? I have two classes in the morning and it's already almost ten…"

"I thought you'd never ask, I'm having *so* much fun but I still have jet lag from my flight!" Lucy responded, relieved.

"I'll call Grace and have her meet us out front. Where's your car? We can drop you off there."

"I actually didn't drive, my license expired while I was overseas so I had my mom drop me off at Lola."

"Oh, I'm sure that Grace can drop you off on our way back."

"Ummm, not until *after* I get to meet your new man," Lucy stated.

"Oh boy, I'm not sure I'm ready for that… or should I say I don't think he's ready for that…."

"Why would you say that?"

"Because I know my best friend, and *she* likes to ask way too many questions," Cara joked.

"I'll be good, I promise!" Lucy said as she held up her right hand as if she was pledging an oath.

"Fine, but I need to call and warn him…"

70

Cooper Madison had just finished his third beer of the night as he finished watching a Cleveland Indians game on TV. They were in the middle of a road trip, and on this night they were playing at the home of the Texas Rangers.

It was one of the few times Coop had actually sat through an entire baseball game since walking away from the game. Despite their subpar record, he was impressed by the Indians roster. There were a lot of young players like Victor Martinez and Grady Sizemore who had the potential to be superstars, and manager Eric Wedge was well-respected by his players. Most analysts felt that the Indians were one front-end-of-the-rotation pitcher away from being contenders.

Due to the time difference, the game didn't end until just before Cara was back at his place. She had called him a few minutes earlier to inform him that she had arrived back to the Westcott and was bringing her best friend, Lucy Eckert, up to meet him.

Coop wasn't thrilled about having another new person at his apartment. Prior to meeting Cara, the guest list at his apartment was as exclusive as it gets. Nonetheless, he pretended that it didn't bother him when Cara apologized for the impending intrusion.

After throwing away his beer bottle, Coop made his way to the elevator area outside his penthouse suite door. He watched the lever on the vintage elevator floor indicator slowly make its way up to his floor. While he wanted to meet Lucy, he wasn't really sure that he wanted a long evening of socialization and small talk.

Maybe I'll be able just to quickly meet her out here?

When the elevator doors opened, Coop was taken aback by what he witnessed. Cara, accompanied by her petite friend, had a huge smile on her face and the two were giggling so hard that their faces were red. He had yet to see Cara in this way, and it made him happy to see her so happy.

"Y'all better let me in on the joke," Coop said.

"Oh my god! I'm sorry, we just were talking about this kid from high school who used to pick his ear wax and eat it during class. We named him the Earl of Earwax!" Cara said as she held her stomach from laughter.

"I see..." Coop replied with a smirk.

"You had to be there, it was so gross!" Cara insisted.

"I'll take your word on it..."

Cara gathered herself and introduced her friend to Coop.

"Lucy, this is Cooper Madison... Coop, this is Lucy Eckert."

"Pleasure to meet you, Lucy. Cara has said a lot of nice things about you," Coop said as he shook her hand.

"Likewise," Lucy replied with a smile.

"So, y'all have fun?" Coop asked.

"Oh my god, so much fun!" Cara answered.

"Totally, and thanks so much for the VIP treatment at Lola. You really didn't have to do that, but it was amazing!" Lucy said.

"Well, it was my pleasure. I just wanted to make sure y'all had a good time. Really, I just called Simon and he took care of the rest."

"Who's Simon? Is he your butler or something? Please tell me you have a butler named Simon," Lucy deadpanned.

"Lucy, stop it," Cara playfully admonished her friend before turning back to Coop. "She's messing with you, I told her who Simon was on the way over."

"Oh, I'm sure he can take it, *Carebear*... So, you gonna invite me in or what?" Lucy asked Coop, who wasn't quite sure how to respond.

"I'm sorry Coop, just ignore her *tough chica routine*," Cara chided.

"It's fine… I kinda like it. Come on in," Coop answered.

"Whoa… I never imagined a place this nice existed in Cleveland!" Lucy exclaimed as she entered Cooper Madison's eleventh-floor penthouse suite.

Coop just smiled at Cara as Lucy made her way toward the balcony doors.

"C'mon, let's go out here!" Lucy said as she opened the doors to the balcony.

"Good idea!" Cara replied.

"Not you, Knox. Just me and Babe Ruth. We need to chat. Don't worry, I won't steal your man," Lucy instructed.

"Lucy, *no*, you promised you wouldn't do this!"

"Uh, do what, exactly?" Coop interjected.

"Relax, you two, I'll be nice," Lucy said, softening her voice.

Coop gave Cara a look of surprise as Lucy grabbed him by the hand and started to pull him outside.

"We'll only be a few minutes. Go freshen up for your man or something," Lucy declared.

Cara mouthed the words *I'm sorry* to Coop as Lucy closed the doors, leaving the two of them alone on his balcony.

"Wow, this is great. Have a seat, we need to talk," Lucy said to a bewildered but intrigued Cooper Madison.

"Yes, ma'am…" Coop replied, feigning surrender.

"Look me in the eyes, dude. You need to look me in the eyes, right now, and promise me that you're not just going to use my best friend and then break her heart," Lucy demanded.

"Can I ask you a question, first? If I was a janitor or a school teacher would you be asking me this question?"

"Fair enough… I'm sure that you get this type of suspicion a lot... " Lucy responded.

"Listen, I am not a naive man... and I will never be crazy enough to think that anyone should ever feel sorry for my success, but you know who *hasn't* made me feel like she doesn't trust my intentions? Cara."

"Yes..." Lucy replied.

"Yes?" Coop asked, puzzled.

"Yes. Yes, I would ask you if you were a janitor or a teacher or flipping burgers. She is my best friend, so I would ask anyone."

"Oh..."

"So, back to the question at hand?"

"I'll tell you the same thing I'd tell anyone, including Cara. I don't know what this is, or where it's going. What I do know is that I can't imagine doing anything other than finding out just that. I really like Cara. A lot. But, we are still just getting to know each other, which is hard enough in any relationship, let alone a heavily scrutinized one," Coop replied.

"Oh…"

"You know what, though?" Coop asked.

"No, what?" Lucy replied.

"It's reassuring to see so many people who truly care about her. She must be as amazing as I already think she is."

Lucy softened.

"You have no idea… she is the best person I know. She's the total package, dude. But, she's not perfect, so don't put that pedestal too high. It's not fair to either of you."

"Fair enough…" Coop replied.

"You know, I'm a little surprised…"

"About?"

"How quickly Cara has let things progress with you. If anyone who knows the two of us would've predicted that which one of us would be the one involved in a whirlwind romance, it definitely would not have been Cara."

"Why's that?"

"She's the most cautious, level-headed person I know. And she could care less about money or being famous. The closest I have ever seen her get to letting that wall down was with Kenny, and she's regretted *that* ever since."

"That seems to be the general consensus about her ex..."

"You have to kiss a lot of frogs before you find your prince, right?"

"Perhaps…"

"I'm sorry, I really just am worried my friend is going to get hurt. She's had to deal with enough of that in her life the last five or six years."

"That makes you a pretty darn good friend, then."

"Maybe, but I'm pretty sure she is going to be mad at me for talking to you out here."

"She'll get over it, we've already been through this routine a few times during our short time together," Coop laughed.

"Her brothers?" Lucy asked.

"Amongst others," Coop replied.

"I guess everyone is just worried about your intentions."

"I don't have anything but the best intentions, Lucy, but I can't promise I'm going to be Cara's prince. I don't need that kind of pressure."

"Well, even if you're not her prince, just don't end up being another frog."

71

"You're not mad at me, are you?" Cara Knox asked as she sat at the foot of the bed, a cup of coffee in hand.

"Mad? Why on earth would you ask me that, girl?" Cooper Madison said as he stretched his arms over his head.

It was just past seven in the morning and Cara had been up for an hour while Coop slumbered away in his bedroom.

"Because I crashed last night before you even were done talking to Lucy out on the balcony. I barely remember you coming inside."

"Yeah, you were out like a light. But, you did look really cute with that lil bit of drool coming out of the corner of your mouth," Coop teased.

"Oh, you want to talk, Sir Snores-A-Lot?"

"I don't snore… that's erroneous!"

"Keep telling yourself that!" Cara laughed.

"Lucy didn't want to wake you up, so she slipped out after we came back inside."

"Lucy sent me a text saying that you got her a car to take her home. I appreciate that. Hopefully, it wasn't too painful…"

"It was fine, you just have a lot of people that care about you is all."

"I'm sure it's getting old, though."

"Nah… keeps me on my toes."

"Listen, I'm not going to class today…" Cara changed the subject.

"Why's that? I thought everything went well yesterday?" Coop replied, puzzled.

"Oh, it did. It went better than I imagined. I just really wanted to spend the day with you. I was thinking last night that you've done so many nice things for me recently, like planning the VIP table last night at Lola, and I wanted to try and plan something nice for you."

"Oh… well, aren't you precious," Coop said as he sat up. "What'd you have in mind?"

"Well, it's a surprise. You're not the only one with surprises, you know! We're going on a 'Mystery Trip'..."

"Look at you, girl!"

"I think you're going to love it, and don't worry, you won't have to worry about anyone popping out of bushes where we're going…" Cara said with a wry smile.

"Oh, that's just not fair! You gotta give me a hint!"

"Nope… Did you give me a hint that you were going to show up at Gabby's party? Or that you paid for an *amazing* five-course meal at the hottest restaurant in town?" Cara responded.

"Touché… touché…"

"I made you coffee, but first, we need to hop in the shower and get dressed."

"*We*…? I like this 'Mystery Trip' thing already!"

72

"Are you sure this is gonna work? I mean, I don't need the Russian mob after me," a visibly nervous Ernie Page said to Detective Jason Knox as they sat in the detective's unmarked police cruiser at Edgewater Park.

"Not if you don't calm down and stop shaking so much. Tick will smell that fear a mile away and this whole operation will be ruined. Don't forget, your cooperation as a C.I. in this matter is what's going to keep you out of jail and your wife from finding out about your extracurricular activities," Jason admonished his newest confidential informant.

Jason had already prepped Ernie back at the 1st District station and fitted him with a wire to record his pending interaction with Tick. After meeting with Ernie the day before, Jason went to his superiors and filled them in to get the necessary warrants to conduct a sting of both Tick and the motel.

Accompanying Jason and Ernie were two plainclothes detectives who were wearing earpieces. They were going to blend in with the other people at the park while listening for orders from Jason.

The plan was that Ernie would repeat his actions from the prior day by buying ice cream and writing his phone number on the Styrofoam container before leaving it for Tick. It was an unusually warm September morning, even hotter than the day prior, but there was a nice breeze off the lake.

"Why can't you just have one of those two guys do it?" Ernie had asked when briefed on the plan.

"Because Tick already knows, for a fact, that you're not a cop. We can't take any chances with him. You're the closest thing we have to a sure bet."

"Won't he know that I'm the snitch after you bust him, though?"

"That part won't matter, trust me. You leave that to me."

"Forgive me for finding that hard to believe. I just don't want to end up in a ditch."

"Well, Ernie, you're kinda screwed either way. Like I told you yesterday, those Russians are going to blackmail you, regardless. Your only chance at keeping that from happening is by letting us do our job, which believe it or not, includes protecting you after the fact."

"Goddamnit, I feel so stupid. I never should've let my other head do the thinking."

"Nobody's perfect, Ernie, but you have the luxury of trying to help fix that mistake. You should feel lucky," Jason smirked.

"Oh yeah, *so* lucky. I'm gonna go play the lottery after this," Ernie said, his voice dripping with sarcasm.

"There's our guy, right on cue," Jason said, pointing towards Tick, who was making his way towards the same picnic table he sat at the day before.

"You can't see the wire, right?" Ernie asked, just as he had five times already after being fitted with the surveillance device.

"Ernie, relax… even if he did see the wire, we are making the arrest regardless. You'll be fine," Jason reassured him.

"If you say so…"

"Alright… you ready?" Jason asked one final time.

"I think so…"

"Good. Go get 'em, tiger. Remember, just do exactly what you did yesterday. The only reason you have the wire is in the event he talks to you first," Jason said, giving his instructions one final time.

Ernie nodded and exited the vehicle. He took a look around before he began his walk towards the concession stand, which stood about 75 yards away from the detective's car.

"Alright boys, Echo is on the move. Give the signal if you copy, over…" Jason said into his radio, Echo referring to Ernie. He had also instructed the two plainclothes detectives to signal that they could hear him through their earpiece by taking the hats that they were each wearing off for a second, bending the brim, and then placing them back on their heads. Jason watched through his binoculars as each of them complied.

The two detectives had positioned themselves at separate picnic tables on opposite sides of the pavilion. They not only had eyes on Tick, but they also were in clear view of Jason, who was watching from his car and ready to radio when necessary.

All three detectives kept an eye on Ernie as he tried his best to casually approach the concession stand.

"Tap your fingers on the table if you think Ernie is shitting himself right now," Jason said into his radio. Both detectives discreetly began tapping. Jason chuckled.

If he wasn't such a scumbag, I'd feel sorry for him...

After waiting his turn and then paying, Ernie received his ice cream order and after casually walked over to Tick's table and had a seat. Jason, through his binoculars, watched as Ernie nodded at Tick, who also gave a quick nod in return as he took a long drag off of his cigarette.

True to form, Tick said absolutely nothing to Ernie. If anyone else had been walking by they likely would have assumed that it was just strangers sharing a table by the lake.

Jason watched as Ernie consumed his ice cream and then discretely wrote his cell phone number on the container. He set the empty foam cup on the edge of the picnic table so even the slightest hint of breeze would knock it off to the ground. He then nodded at Tick, stood up, and began walking back toward the parking lot.

"Echo is on the move… the package is in place… standby for pickup… over," Jason said over his radio to the two detectives who were standing by. Per the plan, Ernie would return to Jason's unmarked cruiser, which he had just moved to a new spot out of Tick's line of sight. In the event he was watching, Jason told Ernie where the cruiser would be located after he left Tick.

"Do you think he saw me?" Ernie asked, out of breath, as he entered Jason's cruiser.

"Not unless he has X-Ray vision. Now we wait..." Jason said as he held up Ernie's cell phone.

"What if he doesn't call?" Ernie asked.

"He will, and when he does I'm going to put you on speaker and you say exactly what you said the day before.

Ernie nodded in agreement, beads of sweat dotting his forehead.

Even though Jason no longer had eyes on Tick, his two plainclothes detectives did. While all of the radio communication had been one-way originating from Jason, each of the detectives also had the ability to radio back if necessary.

Jason had instructed them to stay silent earlier just to be safe, but also instructed them to notify him if Tick picked up the ice cream cup.

"Alpha, this is Bravo, copy?" a voice came over Jason's radio.

"10-4 Bravo, over," Jason replied.

"Tango is on the move… package retrieved… dialing phone… over."

"10-4, standby for pickup, over," Jason said as Ernie's phone began to ring. The screen read "Unknown Caller".

Jason gave Ernie a nod, opened Ernie's well-used flip phone, and pressed the speaker button.

"Hello?" Ernie answered.

"Round two, huh?" Tick's voice came out of the phone's small speaker. Jason would've recognized that voice even if he wasn't expecting to hear it.

"Yessir, I appreciate you setting me up with her," Ernie replied.

"Whoa… I don't know what you're talking about, if you catch my drift. I just gave you directions to a nice motel."

"Oh, right, of course. Do you know if there are any, uh, vacancies today?"

"Not sure about today, but you should definitely ask about December 8th. See what's available."

This caused Jason to pause.

December 8th? Why a different date? There must be some sort of significance to these dates.

"Ok, same place, right?" Ernie asked.

"Same place. Enjoy," Tick responded as he ended the call.

Jason closed the flip phone and picked up his radio.

"Bravo, Charlie, this is Alpha… Tango is ready for extraction, over," Jason informed the two detectives who were waiting for the orders to arrest, or extract, Tick, on charges of prostitution. Jason found it ironic that Tick was going to be extracted.

Man, I wish I could see his face when they cuff him…

"10-4," came back over the radio twice, once from each of the two detectives.

As much as Jason wanted to place the handcuffs on Tick himself, he and Ernie still had a visit to make to the motel, where Jason had a SWAT team awaiting orders nearby.

"Are you ready for Act II?" Jason asked Ernie, who just nodded as he gazed nervously ahead.

73

"Hey Clarence, can I ask you a question?" Cooper Madison asked the owner of CW Security Solutions as he rode in the back seat of the Escalade next to Cara, who was grinning ear to ear.

"Of course," Clarence responded.

"Who's paying you for your services today?"

"That would be you, Mr. Madison."

"But, you won't tell me where we are going?"

"No, sir… Cara told me I'm not allowed to."

"Is *Cara* paying you, Clarence?"

"No sir, you are," Clarence deadpanned with a smile.

"Then why won't you tell *me* where we are going?" Coop begged.

"Well, sir, you hired me to protect Miss Cara Knox at all costs… And she told me that she had a secret to protect, so I guess I am just following orders…"

Cara broke out in laughter in the seat next to Coop, who threw his hands up in surrender.

"This is ridiculous, y'all!" he sighed.

"Don't worry, we will be there soon enough," Cara reassured.

"Not even a hint?" Coop pleaded.

"Man, you really are a control freak, aren't you?"

"Only on days that end in the letter 'Y'..." Coop replied.

"Now I wish I would've picked somewhere further away. We've only been in the car for twenty minutes you big baby!"

"How much longer?" Coop asked.

"Just a few more minutes. *Relax*," Cara said as she held his hand with her left hand and patted the top of his shoulder with her right.

Clarence exited the freeway and turned onto Route 17, which stretches just over twenty miles and runs east-west from North Olmsted to Bedford Heights. It's such a long stretch of road that it actually goes by three different names depending which part of the route you are on. From east to west it takes on the names Libby Road, Granger Road, and then finally Brookpark Road, which is where Clarence's Escalade was heading near the airport.

This particular stretch of Brookpark Road, which is home to numerous strip clubs and abandoned buildings, would best be described as seedy. Some of the motels near the strip clubs actually had hourly rates for prostitutes and their clients to use. Drugs were rampant and readily available up and down Brookpark Road, along with the violence that typically accompanies the sale of those drugs.

"Are you taking me to a strip club?" Coop jokingly asked Cara as they drove past one of the many "Gentlemen's Clubs" on Route 17.

"Don't you think it's a little early for you to meet my coworkers?" Cara deadpanned without missing a beat.

"Well, that explains all the glitter…" Coop replied, not to be outdone.

Clarence just shook his head and laughed in the front seat as he listened to the young couple trading barbs.

The Escalade continued down Brookpark Road, and the further west it went, the nicer the scenery became. Aside from a few rundown and possibly vacant motels, most of the buildings they began to see belonged to industrial companies that boasted large steel warehouses.

Clarence turned into a parking lot just past one of those industrial buildings and a rundown motel. At the entrance to the parking lot was a large neon sign that read "Amazing Adventure Park - Indoor Go Karts, Laser Tag, and Arcade".

"*Indoor* go karts? Sweet!" Coop declared.

At the end of the large parking lot stood a large steel building with a steeply pitched roof and another giant sign on the front. The sign was an exact replica of the one at the entrance to the parking lot, except below this sign was a white vinyl banner that read, "Going Out of Business - Last Day - September 15th" in huge red letters.

Save for two other cars, the parking lot was empty. As the Escalade approached the entrance to the building, Coop could see that the "Hours of Operation" sign indicated that Amazing Adventure Park wasn't supposed to open until later that afternoon.

"I love go-karts and laser tag, Cara, but unfortunately it looks like it's closed," Coop informed.

"Well, it is closed, to everyone except *us*..." Cara replied coyly.

"Come again?" Coop asked, puzzled.

"Lucy's parents own this place, and I asked them if they'd let us come in and have some fun before they opened."

"The hippies own a go-kart place?" Coop asked.

"*Former* hippies, they crossed over to the 'Dark Side' when they had kids," Cara replied.

"That'll do it, I suppose. It's a shame they're going out of business, though," Coop said as he gestured toward the sign.

"They're actually making a *killing* on the sale of the land to a big manufacturer, so don't feel too bad for them. They had a nice run of over two decades. We had lots of great times here as teenagers. It was *the* place to be on the weekends and in the summer," Cara said, a hint of nostalgia in her voice.

"Hippies turned opportunistic capitalists!" Coop laughed.

"Come on, let's go inside. You'll get to meet Brenda and Nelson," Cara said, referencing Lucy's parents.

"I must admit, those are not the names I was expecting. I was thinking something like Willow and Leif," Coop laughed as he followed Cara into the building while Clarence remained just outside the entrance in his SUV.

74

"Nice job, fellas… tell our friend that I look forward to talking with him back at the station," Jason said before ending the call with one of the plainclothes detectives that had just placed a *very* surprised Tick into custody.

Jason looked over at his passenger, Ernie Page, who was doing his best to keep it together. In less than an hour, he was going to help the Cleveland Police Department infiltrate a prostitution ring controlled by the Russian mob. He couldn't help but think that he was about to regret his decision to help the detective.

This is not going to end well for me…

"Hey, relax, all you have to do is go in and do whatever you did before. Well, minus the sex," Jason chuckled.

"Very funny…"

"Seriously, though, just pay the money, get the room key, and then walk over to the room. That's when you will see the cavalry coming in hot. Once you do, get down on the ground and cover your head. We are going to arrest you just like the rest of them so they won't know it's you that sold them out."

"Oh, I still think that they'll have an idea. Then I'm a dead man," Ernie replied.

"If this thing leads to where I think it does, you won't be a blip on their radar even if they do think it's you. They'll have a lot more to worry about," Jason said, implying that this was about more than hookers and pimps.

"Is that *supposed* to make me feel better, Detective?"

"Ernie, if I was worried about your feelings I would have become a therapist or something."

Ernie's shoulders fell a little as he sat in the passenger seat, contemplating a way out of the situation he found himself in.

Maybe I can just jump out of the car while it's moving?

Jason pulled into a parking lot about a mile down there road from the motel that Ernie would soon be visiting. Awaiting him was a staging area that included an armored police vehicle and a dozen SWAT officers in full gear armed with AR-15 rifles.

Joining them was First District Commander, Michael "Mick" McCarthy, who met Jason as he exited his vehicle.

"Well, Detective Knox, looks like we didn't get dressed up for nothing!" Mick said as he shook Jason's hand. His voice was a mixture of excitement and adrenaline, which was pretty typical for any cop about to make a bust.

"Sure looks that way… Hopefully, they'll give us some insight on the dead Russian girls that keep washing ashore, too," Jason said, lowering his voice.

"I apprised Chief Johnston of the situation. He's very excited to get a press release out as soon as we're ready to. Especially if these Russians have any ties to the EPK case," Mick whispered to Jason.

"Trust me, Mick, if there's a link between the two I'll be even more excited than the Chief," Jason whispered back.

"Well, alright then. The boys are all set and we have this jackass's car over here for him to drive to the motel," Mick said as he nodded toward Ernie, who was still seated in Jason's cruiser.

"Perfect, I'll be parked across the street in the parking lot of the Five Star Packaging building. I'll have eyes and ears on Ernie, the motel, and will be in direct contact with you and the team. Once I see Ernie exit the motel office with the key, I'll give the green light to go in," Jason confirmed.

"We'll be ready and will be coming in hot. Make sure this douchebag gets his ass down so we don't accidentally shoot him and protect future car buyers," said Mick, jokingly.

"I already prepped him and told him that he will be cuffed just like the rest of them and to keep his mouth shut."

"Well then, let's go catch some bad guys!"

75

"I think I just lived out every boy's dream! A go-kart track all to ourselves," Coop said as he climbed out of his kart.

"You totally cheated though, the sign said 'No Bumping'..." Cara replied as she pointed to the rules hanging above the indoor track.

"Oh, hell, that was just a love tap! You're such a sore loser!"

"Sore loser? You spun me out in the last turn when I had the lead!"

"Excuses are like armpits, Cara. We all have them and they all stink! Now pay up, girl," Coop said as he puckered his lips.

"For the record, I'm only awarding you this kiss under protest," Cara replied as she planted a long kiss on Coop.

"For the record, I'm fine with that," Coop replied after the kiss as he held her in a hug.

"What's next kids?" the voice of Brenda Eckert interrupted the young couple.

"How about a game of laser tag?" Coop asked Cara.

"Only if you don't cheat!" Cara replied.

"I wouldn't dream of it…"

Just then the entrance doors of Amazing Adventure Park burst open and Clarence Walters came charging towards Coop, Cara, and Brenda. Nelson Eckert was so startled by the sound of the doors being flung open that he came running out of his office near the entrance to see what was happening.

Clarence was visibly concerned as he ran towards the group.

"We got to go, NOW!" he yelled to Coop and Cara as he neared.

"Go? But we just got here. What's going on?" Coop asked.

"Something big is happening next door at that old motel. I just saw a SWAT team run in and heard shots fired. We need to evacuate this building NOW!" Clarence ordered as he grabbed Cara by the arm and instructed Coop to follow.

"What about Brenda and Nelson?" Cara yelled as Clarence dragged her toward the door. She could see that he had pulled his SUV up to the door and that the rear passenger door was open just a few steps outside the doorway. It was there that they could hear the loud pop of gunfire that had previously been inaudible over the sounds of the arcade games near the go-kart track.

"Lock up behind us and take shelter in your office. Don't open the door for *anyone* except the police. If the police come you'll know it's them," he instructed.

Nelson and Brenda each nodded as Clarence stopped at the front door. He looked through the glass doors to make sure that they would have a safe exit before turning and giving everyone further instruction.

"Okay, I will open this door and step out first, you two will keep your heads down and jump right into the backseat where you will remain down until I tell you otherwise. Understand?"

"Yessir," Coop answered as Cara nodded.

"If anything should happen to me, Coop, you need to jump in the front seat and get Cara out of here. Don't stop for anything or anyone. That includes me. Just *drive*. I'll be fine."

Clarence turned towards Nelson and Brenda.

"You two, as soon as we are out the door you lock it and get in your office. You understand?"

They nodded nervously in agreement.

"Okay, on my command…" Clarence said as he shoved the door open and formed a barrier using his body between the open door of the Escalade and the action going on at the motel next door.

"Go, Go, Go!" Clarence yelled as Cara and Coop each dove into the back of the SUV. As they huddled on the floor of the backseat they could hear Clarence slam the door shut as the gunshots sounded like they were coming from only a few feet away.

"Oh my God!" Cara yelled as two more shots sounded as if they were fired right next to the backseat.

"Calm down, I got you," Coop said as he positioned his body on top of Cara's, his hands over her ears.

Just then they heard the sound of the driver's side door open and close quickly.

"Stay down! We're moving!" Clarence yelled as they felt the Escalade accelerate quickly. Coop and Cara felt the weight of the vehicle swing sharply to the right as Clarence made a sharp left turn, presumably out of the parking lot and onto Brookpark Road.

The sound of gunshots faded before they could no longer hear anything other than the sound of the SUV's engine humming through the floorboards.

"Okay, you can get up now, we're on the highway," Clarence said after what seemed like an hour later, but in reality was only a few minutes.

Coop pushed himself up off the floor of the Escalade and helped Cara get up into the seat next to him.

"Are you okay?" he asked as she looked at him, tears of fear still present in her eyes.

"What the *hell* just happened?" Cara asked no one in particular. She was shaking and began to sob as the reality of what just happened set in.

"You're okay, it's gonna be okay," Coop said as he pulled her head to his chest and wrapped his arms around her.

Clarence pressed the button on his earpiece.

"Alpha, this is Baker... we are on the interstate and clear… find out what the *hell* that just was, please? Over."

"I'll tell you what it was," Coop announced.

"What?" Cara asked, her head still pressed firmly against Coop's chest.

"That was Clarence being a hero and getting us out of a very dangerous situation. That's what that was…"

"No, sir, the heroes were next door fighting the bad guys," Clarence responded.

"Them too, but you were amazing, Clarence. I don't know how you remained so calm. You're the man," Coop said.

"Well, I've had a lot of practice over the years. I used to be one of those guys in the SWAT gear storming the building."

"See, you are a hero," Coop declared.

"Just doing my job," Clarence said.

"Well, let me tell you, you're getting a raise after today."

76

Detective Jason Knox was not certain if he should feel upset or relieved at how things had just unfolded at the motel sting. Everything was going smoothly until Ernie Page exited the motel, presumably towards one of the rooms occupied by prostitutes.

Only Ernie was running for his life.

The sound of gunshots came from within the office and a man fitting the description Ernie gave of the Russian from the prior day came running out after him with a gun.

As the Russian exited the office he saw the armored SWAT vehicle approaching with officers since Jason, per the plan, had just given them the green light to go in.

Goddamnit, Ernie…

Upon seeing the SWAT team approaching, the Russian immediately ran inside the motel office to alert his accomplices that trouble was coming. The SWAT team was met with gunfire coming from the window of the office as they pulled into the driveway of the motel. Ernie, as planned, immediately laid down on the ground and covered his head as the chaos ensued.

The officers took cover behind their armored vehicle for a few minutes as the bullets began to ricochet off of the vehicle's heavily plated exterior. As planned, the SWAT officers would not return fire unless absolutely necessary.

The assumption that Jason and Mick had made was that the Russians, while likely armed, would not have an extensive arsenal or cache of ammunition. If they decided to fire at the armored vehicle, which was a futile effort unless one possessed a rocket launcher, the team would let them unload their guns before attempting to breach. Officers were told only to return fire if an immediate threat presented itself, like one of the occupants exiting the building or firing in the direction of anything other than the armored vehicle.

The plan worked, and Jason next ordered the SWAT officers straight into phase two of the operation, which was to breach the building and apprehend the suspects. The SWAT team was ordered to avoid lethally neutralizing any of the suspects unless absolutely necessary. Jason needed them alive, and it wasn't just to answer questions about Russian prostitutes.

The vehicle, fitted with an extended steel battering ram, drove into the motel's office. This provided a few moments of cover for the members of the team who were designated to evacuate the girls from each room, "arrest" Ernie, and provide cover for the remaining officers trying to breach the office.

After taking out a large chunk of the motel office's front wall, the armored vehicle reversed its course and exposed the gaping hole that it had left in its wake. At that moment, two of the officers fired canisters of tear gas into the opening as a few more sporadic gunshots came from within, before ceasing altogether.

As Jason watched the operation unfold from his position across the street, he couldn't help but marvel at the SWAT team's level of efficiency. He was so focused on the motel that he never noticed the black Cadillac Escalade speeding away from nearby Amazing Adventure Park.

The SWAT team, using the PA system on the armored vehicle, ordered the motel office's occupants to lay down their weapons and exit the building with their hands up. After some yelling and a few tense moments, the Russian who had first alerted the others that SWAT had arrived came out with his hands up. He was immediately detained by one of the officers as two more provided watch, their guns aimed at the large opening in the front of the motel.

After some more yelling from inside, a mixture of Russian and English vulgarities, three more male suspects exited the building before being placed into custody. A sweep of the building concluded that there were no more occupants in the office to detain.

The four suspects from the motel, all of whom appeared to be Russian, were placed in the back of four separate police cruisers that had arrived on the scene shortly after they surrendered.

Ernie, who was unharmed but shaken, was placed in the back of a fifth cruiser. Jason had instructed that officer to remain on the scene until instructed otherwise.

In all, seven of the eight rooms had a girl in them, some of whom appeared to be under the age of consent. All of them informed officers through broken English that they were of Russian or Ukrainian descent.

The girls were all placed in protective custody and transported to MetroHealth Medical Center for physical and mental health evaluations. Jason knew he would eventually sit down with each girl and see if they knew anything about the EPK victims, but first, they needed to be provided with medical care and a feeling of security.

After the four cruisers containing the Russians departed for the 1st District precinct, Jason walked over to the cruiser that a handcuffed Ernie Page was sitting inside. He opened the back door and pulled Ernie out before uncuffing him.

"Man, you are one lucky son of a bitch. I thought for sure one of those Russians was going to pop a cap in your ass. Goddamnit, Ernie, what the hell stinks?" Jason chided.

"I...I may have shit my pants a little... during the shooting," a visibly shaken Ernie responded.

"Well, that explains the smell. Hopefully, you have a change of clothes back at your crappy car dealership you can change into before you go home and pretend that none of this happened. No pun intended…"

"How am I supposed to do *that*? I was almost killed today!"

Jason grabbed Ernie by the shirt and pulled him close to his face.

"Listen to me very closely, Ernie. If you are smarter than I think you are, you'll go home to your poor wife and *never* tell anyone about what happened today. Not your brother, not your drinking buddies, nobody. I'm going to do my best to keep you from having to testify against these guys because the Russians don't take kindly to eyewitness informants. The fewer people who know you were involved today the greater the chance that doesn't happen. Are we clear?"

"Okay… we're clear, we're clear… just let me go," Ernie pleaded.

Jason released him and gave him the car keys that Ernie had dropped inside the motel before he got into his vehicle and drove away.

Time to go interview some Russians…

77

"So much for me planning a *special* day," Cara said as they sat at Coop's kitchen table. They each had a beer in front of them, hoping to calm their nerves down from the day's prior events.

"Yeah, I wish you would've told me that I needed my bulletproof vest… I would've worn it," Coop replied, jokingly.

"Very funny…"

"Gotta laugh or we'd cry, right?"

"Thank God Lucy's parents are okay…"

"Clarence just texted me that he is with them now. They're shook up but will be okay. He's going over what we talked about on the way back," Coop said, referencing Clarence's plan to make sure that Brenda and Nelson Eckert did not talk to anyone, including police, about Coop and Cara being in their business at the time of the shooting. If the police gave them a hard time, Clarence said that he would handle it for them.

"Can I talk to Lucy about this? I have to, I could never keep this from her," Cara had asked Clarence.

"As long as you can trust that she won't talk to anyone else about it," Clarence answered.

"What about my brother? I wonder if he was there?" Cara asked as that possibility hit her.

"Let me talk to Jason, first," Clarence said. He was pretty certain that he'd seen Jason's unmarked cruiser as he sped away from the scene.

Cara took a sip of her beer and sighed.

"I feel like I'm living in an alternative reality right now… and to think I used to feel that my life was too boring," she laughed.

"I'm sorry," Coop replied.

"Why?"

"Because all this crap has happened since you met me. Paparazzi, CMZ, bodyguards, and now shootouts. I'm the common denominator in your recent struggles."

"Don't do that to yourself…"

"It's the truth, Cara… If something would've happened to you today, it would've been because I came into your life."

"First of all, I could get shot waiting for the RTA bus. Secondly, I made the plans for the day, remember? Thirdly, I don't think either one of us can take credit for the fate that brought us together."

"It was fate, wasn't it?" Coop said as he reached across the kitchen table and put his hand on hers.

"I can't think of any other reason," Cara replied as she gave his hand a gentle squeeze.

"I hope you think I'm worth it… the headaches and the chaos…"

"You already were… that first night at Coe Lake… when we said…"

"Nothing…" Coop finished her sentence.

"Nothing…" Cara replied.

78

"Listen, I know you don't want to talk. But, you're going to go to prison either way. How long you go away for and what you get charged with all depends on what you're willing to give me. *Today*. Right now. If you don't, I'm going to make sure that they try you for multiple counts of attempted murder of a police officer, prostitution, and narcotics. If you give me what I need, and it pans out, you may just live long enough to see the outside world again before you're too old to enjoy it," Detective Jason Knox said to the man sitting in an interrogation room at the 1st District headquarters.

The man, whom they already pinpointed as the leader of the motel operation, sat across from Jason with a cold gaze. He had been identified, via the passport the police found on the scene, as Vladimir Popov. One of the other suspects had already talked, giving nothing of substance, but he did admit that they all spoke English.

Still, Vladimir Popov said nothing.

"Fine, have it your way, Vlad. I'll get one of your boys to talk, especially when I tell them that you'll be taking the brunt of the charges as their leader. Hell, they might not even serve time if they flip. Hope you never treated any of those guys poorly…"

Jason began to walk away before Vladimir's voice was heard for the first time since sitting down in the room.

"Nyet! No!"

"Excuse me? You having a change of heart?" Jason asked.

"Turn recorder off," Vlad said as he nodded toward the device.

"You don't get to make the rules, Popov. This isn't Moscow."

"Turn recorder off, and video too. I talk. Otherwise, no."

Jason, against his better judgment, couldn't resist finding out what Vladimir Popov had to say. He pressed stop on the audio recorder and powered the video camera off.

"You have one minute. Go."

"Give me pen and paper," Popov demanded in broken English.

Jason slid his notepad and pen across the table.

"Clock's ticking, Vlad."

"I give you this, you solve EPK murders. You drop attempted murder and narcotics charges," Vlad said as he folded up the piece of paper he had just written something on.

"Vlad, I haven't said anything about the EPK murders, so why are you offering that?"

"Cleveland Police don't care about my business. Many of my customers are cops. Never had problem. Then today, SWAT comes. Why SWAT? For prostitutes? Nyet! You're after something bigger. EPK kills Russian girls. We're Russian. We have girls. You think it's us. But, it's not..."

"Okay, slow down, Vlad. That's an awful lot of conclusions you're trying to jump to..."

"Isn't that what police do every day?" Vlad laughed.

"Ok, before I even entertain the thought that you know *anything* about the EPK case, you need to know that I can't make the promises you're asking for. But, if you do give me the EPK, I will do what I can to get the attempted murder dropped."

"Do I have your word, Detective? If you break promise. People will find you. Your wife..." Vladimir said as he stared at the wedding ring on Jason Knox's left ring finger.

"How do I know you won't do that anyway?" Jason asked. This wasn't the first, or last time, he had been threatened.

"Because I want to help you catch EPK. It's personal."

"Okay, but I need to know why you'd be willing to offer it up without a lawyer and so early in the process. To be honest, Vlad, I was planning on breaking you and your boys down for days, even weeks if I had to. Why are you willing to show me your cards now?"

"Because, today, we're after same thing," Vladimir Popov said as he slid the folded piece of paper towards Jason.

Jason slowly opened it up, and when he saw the name Vladimir Popov had written his stomach dropped.

"So, Detective… Do we have deal?" Vlad asked, coyly.

"Is this for real, Vlad? Because if this isn't, I'll make sure you die in prison," Jason answered, clearly shocked by what he had just read.

"I told you, today we're after same thing. Come close so I can whisper," he gestured to Jason, who leaned in as Vlad whispered in his ear for the next few minutes.

Next door, in the adjacent interrogation room, Jason could hear someone yelling through the walls.

"I want my lawyer!" Timothy "Tick" Braun yelled at Mick McCarthy, who was trying his best not to lose his cool.

"How's the arm, Tick? Still sore?" Mick said, ignoring his request.

"Oh, you mean the arm that *bitch* broke?"

"She's not a bitch, you're just mad that a chick kicked your little ass."

"Oh, what's the matter? Were you tapping that, *Commander*? Does your wife know?"

"Ask your mom, oh wait… sorry about that, Tick. She hates you, too."

Mick hated that he was stooping to Tick's level. In fact, he rarely ever did interrogations anymore since his promotion to Commander. But, this was *personal*. He'd wanted a run at Tick ever since he walked last year after his case was thrown out.

Just then, Jason Knox pounded on the door and signaled for Mick to come out into the hallway.

"What's up? I was just about to bust his balls some more for getting his ass kicked by a chick!" Mick said loud enough for Tick to hear him as he closed the door.

"Look at what Vladimir Popov just gave me. He said it'll solve the EPK case. He wants the attempted murder and narcotics drugs dropped, though."

Mick looked up solemnly at Jason after he read the paper.

"If this is true, I'll get the DA to drop the attempted murder and drug charges myself. We gotta go."

Jason nodded, and the two ran off in the direction of the department's bullpen area where they could fill the other detectives in on their recent discovery.

Tick, who witnessed the detectives running off, started yelling even louder to whoever would hear him.

"Yo, where are you going? Get me the hell outta here, man! This ain't funny!"

79

"I don't know where he is, he never came home after work today. Is something wrong?" asked a very startled Ellie Page to the two detectives who had shown up at her door just before dusk to ask if her husband was home.

"When was the last time you spoke to him?" Detective Jason Knox asked.

Alongside him was Commander Mick McCarthy. Uniformed backup and SWAT were on standby around the corner waiting for orders. A quick surveillance of the house earlier indicated that Ellie was likely the only person home.

Another set of detectives and SWAT unit were currently going through Ernie Page's office at Rides 4 Less. Ernie was nowhere to be seen, but his brother and boss, Raymond Page, had been detained for questioning back at the precinct.

Apparently, Ray showed up to Rides 4 Less at around five in the afternoon to get a bank drop envelope from Ernie, but Ernie was not there. The dealership had been locked up and the phones were all off their hooks. Shortly after he made that discovery, Ray had a front row seat to what it's like to have a SWAT team storm his place of business.

Back at Ernie's residence, Ellie was not proving to be much of a help. Jason felt as though she was being authentic, but also blissfully unaware of the monster that shared the same roof with her.

"I haven't spoken to Ernie since this morning when he left for work. He seemed nervous, but wouldn't tell me why," Ellie responded.

If you only knew...

"Is there anywhere that you think Ernie might be? Do you have any other residences like a cabin or vacation home?" Mick asked.

"No... why are you asking me all of this? Is Ernie missing?"

"Yes, he is, Mrs. Page. However, he's missing because he wants to be. We're afraid that he may be a harm to himself and possibly others if we don't find him soon," Jason answered.

"Harm? Ernie? No, no, no... you must be mistaken. Ernie wouldn't ever hurt anyone. He doesn't even own a gun or hunt."

"Please, Mrs. Page, we need your help. If Ernie was trying to hide somewhere safe, where would he go?" Mick asked.

"The only places Ernie ever goes are work, home, and the Corner Pocket. He's a homebody."

"The pool hall?" Mick questioned, in reference to the billiards hall on Cleveland's west side.

"Every single night after work..."

"Ok, Mrs. Page. Thanks for your help. We need to inform you that we have a warrant to search your house, and we are going to have a few officers stay with you in your home for a while, maybe longer," Jason informed.

"A warrant? I... I don't understand. What do you think Ernie did?"

"That's what we're trying to figure out, ma'am," Mick reassured.

"If Ernie, or anyone else for that matter, tries to contact you over the phone the officers will be there with you listening and recording the calls. If you alert Ernie, in any way, that we are looking for him you will be immediately placed under arrest for obstruction. Do you understand, Mrs. Page?" Jason asked.

"Yes..." Ellie Page nodded solemnly.

"We know that this is difficult for you, ma'am, but the best way to help Ernie is to help us find him," Mick said, doing his best to reassure Mrs. Page.

80

"I can't believe I had him, Mick. I freaking had him! Goddamnit!" Jason yelled as he punched his steering wheel.

"Jason, *we all had him*, and none of us saw it either. This isn't on you. Hell, it's not even on us. If you hadn't been doing your job like you were we wouldn't even have a suspect, let alone starting a manhunt for one," Commander Mick McCarthy insisted.

Earlier, after Vladimir Popov slid the folded piece of paper to Jason in the interrogation room, a chain of events went into action that turned the entire department into a chaotic scene.

First, Jason briefed the team on who their newest suspect was, while Mick immediately got on the phone and started the process of securing warrants for Ernie Page's house, office, and arrest.

"Apparently, Ernie Page is a helluva lot smarter than he looks," Jason informed the others, all of whom couldn't believe what they were hearing. Looks of surprise and exasperation filled the 1st District precinct as Jason continued to brief the others.

"I feel like an idiot, but this guy is *smart*, people. I bought the whole pathetic, lonely married guy routine. That being said, I've received information that yesterday was not Ernie's first trip to the motel. He's actually been one of their best clients for quite some time. Apparently, Ernie's entire story about cameras in each room and the girls being drugged was a farce. Mr. Popov said that his girls are free to come and go as they please and that none of them were there against their will. He said that most of them were prostitutes back in Russia working in deplorable conditions. He claims that he would arrange for their entry into the US and provide them with a safe place to ply their trade and earn more money than they would in Mother Russia. Through some sort of degenerate logic, he views his work as a good deed."

"What's the connection to the EPK?" one of the detectives asked.

"Stoya Fedorov…"

Jason's mention of the EPK killer's first known victim led to gasps and whispers before Jason continued.

"This morning we actually interrupted Vladimir Popov and his crew's attempt at vigilante justice. According to Popov, Stoya Fedorov worked for him after coming over from Russia. After she had an emergency appendectomy and was released from Metro, Popov said that he gave her time to recover until she was ready to return to work. He gave her money for food and paid for her to stay at The Roadway Inn."

"The Roadway Inn? Is that the place over on Lorain?" the same detective asked.

"Sure is… right across the street from the esteemed Rides 4 Less used car lot," Jason confirmed.

"So, Popov said *Ernie* killed her?"

"How does he know that?"

"What about the other girls?"

The questions came quickly from the officers who Jason was briefing.

"Popov said that he didn't know the other two victims, only Stoya Fedorov. He also said that he had no idea Ernie had anything to do with her disappearance until yesterday. Apparently, the girl Ernie visited yesterday was a new employee who looked a lot like Stoya. She mentioned to Popov that Ernie insisted on calling her 'Stoya' during their session together. She was also upset over the fact that Ernie had left marks on her neck from where he choked her. Popov decided to find out where Ernie worked, and when he saw that it was right next to the last place he or anyone else had seen Stoya alive, he put a plan in place confirm his suspicions the next time Ernie came by the motel."

"They were planning on doing a little interrogation of their own on Ernie, Russian style. When Ernie realized what was happening he made a run for it out the doors, knowing that we'd be there to save his ass if he made it outside," Mick interjected as he entered the room.

"Vlad said that they were so caught off guard that he made a break for it because they had their guns drawn on them. They barely got a shot off before he was out the door. They figured he was insane… until they saw the SWAT team coming," Jason added.

"Holy shit…what are the odds?" asked one of the detectives.

Jason laughed as he and Mick drove to the Corner Pocket Billiards Club.

"I gotta give it to the guy, he even *shit* himself during the shootout to look more pathetic. I'm pretty certain he drove straight to Rides 4 Less, grabbed whatever cash he could, and took a different car to flee," Jason said.

"Figuring the timeframe, he could be anywhere within a five-hour radius of here. I alerted border patrol in case he made a break for Canada, and also notified airport security to be advised," Mick replied.

"Did we find out from the guys at Rides 4 Less which car he might be in?" Jason asked.

"This might come as a shock to you, but Ray and Ernie don't keep a lot of paperwork on the vehicles that they buy and sell on that lot. Ray said he is there so rarely as the owner that he wouldn't even know which car is missing. Ernie was the brains behind the business and Ray was the silent owner. He said Ernie took everything from the safe, including a gun, and probably a few grand in cash."

"You think we'll be lucky enough to find Ernie betting it all on a game of 8 Ball?" Jason joked as they pulled into the parking lot of the Corner Pocket Billiard Club.

"Not a chance, but maybe one of the people there will be able to point us in the right direction," Mick replied.

81

"Any news, T?" Cooper Madison asked his agent, Todd "T-Squared" Taylor over the phone, as he stood outside on his balcony at the Westcott Hotel. In just a few short hours, Coop would find out if he had cleared waivers and would officially become a Cleveland Indian, at least on paper.

"Looks like it's going to go through. The few other teams that might've claimed you already contacted me and I told them that you wouldn't ever suit up for them if they did," Todd replied.

"Wow, who'd of thunk it?"

"Not this guy, that's for sure. To be honest, I always thought you'd eventually go back to the Cubs. When it becomes official, there will obviously be press releases and statements will be needed. What do you want me to say?"

"No comment…" Coop replied, only half-jokingly.

"Very funny…"

"That I am extremely grateful to the entire Chicago Cubs organization, the players, the coaches, and the fans," Coop replied.

"Wow, you sound like maybe you should come work for me as a PR writer," Todd laughed.

"I could never work for such an abusive boss…"

"What about in regards to the Indians? What do you want me to say to the press?"

"Tell them that while I still do not have any intentions of playing baseball this season, if ever, that I am happy to be part of such a great organization that is definitely on the rise."

"Who *are* you?" Todd joked.

"Good question…"

"Okay, now that we have the media statements out of the way, what do I tell the Tribe's front office?"

"That I don't know..."

"Well, you're going to have to meet with them regardless to sign the paperwork, so why don't I tell them that you look forward to meeting with them and seeing what they have to say?"

"I suppose…"

"Good, stay by your phone in case something changes."

"Will do."

"Peace…"

Coop ended the call on his cell phone and went back to his apartment where Cara was lying on the couch.

"Everything okay?" she asked.

"It is now," Coop replied with a grin.

"What did Todd want?"

Coop sighed and sat down next to where Cara's feet rested on the couch. He placed his right hand on her ankle and sighed before explaining everything that had been brewing in regards to a possible trade to the Indians.

"Are you serious? The *Tribe*?" Cara said, sitting up, clearly excited at the news.

"Does that make you happy?" Coop asked, definitely caught off guard by her joyful reaction.

"I don't know if *happy* is the right word. I guess I just figured that sooner or later you'd probably return to baseball, and if you did that it would be awesome if it was in Cleveland."

"I see… does that mean you'd actually go to a baseball game and watch me play? I know you said you weren't a big baseball fan," Coop chided.

"Oh, I would totally go… they have great hot dogs at the Jake," Cara replied, referencing the Indians home ballpark.

"Brutal…"

"I guess it depends on whether or not I'd have to pay for my ticket…"

"I might be able to work something out…"

"Are you seriously considering playing again? Isn't the season almost over?"

"I don't know what I'm doing, to be honest. But, from what I understand, the Indians want to give me a chance to return at my own pace. Whether that's this year or next, I don't know. I'm not even sure I want to..."

"Well, I'll support you either way... especially if I don't have to pay for a ticket," Cara laughed.

"Wives and girlfriends never have to pay, they even have their own section at each ballpark."

Coop's words came out of his mouth so naturally that he didn't quite understand the surprised look on Cara's face when he said them.

"What?" Coop asked.

"Oh, it's just you said 'girlfriend' and that kinda caught me off guard..."

"Oh... yeah, I suppose I did, didn't I?"

"Sure did..."

"I didn't even think twice about it... I suppose it just felt right. I guess I just already think of you that way... which is totally weird for me because that's definitely not my M.O."

"Mine either, but nothing so far about our relationship has been normal, I guess. I mean, we escaped gunshots today. If that doesn't scream girlfriend material then I don't know what does," Cara chuckled.

Coop got down off the couch and mockingly went to his knee as if proposing.

"Cara Knox... will you do me the great honor of letting me refer to you as my *girlfriend*?"

Cara played along, feigning surprise and holding back fake tears.

"Oh my god! I can't believe this is happening! Yes! Yes! Yes!"

"Oh, thank you, Baby Jesus... I was so nervous!" Coop replied, maintaining the act.

"How do you do that?" Cara asked, dropping the act.

"Do what?"

"Make me drop my guard so quickly, especially when I'm about to make a situation awkward?"

"I dunno, I think I get that from my momma. She was really good at that sorta thing."

"She sounds like she was a great woman, I wish I could've met her."

"Me too, and she was…"

"Well, she raised a great son…"

"Weird, I didn't know I had a brother out there!"

"Oh my god! See! That's what I'm talking about. It's like a Jedi mind trick or something!"

"Wait til you see what I do to you next," Coop said as he leaned in to kiss Cara.

"Can't wait…"

82

The Corner Pocket Billiards Club had been a fixture on Cleveland's west side since the Prohibition Era when it doubled as a speakeasy. Rumor has it that Al Capone once played a game of 9 ball there, but like many tales of that time, it was never fully substantiated.

The Corner Pocket, once a proud establishment, was now just another Cleveland relic that was lucky to still be open. Most of the customers were the same 10-15 regulars who played there every night and accepted the antiquated pool hall for what it was.

New patrons to the hall were often met with a cold response. The regulars were always wary of pool sharks who would travel from town to town hustling the regulars. The irony is that most of those patrons were nothing of the sort, rather they were just looking for a "home" establishment to play billiards. The icy response usually meant one-and-done visits from these patrons, who would move on to find another place to play while the Corner Pocket continued to struggle.

Detective Jason Knox and his commander, Mick McCarthy, were getting a taste of that icy treatment as they approached the bar. Upon entering the rundown pool hall, they were met with watchful eyes and most conversations stopped.

The bartender, an older gentleman with a grey mustache and horseshoe ring of hair surrounding a bald head, walked over to the two new faces at his bar.

"What can I get for you, officers?" the old barkeep asked.

Jason and Mick looked at each other, puzzled.

"Detectives, actually…" Jason said as he and Mick each showed their badge.

"Was it that obvious?" Mick asked.

"When you've been doing this as long as I have, you can spot a cop before they get in the door," the bartender replied.

"Well then, let's get to it. We are looking for one of your patrons, Ernie Page. Have you seen or heard from him today?" Jason asked.

"Nope. Haven't seen him in a few days, actually. Maybe his wife finally put her foot down. I know that some of the guys here sure miss him."

"Why's that?" Mick asked.

"Because they call him 'Easy Ernie' around here. For a guy who plays as much pool as Ernie, he's absolutely the worst regular player I've ever seen. But, that doesn't stop him from, well, you know…" the bartender said, stopping short of incriminating his patrons for gambling.

"We aren't here to bust anyone for gambling on pool, so relax," Jason said.

"Well then, why *are* you here? Ernie in some sort of trouble?"

"Is there anyone here who you'd say is closest to Ernie?" Mick asked.

The bartender leaned in so only Jason and Mick could hear what he was saying.

"Pool halls are dens of thieves, Detective. Nobody ever gets real close to anyone else around here, especially not Ernie. He would usually come in half in the bag. Then he'd finish the job, play pool, lose money, and leave. He's an obnoxious asshole, on top of it, so that didn't help him much in regards to making friends. From what I hear, his own brother doesn't even like him - and he's his *boss*!"

"Did he ever talk about going anywhere else besides here?" Jason countered.

"Not that I can recall, but he did give me this a few weeks ago when he found out it was my birthday."

The bartender turned around and retrieved something from below the back wall of the bar. He discreetly handed it over to Jason before offering a disclaimer.

"This might help, but I dunno. He said he was old pals with this guy and to mention his name if I ever wanted to go out. Said the guy owed him some favors and he'd take care of me."

Jason looked at the business card that was just handed to him by the barkeep. It was a traditional cream-colored business card that read *Jake on the Lake Fishing Charters*. The owner was listed as Jake Kingston and the address was 6500 Cleveland Memorial Shoreway.

"6500… hey isn't that…" Mick started to say after Jason showed him the card.

"Edgewater Park Marina…" Jason finished Mick's sentence for him.

"So, are you guys gonna tell me what this is all about? Everyone in here is going to be asking when you leave, and I don't need anyone thinking I'm some sorta snitch," the bartender said in a hushed tone.

"Tell them that we're investigating his car dealership. Nobody would doubt that for a second," Jason replied, nodded to Mick, and the two left the Corner Pocket Billiard Club.

"So, do you think Ernie is actually there?" Mick asked Jason as the pair drove towards Edgewater Park Marina.

"I don't think we're that lucky," Jason replied.

"Gotta check it out, though…"

"I wouldn't be able to sleep if we didn't."

It was almost midnight of what had been a very long day, but they both felt that they had to follow-up on the lead before calling it a day.

"Do you think Ernie even knows that we are on to him?" Mick asked.

"I guess our only hope is that he doesn't. Maybe he thinks he's running from the Russians, not the cops. He can't know that they told us anything, and as of earlier today he certainly thought that he got away with it when I let him go."

"Maybe if he thinks he's running from the Russians then he'd assume he had some time to lay low before making a break for it."

"He doesn't have a ton of cash on him and the borders have all been notified, so there's a chance you're right. He might ask this friend who owes him favors to use his boat, try to make it to Canada," Jason agreed.

"You would think if that was the case he already would've left, though, don't you?" Mick asked.

"Maybe, but maybe he couldn't get a hold of the guy. Maybe this guy Jake was out on the water for a chartered trip? It was a beautiful day, after all. If we're really lucky then he's still in the area and he doesn't have a clue that it's not the Russians he's hiding from."

83

Ernie Page was exhausted, scared, and unsure of what to do next. He'd been trying to get ahold of his old friend Jake Kingston from one of the few pay phones left in the city for most of the evening. He had smashed his cell phone earlier back at Rides 4 Less, where he managed to get himself cleaned up a bit before also cleaning out the two thousand bucks in cash that was in the safe.

He felt bad about stealing the cash and a car off the lot from his brother, but this was about survival now. He hadn't even called his wife to tell her goodbye.

Ernie Page had been a survivor his entire life. He and his older brother, Ray, were the wards of the state from a very young age until adulthood. Ernie was four and Ray was six years old when their mother gave them up for adoption. Ernie barely remembers being left at the orphanage in Pittsburgh, but he knew it was because his mother didn't want him or his brother anymore.

From that day on, the two bounced around from institution to institution, long before the days when foster families were being used on a regular basis. When Ray turned 16, he and Ernie decided that they would no longer live as wards of the state. After two days of walking and hitching rides, they made it all the way to Cleveland's west side, which is where their new lives began.

Ray lied about his age and said he was 18, and Ernie 16, and they got jobs at the old Cleveland Press newspaper building sweeping floors. They would work third shift each night and find different places to sleep each day until they had enough money to get a room at a fleabag motel not far from their jobs.

Ray, always considered intelligent despite his lack of formal education, managed to work his way up from floor sweeper to working on the printing press. Union wages soon followed, and he and Ernie found a small apartment nearby to live. Eventually, Ernie was promoted himself to working on a delivery truck.

Things stayed that way for the next three years until Ray fell in love with one of the young secretaries in the offices of the Cleveland Press. Within a year they were married and moved into a house.

Ernie, now officially 18, was on his own for the first time in his life. He kept the apartment that he and Ray shared and continued to work on the truck. It was also at this time that Ernie started drinking on a nightly basis. Back then you could get "3-2 beer", or beer that only had 3.2% alcohol by ratio, in Ohio at the age of 18. Ernie, no longer under his older brother's watchful eye, began pounding at least eight to ten of those a day.

Ray, meanwhile, wasted no time starting a family with his wife, Eleanor. They welcomed their first child, a boy, during their first year of marriage. Two more boys followed over the next three years, as Ray continued to work his way up the ladder at the Cleveland Press and became a foreman.

Ernie, on the other hand, seemed to be content with the same job working on the truck he had held for years. Every single day was the same: work the predawn shift on the truck, clock out at two, head to the bar and get sloshed. It was also around this time Ernie began playing pool, albeit not very well.

Ernie loved being an uncle and dreamed of having kids of his own someday. Unfortunately, for Ernie, he was socially awkward around the opposite sex and had he not discovered a local brothel he likely would have still been a virgin when he met his future wife at the age of 22. Despite his new relationship, Ernie's trips to local brothels did not stop. Even though he had a partner at home, it was not what he felt he needed. In fact, after the first few years of marriage, Ernie rarely touched his wife. He only wanted to visit prostitutes.

Ernie loved the control of choosing his partner, and better yet, her not having a right to refuse his advances. His desire to control women was a result of his own mother abandoning him and his older brother, and when he was with a prostitute he was in charge.

Just like any addiction, the need to satisfy it only grows over time. Even when addicts completely stop feeding their addiction, the desire to rarely leaves.

Early on, when Ernie would visit a brothel he found that most of the women he slept with were older than him, and most wanted to tell him what to do. After a few years of that, he realized that he was leaving each trip physically satisfied, but emotionally wanting more.

That all changed on one trip when he was nearing 26 years of age. Ernie visited one of his favorite brothels and encountered a young girl who couldn't have been more than 18 years old. She was nervous and scared, and Ernie could feel the rush of adrenaline that her demeanor gave him. Unlike the older women, she was at his complete mercy. He was in charge.

He loved it.

Over the next two decades, Ernie rode a roller coaster of elation and self-loathing that accompanied each trip to a brothel. Over the past decade, police had done a much better job cracking down on the establishments that Ernie could visit. Adult magazines, movies, and later the Internet, helped, but it wasn't enough. He needed the girl to be present to feed the beast that was inside him.

Since there were fewer places he could go to, Ernie began traveling to places that had much lighter enforcement on prostitution. Once a month he would even take his wife to parts of Canada where prostitution is legal, and actually get two rooms so he could do what he needed to as his wife played her beloved penny slots in the casino.

She never knew, and even if she did, their marriage was one of convenience. After they found out that they could not conceive a child, they decided not to adopt and just live their lives as married adults. They had even been sleeping in separate bedrooms for the past 15 years.

A few months ago, Ernie thought his luck had finally changed. A new brothel had opened up not far from where he worked and they had an excellent system in place to keep from getting caught. It was located in an old motel, and you had to complete a tedious list of activities to even get the right question to ask at the front desk. If you showed up without the proper date to ask about, then you were turned away. After a little research, Ernie soon realized that the random dates he was given were actually significant dates in Russia's history.

Russians, scary Russians who seemed to be connected to the mob, ran the brothel. To Ernie, that made him feel strangely safe about frequenting there. The best part, for Ernie, was that the majority of the girls were *young* Russians.

Despite being married, the first time Ernie truly fell in love was with one of those young Russian girls from the motel brothel. Her name was Stoya, and she was gorgeous. Better yet, she learned quickly what Ernie was looking for, and she did her best to play the part. She would take on a new persona with each Wednesday visit, but each of those personalities she portrayed was that of a girl who needed to be told what to do.

She was the first girl he visited there, and the only girl, until one day she was gone.

"What do you mean Stoya isn't here? She's *always* here on Wednesdays," an agitated Ernie asked at the time.

"Medical emergency. She will be back soon enough. Today, you pick different girl," he was told by one of the Russians working there.

But, Ernie didn't *want* a different girl. He wanted *his* girl. He decided to leave the motel that day without visiting one of the other options. A week went by, followed by another, and Ernie checked in at the motel every Wednesday to see if she had returned.

During the third week of Ernie's forced celibacy, luck found him once again. He had just returned from giving a test drive when he saw her. Not only did he see her, but also she was walking into the door of one of the motel rooms across the street from Rides 4 Less.

She didn't look the same. Her hair was up in a ponytail and she was wearing pajama pants with a t-shirt. She definitely did not have any makeup on, either.

Ernie did not care.

He wasted no time walking across the street and knocking on her motel room door. A very startled Stoya answered, obviously not as happy to see the man who stood before her.

"Ernie? What you do here?" she asked in broken English.

"Stoya, I missed you so much. I never thought I'd see you again… I… I work right across the street," Ernie answered, gesturing towards Rides 4 Less.

"Okay, but why you here?"

"I dunno, I suppose I just couldn't help myself. I saw you across the street and I missed you so much. I haven't even seen another girl. I promise! I only want you. Is this where you're working out of now?" Ernie said, oblivious to Stoya's body language, which was a mixture of fear and repulse.

"Ernie, I had surgery. I not working until next week. I see you then, okay?"

"No way, I need to see you now. We don't even have to have sex. I just need to see you. Oh man, I sound pathetic…"

Ernie, realizing he sounded pathetic, changed his tone immediately from that of a beggar to the way he spoke to her at the brothel. Maybe that's what she was waiting for, he thought.

"I don't think you understand, *young lady*, this isn't a *choice*. Now let me in," Ernie demanded of Stoya, just like he would have countless times before. Only this time, Stoya wasn't playing along.

"Ernie, you must go. Now. We are not at other motel. I need time. I will see you soon. I promise. Just go now," Stoya answered.

Her reluctance caused a fire to flash within Ernie's eyes that she had never seen before, not even when role-playing. This was a look of betrayal… and hatred.

"Get the hell inside," Ernie grunted as he pushed his way into her motel room before locking the door behind him.

"Ernie! Stop!" Stoya screamed as loud as she could, hoping someone would hear her. The volume of her voice only angered Ernie more, and he displayed that anger in the form of a backhand to her face as she struggled to get up. This caused her to tumble back to the floor, blood beginning to pool up in her mouth.

Ernie climbed on top of the trembling girl who laid before him. The girl that he loved. The girl that he had been waiting his whole life for. The girl that he had just realized moments before was a fraud.

Just like his mother, she had abandoned him.

Unlike his mother, Stoya had to pay for her betrayal.

He watched as the fear in her eyes vanished, replaced by a cold distant stare as he choked the life out of the one girl he thought would always be there for him.

84

Back at Edgewater Beach Ernie finally felt it was dark enough to sneak onto his friend's fishing boat. Jake Kingston was one of Ernie's only true friends, and he had even given Ernie a spare key to his boat to use on the days that he didn't have a charter scheduled.

Ernie had really helped Jake out when he was going through his divorce. He managed to get Jake a car from a dealer-only auction for pennies on the dollar and cosigned on the lease for his apartment. Owning a cash-only fishing charter didn't exactly give Jake a great credit rating.

Jake was always grateful to his old friend, even though he never really felt he *knew* him. They had met back when they were both teenage dropouts sweeping floors at the old Cleveland Press. They would frequently play pool together and get hammered on 3-2 beer. Even when they both got married and moved on to new jobs, they stayed in touch, occasionally playing pool together at the Corner Pocket.

Despite all of that, Ernie always seemed to limit what Jake would get to see of him. Jake used to joke with his ex-wife that if he found out someday that Ernie was hiding a secret family somewhere or the police found bones in his backyard he wouldn't be surprised. It wasn't that Ernie ever did anything to elicit that kind of observation from Jake, rather it was simply that it seemed like he was definitely hiding something from his only real friend.

Even though he had the keys to the boat, Ernie never took Jake up on the offer until the day he ended Stoya's life. As soon as he realized what he had done to the girl he had obsessed over, Ernie became hysterical. He tried to wake up her lifeless body on the floor of that motel room, but there was nothing left to wake. She was gone, and he had killed her.

He spent the next few hours in her motel room waiting for nightfall beside her lifeless body. He even prayed for forgiveness despite being a lifelong atheist. He also prayed that she wasn't expecting any visitors that night. Despite recent events, Ernie had never physically harmed another human in his life. He certainly wasn't going to be able to do it again if someone showed up at her door.

Thankfully, for Ernie, nobody had visited by the time it was dark enough to try and transport her body. Ernie ran across the street to Rides 4 Less and grabbed the keys to a van that was for sale from the office. Since Stoya's room was on the first floor next to the parking lot, he knew there was a good chance that he'd be able to back the van up and place her in the back without garnering any attention.

After rolling her body up in a bedsheet, Ernie carefully surveyed the area outside her motel room before he quickly carried her to the van and laid her down in the back. He quickly shut the doors to both the van and the motel room, which he felt he made sure had no trace of him being there, and began his journey to the Edgewater Park Marina.

The weather was rainy and chilly that night, so it was no surprise to Ernie that he found Jake's boat tied up to the dock. He parked the van by the boat launch and drove the boat near the ramp used to place boats in the water. After making sure that nobody else was around, Ernie pulled Stoya's lifeless body out of the van and carried her to the back of the boat where he then laid her down gently.

After returning the van to the parking lot, Ernie hopped in the boat which he had tethered next to the launch ramp and began his journey out to the middle of Lake Erie, which actually reaches a depth of 210 feet at its deepest point. Ernie figured if he made it out far enough he could use one of the heavy rocks he had grabbed from the area near the boat launch to weigh her down and dump her body overboard.

After about 30 minutes of traveling north through mildly rough water and rain on Lake Erie, Ernie shut the boat's engine off and prepared himself for what he was about to do. Ernie wept as he lifted her body, which was still wrapped in the motel sheet and had a heavy rock wrapped up next to it inside the homemade cloth coffin. He told her that he loved her and begged for her forgiveness as he watched her body disappear beneath the dark water of Lake Erie.

The next day Ernie tried to keep to his normal routine. He knew chances were that nobody saw him with Stoya, but he also wanted to keep an eye on her motel room across the street to see if anyone noticed she was gone.

What Ernie didn't know was that Vladimir Popov had pre-paid for her motel in cash, and there was no record of a Stoya Fedorov staying at the motel. As far as the motel was concerned, there was never going to be any reason to think anything had happened.

That is, until Vlad showed up looking for her that day.

Ernie's stomach did flips from his view across the street as he watched the Russian that he had seen so many times at the motel brothel pound on her door. He then watched Vlad go to the motel office and later return with an employee who opened the door to Stoya's room. After entering the room, an angry Vladimir Popov came out and appeared to be asking the motel employee questions.

He knows something happened to her.

What Ernie also didn't know was that Stoya had promised Vlad that she would call each morning and also that she would not go anywhere without telling him. Even though Vlad knew something wasn't right, he played it off to the motel employee and told him to keep her room waiting for her in the event she had just wandered off to go to the store or something.

The fact that Stoya was in the country illegally and working at his brothel was all the reason Vlad needed to hope for the best, but also to keep the police and anyone else out of it.

Just then Ernie's phone rang. It was Jake.

Shit...

"Hey, Jake, what's up?" Ernie managed to ask as normally as possible.

"Ernie, did you finally take me up on my offer to use the boat last night?" Jake asked.

"Uh... yeah, sure did. Sorry I didn't tell you."

"Well, it's about damn time you did!"

Ernie felt a sense of relief as he heard Jake's words, and even more so as he saw the Russian leave the motel in his car.

"Hope I left it in good shape for ya..."

"Yeah, looks great. But you sure could've picked a better night to go out. You probably were miserable out there in the rain!"

"Yeah, I realized after it was too late. I just needed to get out and clear my mind. Rough day at work..."

"I hear you, man. Listen, you know you can take her out anytime I'm not using her, got it?"

"Absolutely, and thanks, Jake."

"Nonsense, I owe you big time, still, buddy. See ya later at the Corner Pocket?"

"Yeah... sure. See you then..."

Ernie took a deep breath of relief after hanging up the phone.

Maybe I'll get away with this, after all...

Ernie's anxiety over being caught lessened each day that passed without any sight of a police car or visits from scary Russians. He even visited the brothel the very next Wednesday, as usual, and asked for Stoya. The Russians lied to him and said she was still dealing with a medical issue.

They have no idea...

This time, he stayed and visited a new girl. He found that as long as he thought about Stoya he could continue going to the motel for his weekly visits.

Somehow, be it luck or divine intervention, Ernie felt that what he did to Stoya would be a secret that only he would take to his grave. Life returned to normal, for the most part, and he even felt as if he were a more confident man because of it.

Until the day Stoya's body washed ashore.

Despite his best efforts to weigh her body down with the heavy rock, Ernie failed to take into account the pure strength of

Lake Erie's undercurrent. Within a few weeks of his one and only boat trip, the powerful lake managed to free her body from the tightly wrapped sheet and her badly decomposed body washed ashore at Edgewater Beach.

Ernie's feelings of fear and anxiety returned in full force. He wondered each day if someone would show up at his door to arrest him. He feared that maybe they would find some sort of evidence on her body that he was with her the night she died.

Then a second body washed ashore. Not long after that a third.

The media was even saying that there might be a serial killer out there targeting girls near Edgewater Beach. The emergence of these two unidentifiable bodies and the possibility of a serial killer actually made Ernie feel a little better about his situation.

Because he didn't kill those two other girls.

Whoever did sure wants everyone to think that I did, though...

Just like before, Ernie's anxiety dissipated over time. In fact, until Detective Jason Knox paid him a visit at Rides 4 Less he thought he was completely out of the woods. Once he realized that they weren't after him, specifically, but rather the Russians, Ernie truly began to feel bulletproof.

If I can get through this, and those Russians get popped, the only people who would ever suspect me for Stoya's death will be dead or in prison...

Everything was going as planned on the day of the motel sting until Ernie walked into the office to get the key, as instructed. As soon as he entered the office, Ernie was greeted by Vladimir Popov holding a gun in his hand and telling him to sit down.

"Hello, Ernie. Let's have chat…"

"A chat? About what?" Ernie asked, still unsure how they must have known he was working with the police.

Why else would they have a gun?

"Oh, just a little chat about Stoya…" Vlad let his words hang in the air, and Ernie's non-verbal reaction was all he needed to confirm what he suspected: Stoya Fedorov's murderer was Ernie Page.

Ernie, knowing that the SWAT team was outside, decided to make a break for it. He was a dead man regardless and this was his only chance out. If he could get outside without getting shot then he might have a chance. Even if Vladimir told the police that he killed Stoya, they wouldn't believe him. Ernie would just deny it, anyway.

Ernie took a deep breath and then fled out of the office door as fast as possible, knocking over the Russian who was trying to guard the door behind him. Vlad got a couple shots off, all of which somehow missed Ernie as he ran out of the office.

Vlad gave chase out the door, knowing that Ernie wouldn't be able to outrun him. What Vlad didn't expect was to see a SWAT team approaching in an armored vehicle as he chased Ernie.

Without hesitation, Vlad ran back inside and alerted his crew that the police were here and to open fire on them. Vlad was hopeful that would buy him enough time to shred the little bit of evidence of the brothel's financials that were in the office.

His plan worked. While the others were firing shots at the armored vehicle he was able to shred the only papers that possibly could prove that they were running a brothel. He made sure to destroy all of the customer information that they had, including the police officers that frequented the girls at the motel. They would be of much more help to him if they weren't in jail, too.

Outside, meanwhile, Ernie was laying on the ground and covering his head. He had fully expected to get shot in the back as he ran outside, but miraculously that didn't happen. What did happen was his disbelief that he was actually happy to see the police for once. Unfortunately, for Ernie, he must have been so surprised that he defecated in his pants while the shots were whizzing by him. At first, he was really embarrassed, but then he realized the more pathetic he looked to the police, the better.

I'll play the pathetic card, and if I get out of here I'm gone for good...

When Detective Knox released him, Ernie knew that his time may be limited before the Russians talked. Even though the police likely wouldn't believe them, they still would follow up with Ernie.

That was a chance that Ernie didn't want to take, so he decided to cut his losses and make a run for Canada on Jake's boat before the authorities caught up with him. Unfortunately, for Ernie, the boat wasn't at the dock and he couldn't get ahold of Jake to see when it would be back. Sometimes Jake and other charter captains would go for nighttime charters because the fishing on Lake Erie was sometimes best in the dark.

This is obviously one of those nights...

Ernie decided to sit in his car, which like most of the cars on the Rides 4 Less lot had very little gas left in the tank, and wait for Jake's boat to return. He couldn't think of anyone that would even know about his connection to Jake's boat outside of a few people and felt none of them would likely talk to the police on the outside chance that they were even questioned to begin with. Even his very own wife, Ellie, didn't know.

Ernie felt tonight as if he had the small luxury of waiting for his getaway boat to return, and then he'd once again rely on the same instincts that he had always used to survive.

85

"How's the newest member of the Cleveland Indians doing?" Todd "T-Squared" Taylor asked his most coveted client. It was just after midnight and Cooper Madison had cleared waivers in a deal that would send him to the Indians.

"I'm assuming this means it went through?" Coop replied. He and Cara decided to stay up until at least midnight so that they'd know for sure if the deal went through.

"Yessir it sure did, and the Indians front office really is looking forward to meeting with you tomorrow."

"Don't you mean today? It's past midnight."

"Not where I'm at. *Vegas* baby!"

"Gambling away all the money I've made you?"

"T-Squared only *wins*, baby!"

"Yeah, yeah, whatever. Even a broken clock is right twice a day."

"Speaking of clocks, can you be down at the Jake at noon? I'll be catching a redeye here in a couple hours and will meet you there."

"Yeah, I'll be there. I just hope that you made it clear that there's no guarantee that I will ever pitch for them."

"They know that, but we need to hear them out."

"Good deal, be safe and come back before you're broke."

"T-Squared only WINS, BABY!"

Coop could hear his agent yelling what apparently was his new motto as he hung up the phone.

"So… are you an Indian?" asked Cara, who was sitting with her legs lying across his on the couch.

"Apparently…"

"So… what's next?"

"I have to meet with them at noon at Jacob's Field. I'll have to take a physical and sign some paperwork to make it official."

"Do you think they'll try and talk you into playing this season?"

"Oh, I'm sure as the moon."

"What are you thinking?"

"I dunno…"

"Well, you will. You'll know after a few minutes of meeting them if you'll ever want to play for them."

"A few minutes, huh?" Coop asked.

"Yup…" Cara replied.

"How's that?"

"It's science…"

"Science?"

"Yup…"

"Explain, please…"

"Well, it's kinda like choosing a mate. They say that humans subconsciously decide within minutes of meeting whether or not they would want to reproduce with the other person," Cara asserted.

"How long did it take with me?" Coop asked.

"Twenty-four hours…" Cara said, coyly.

"Ouch!" Coop replied.

"I'm kidding… it was only nineteen hours…"

"Very funny…"

"How about you?" Cara asked.

"Before we ever spoke," Coop replied.

"Before we ever spoke?"

"When I saw you through the peephole the first time you delivered food to me."

"Really? I didn't even know you saw me. All I heard was your deep southern drawl coming from inside."

"Really. You're insanely gorgeous."

"Well, I disagree, but thank you."

"Welcome…"

"I have an admission to make," Cara said.

"What's that?"

"I knew before we ever met, too. Well, at least before we met in person…"

"Really?"

"It was when I looked you up on the internet because I didn't know who you were. I saw those eyes of yours and, yeah… I knew then…"

"Well then… I think we should go into my bedroom and test out that theory."

"Um, I think we have already done that. Multiple times…"

"A true scientist has to test and retest his theories over and over…"

"Well, then… we better get to the lab, Dr. Madison…"

86

"Put the gun down, Ernie!" Detective Jason Knox screamed at the most wanted fugitive in Ohio.

Minutes earlier, Ernie Page saw his childhood friend Jake Kingston pulling his boat into the Edgewater Park Marina and he got out of his car to meet him at the dock. Ernie was going to wait for Jake's charter group to get off the boat and then inform him that he was going to take her for a late night spin to clear his mind. In reality, he was going to drive as far north and as fast as he could until he reached Canada.

What Ernie didn't see was the unmarked police cruiser pulling in to the parking lot as he walked toward the dock. The detectives inside the cruiser couldn't believe their eyes when the man they feared had already fled the country was just steps away from them.

Commander Mick McCarthy immediately radioed in for back-up and let dispatch know that they had located Ernie.

"Unbelievable," Jason said to Mick when he witnessed Ernie walking along the edge of the dock.

"He obviously thought he was only running from the Russians and not us," Mick replied.

"How are we going to do this?" Jason asked as he gestured towards Jake's charter group which was just now exiting the boat.

"We can't risk him getting in that boat, but we also can't risk him taking a hostage. His brother said that he likely has that gun from his safe on him, too."

Jason and Mick decided that they'd wait to try and sneak up on Ernie and get close enough to him to safely fire their guns if need be. Jake's boat was about fifty yards from the parking lot, so Jason figured that they might be able to get halfway there before they were spotted, which is exactly what happened.

After the last of Jake's charter group had exited the boat and headed towards the parking lot, Ernie greeted him. His back was to the parking lot, so Jason and Mick were hopeful that he wouldn't see them at all as they approached him.

"You really want to go out on her this late? Must have had a fight with Ellie, huh?" Jake asked his old friend.

"Yeah, man… real tough week. I just need to feel the open water," Ernie replied.

Jason and Mick were about halfway to Ernie when Jake noticed them walking up. They had decided not to draw their guns out until they were close, so Jake had no idea who they were.

"Are those guys going out with you, too?" Jake asked Ernie, who spun around to see Jason and Mick approaching. Ernie immediately pulled the .38 caliber pistol he had tucked into his belt and aimed it at the detectives, who also drew their firearms.

Ironically, Ernie detested guns, but he knew that there might come a time when he would actually need it to survive. That time had come.

"Put the gun down, Ernie!" Mick yelled as he and Jason continued to slowly approach.

"Ernie, what the *hell* is going on?" Jake asked, in total disbelief at what he was witnessing.

"Get away from here, Jake!" Ernie yelled at his friend, who immediately hopped in his boat and got down in case bullets started flying.

"Ernie, drop the gun, man. This isn't going to end well for you!" Jason yelled, still slowly approaching his suspect.

Ernie didn't budge. He kept his pistol pointed in the direction of the two approaching officers, who had begun to separate from each other so he'd have two targets to try and cover with his gun.

"I'm not the monster you think I am!" Ernie declared while alternating his aim.

"Nobody said that, Ernie! We just want to talk to you, but you're complicating things!" Jason replied.

"Oh yeah? I know why you're here. You think I killed all those girls. You think I'm the EPK killer!"

"We don't think anything, yet, Ernie. That's why we just need to talk to you, so put the gun down!" Mick ordered.

"The other two girls… I didn't kill them! Only Stoya…" Ernie confessed.

"See, Ernie, that's why we need to talk to you. You can tell us what happened and set the record straight," Jason replied as he tried to calmly coax Ernie.

"There's nothing else to say… I killed Stoya. It was an accident! But I did *not* kill those other two. Somebody's sure trying to make it look that way, though. Real convenient for them, huh? Probably those Russian pricks!" Ernie yelled, still pointing his gun at Jason and Mick who were now ten yards away.

"We believe you, Ernie, just put the gun down," Mick pleaded, also lowering his voice like Jason.

"No… no, you don't… nobody else will, either…tell Ellie I'm sorry..."

Ernie raised the gun to his temple and pulled the trigger before Jason or Mick could stop him. The sound of the gunshot was deafening as it reverberated off of the boats that lined the docks.

"Ernie!" Jake Kingston jumped out of his boat and was the first to reach his old friend. It was too late.

Ernie was gone.

87

"Cara, hey, your brother is on the news! Come quick!" Cooper Madison called out from his bedroom to Cara, who was in the kitchen pouring herself another cup of coffee.

"Jason? What happened?" she asked as she came running in, hoping that it was for a good reason.

Coop turned up the volume on the large plasma television, which was tuned to a local news show and the graphics read *EPK Murders Press Conference.* Chief Horace Johnston, also known as "HoJo", was on the screen in his dress blues giving a press conference outside city hall. A very tired-looking Jason Knox and Mick McCarthy stood in the background.

"Through the tireless work of the Cleveland Police Department, especially by Commander Michael McCarthy and Detective Jason Knox, I am happy to announce that the city of Cleveland can sleep a little safer tonight. At approximately 12:35 am, after a daylong manhunt, the man we believe to be the Edgewater Park Killer was located and confronted by the two brave men standing behind me. The man, who we have identified as 53-year-old Ernest Page, admitted to the murder of Stoya Fedorov before taking his own life. Please take a moment and remember the three young women who lost their lives at the hands of this man. A man who took the cowardly way out. I will gladly take any questions you have at this time, with the understanding

that it is still very early and we may not be prepared to answer all of your questions at this moment."

A flurry of reporters took Chief Johnston up on his offer all at once and questions started flying fast.

"Did he admit to killing the other two victims?"
"Are there any other suspects?"
"Is there any link to the shootout at the alleged brothel motel yesterday?"
"Are there any other victims?"
"Does he have a wife? Is she a suspect?
"How did you determine it was him?"
"Were there any other witnesses?"
"Can we talk to the detectives?"

Out of all the answers that Chief Johnston gave to the reporters, one of the only ones that Jason was happy with was when he told the reporters that he and Mick were not available for interviews at this time.

He doesn't want me talking...

The other questions were mostly answered vaguely or not at all. In reality, Chief Johnston knew it didn't matter what he said. In cases like this people want justice, and justice was served.

In the hours between the self-inflicted gunshot wound that ended Ernie Page's life and the press conference, Jason had tried to convince his boss that Ernie may not have been the EPK Killer. Chief Johnston, desperate for an ending to the nightmare that had become the EPK murders, was not having any of it.

"Just because he didn't admit to them doesn't mean that he didn't kill them. This guy has all the traits of a serial killer - lonely, older, abandonment issues. It's a slam dunk. I'm not going to waste taxpayer dollars looking for a killer that's already dead, and neither are you, Detective," Chief Johnston informed his detective.

"With all due respect, sir, I'm just saying that maybe the press conference can wait until we have followed up on the possibility that he isn't the EPK," replied Jason.

"Well, Detective Knox, with that same due respect I will gladly remind you that it's not your job to make those decisions."

Chief Johnston did not give Jason a chance to respond as he walked away with the confident stride of a man who was just about ready to permanently etch his name in Cleveland history forever.

After it concluded the television station cut away from the press conference to commercial. Coop changed the channel to one of the other local stations. Then another. They all were proclaiming the end of the EPK case.

"Hol-lee crap…" Cara said, her eyes fixated on the screen.

"Your brother is the MAN!" Coop exclaimed.

"I knew he'd catch that bastard. Oh my God, I'm so proud of him! I want to call him, but he's probably exhausted. Do you think that's what we saw yesterday?"

"Yes ma'am, I'm figuring we were right next to a real-life serial killer yesterday."

"I have to call my mom!" Cara ran off to the kitchen to get her cell phone and called Joanne from the balcony outside.

Coop could hear her talking to her mom through the window. The pride in her voice made him happy. He wanted her to be proud of him like that someday. He glanced at the clock and realized that he only had a couple hours until he had to meet with the Cleveland Indians front office.

Then he felt it.

He wasn't sure if it was the adrenaline from seeing Jason's big arrest or the desire to make Cara proud, but he definitely felt it.

Cooper Madison felt the need to compete again.

88

Detective Jason Knox returned home later that morning after being awake for nearly thirty straight hours. As he set his keys on the kitchen table his daughter Gabby came running in to greet him.

"Daddy! I saw you on the TV!" she squealed as she jumped up into his waiting arms.

Jason's wife, Erica, followed Gabby into the kitchen and wrapped her arms around both of them. She held on longer than normal, and Jason could tell that she had been worried.

"You actually let her watch the EPK press conference?" Jason asked, surprised. His wife typically was the one to shelter Gabby from the evils of the world.

"Relax, I turned the volume off. She just wanted to see her daddy on TV. I told her you were a hero," Erica answered.

"Grandma and Grandpa saw it, too, Daddy! They called mommy and told her," Gabby added.

"Did they? What did they say, Mommy?" Jason asked his wife.

"That they were *very* proud of their son. Your mom said that your father even asked for the phone to call Ed and some of the other guys from work that he hasn't talked to in forever. She said she hadn't seen him talk that much on the phone in years," Erica replied.

"Really? I can't picture that," Jason chuckled.

"Well, he did. He is so proud of his boy. We all are. You captured the *freaking* EPK, babe. Do you know how amazing that is? Has it set in?" Erica asked as she pulled Gabby off of Jason, who then ran off into the family room.

"*Alleged* EPK Killer, but I've been too tired and too busy to let anything except exhaustion set in," Jason answered, making sure Gabby was out of the room.

"What do you mean *alleged*?" Erica asked, confused.

"I just still have some doubts, is all."

"But they said he admitted to killing that Russian girl, right?"

"Yeah, he did. I heard it with my own ears, too."

"So what's the issue?"

"The issue is he swore to us that he didn't kill the other two Jane Does. Right before he pulled the trigger."

"So what? That doesn't mean he didn't kill them."

"True, but why would he care if he was just going to kill himself anyway? Most serial killers *want* the whole world to know what they did, especially after they're caught. He had every reason to take the credit for the killings and go down in history as the EPK Killer. Why wouldn't he?" Jason asked.

"Maybe to protect his family?"

"He barely had one. Just a wife who probably hated him, a brother, and no kids."

"Well even if he *only* killed one girl, you're still a hero because he probably would've done it again," Erica reassured her husband.

"I know, and I appreciate you. Maybe I'm just tired, but I can't shake the feeling that he isn't the EPK Killer. The other two victims had been mutilated with a knife, while Stoya had only been strangled. I'm just worried that there's still a killer on the loose and we just cleared his name… Honestly, it doesn't matter anyway. The Chief has already made this the 'HoJo Show', as if he actually did anything, and that show won't allow for an alternate ending."

"Well, to change the subject a bit… I have a confession to make, too, Detective Knox," Erica said as she wrapped her arms around her husband.

"Oh you do, huh? What do you have to confess?" Jason played along.

"That seeing my husband on the TV today made me…" she finished the sentence in a whisper in Jason's ear as his eyes widened.

"Oh my…" he replied when she finished her secret confession.

"Unless you're too tired, that is…" Erica said as she slowly led him out of the kitchen towards the hallway that leads to the bedroom.

"What about Gabby?" Jason said.

"She's watching TV, she'll be fine. I guess we'll just have to lock the door while I plead my case and beg for leniency..."

"Feeling a second wind coming on, I think…" Jason announced as the two closed the bedroom door behind them.

89

"Can I ask your advice on something?" Cooper Madison asked Clarence Walters, who was driving him to meet with the front office of his newest baseball team, the Cleveland Indians.

"At your own peril, I'm a brutally honest person," Clarence replied.

"Well, good, because that's what I need to hear."

"Lots of people say that, but when it happens they don't like it."

"Well, I can assure you I will."

"Go ahead, then."

"If you were in my shoes, would you ever play baseball again?"

"That depends on whether or not I needed it."

"Needed it? Like for the money?"

"No, not for the money," Clarence chuckled.

"I was going to say, I'm pretty much set there for a couple lifetimes, thankfully. What do you mean by need?"

"Do you *need* baseball? The game itself. Not the fans, or the fame, or even the cameras. Do you *need* baseball in your life to be happy, like you need air to breathe? If you *need* baseball to survive like you need air to breathe, then I'd say yes. If you don't, well, then you don't," Clarence responded.

"Wow, that's pretty much the best answer I think anyone could've given me. You should write a damn advice column. You could call it 'Dear Clarence' like that lady does," Coop said, only half joking.

"The newspaper couldn't afford me," Clarence laughed.

"You know... I guess I haven't been happy, for obvious reasons, since I played ball. Well, except for Cara. I'm happy with her, man. She kinda rescued me, I think. I didn't realize just how unhappy I was."

"She's a sweet girl, for sure."

"Yeah she is, and just a real person, you know? I feel like I have met more 'real' people in the past week than I have in the past decade. All since I met her. I forgot what that was like."

"Maybe she is the reason that you're realizing that you miss playing now..."

"How so?" Coop asked, leaning forward from the back seat of the Escalade.

"I see it like this, okay… There are certain people in our lives that are like keys that can be used to unlock the parts of ourselves that would otherwise never see the light of day. In your case, Cara is like the key that unlocks the part of you that you used to be, but have locked away since you stopped playing."

"Whoa… that's some deep stuff right there Clarence. Are you sure you're not a therapist or even a motivational speaker on the side?"

"Don't do that, man," Clarence replied, sternly.

"Do what?" Coop asked, taken aback by the response.

"Deflect. I'm guessing you always deflect like that to avoid confronting your feelings."

"I do… I guess it's my way of dealing," Coop answered.

"It's *okay* to have the focus on you, sometimes. I know that sounds like a weird thing to say to someone who has lived in the spotlight for his entire adult life, but that ain't real, man. You have always had people heaping praise on you for what you can do on the field to the point that you feel guilty because you know that type of praise is only because of your physical gifts. So, when a person gives you praise for something that has nothing to do with baseball, you feel like you have to deflect to balance out all the stuff you don't think you deserve."

"You're right, Clarence. That's exactly how I feel, man…"

"I know, brother, and I don't blame you. I can't even begin to say that I can relate, but that doesn't mean I can't have empathy."

"I guess you're one of those keys, huh? You're helping me unlock the fact that I need to start recognizing that it's okay to separate the two…"

"Now you're feeling me, Coop!"

"I'm not trying to deflect here, but, who are some of your 'keys' that you've had in your life?" Coop asked.

"My wife, Evelynn, for one. I was an angry young black man when I met her. I won't get into it, but she helped unlock the part of me that wasn't always assuming that people were out to do me wrong."

"That's pretty amazing."

"She is amazing," Clarence confirmed.

"Anyone else?" Coop asked.

"Cara's brother, Jason."

"Jason? How so?"

"He wasn't like most of the cops I knew. He definitely is not an alpha male, which is probably what makes him a great detective. He barely has an ego, but he's also confident and tough. He's one of the best dudes I know."

"He definitely seems like it, and I know how much Cara loves him."

"And he loves her, man."

"Anyone else? This has been great, man."

"My daughters, for sure. They softened me some more and taught me how to love unconditionally. That's something you won't ever know until you become a father."

"I hear that a lot, and I believe it."

"God willing, someday you'll know for yourself."

"What about Grace?" Coop asked.

"Grace Brooks?" Clarence replied.

"Yeah, is she a 'key' in your life?"

"Absolutely, man. She opened up that part of me that allowed me to have empathy for people who had an unfair hand dealt to them."

"Unfair? How so?"

"She was a great cop, man. Notice how I didn't say a great *female* cop? She was just a great cop. One night she was chasing a drug dealer who tried to flee during an arrest. He was a little guy, a real asshole. His nickname was Tick because he was so small and would get under your skin."

"Sounds like an appropriate nickname, then," Coop agreed.

"Oh, you better believe it."

"What happened?"

"Well, Tick takes off running and Grace is in pursuit. She manages to catch up to him and tackle his little ass. Instincts kicked in and she used some of her MMA skills to put him in an armbar to restrain him. She didn't know if he had a gun, you never know to be honest. Well, he kept fighting to get free and she applied more pressure on the hold and pulled his goddamn elbow out of the socket. I mean like, *pop*!" Clarence emphasized.

"Holy shit! That's awesome!"

"You'd think, right? But, it wasn't. Not for Grace, man. They said it was an excessive use of force and she was going to have to do all sorts of bullshit just to keep her badge. The worst part is that little bastard got off because of it."

"Are you kidding me?"

"Wish I was..."

"So did she keep her badge?"

"She could have, but she decided not to. She shouldn't have *had* to. That's when I offered her a job to work for me."

"Well then, I guess you are a 'key' to her, too. You're allowing her to see that you believe in her," Coop stated.

"I'd like to think that," Clarence replied.

"I think it's safe to say."

"So, back to Cara. I feel she's a key to you learning to be a real person again, not just a ballplayer."

"I think she's even more than that. I've never had this happen to me so quickly, and maybe it's not realistic, but I feel like I already love her. How's that even possible? Shouldn't love take longer than a week to happen?"

"No sir, I fell in love with my wife before we ever spoke."

"How so?"

"Evelynn was working as a social worker for a few of the families that were on my beat when I was a rookie. She was beautiful, man. I used to hope that I'd get dispatched to one of those houses when there was an issue in the hopes she'd be there. She was so damn kind, too. Some of the people that she had to work with were just awful, man, but she was so good at making them feel like she cared. One day, I saw her get between some dude and the wife he was beating up on a daily basis. As I pulled up to the front yard, I see all 110 pounds of Evelynn telling this asshole that she wasn't going to let him touch that wife of his ever again, and that he'd have to get through her first. I came running up just as he was about to test her and flattened his ass. I made sure to follow up with her later to make sure she was okay, and we just went from there. But, I knew I loved her, man. I knew when I saw her step in front of that abusive husband to protect a woman that she barely knew. That's all I needed to know. Game over, brother!"

"Wow, that's amazing, Clarence. She must be an amazing woman."

"She is, Coop. But you know what? She's not perfect. And neither am I. But the love we have for each other and our children *is*. The best part was that before I met her I was convinced I wanted to be a bachelor for life."

"It's funny you say that. My daddy used to always tell me that I'd fall in love someday when I stopped looking. He'd say, 'Those who hunt for love go to bed hungry'..."

"Sounds like a smart man," Clarence said.

"Yessir, he sure was. I miss him."

"I have a feeling he's really proud of you, even still."

"I hope so..."

"I think if you want to feel that close to him again that there's only one way to find out."

"How's that?"

"Do whatever it is that will make you the happiest version of yourself. As a father, all I ever want is for my kids to be the happiest that they can be. So, while I never knew your father, I'm certain that he wanted the same for you. Maybe if you reach that point you'll feel him with you."

"I think he'd want me to play ball again..."

Clarence let Cooper Madison's words go unanswered because he knew that his passenger wasn't trying to elicit a response.

A few moments later as Clarence pulled his SUV into the player's parking lot outside of Jacob's Field, Cooper Madison wondered if this would be the first of many trips here.

90

Three weeks later on October 1st, there was an electricity inside a sold-out Jacob's Field. From 1995 to 2001, Cleveland was used to having sellout crowds, 455 of them to be exact. However, it had been a long time since The Jake had been at capacity during the subpar 2006 season.

Tonight, even though it was the final game of the regular season against the Tampa Bay Devil Rays and there would be no postseason playoff games to look forward to, Tribe fans had a reason to be excited.

Cooper Madison was scheduled to make his first Major League start in over a year. After trading for his rights, the Indians had sent Coop down to get back into pitching shape with their AA affiliate, the Akron Aeros. After the first two weeks of throwing and getting back into shape, he made two relief appearances.

In the first game in front of a standing room only crowd at Akron's Canal Park for one of their AA playoff games, Coop entered the game in the 7th inning with the Aeros clinging to a one-run lead with two outs.

As he walked to the mound that night, he thought for sure that it was going to feel a whole lot stranger than it actually did. Instead, he felt at peace as he toed the rubber to face his first batter. As he rocked back into his windup the sellout crowd went silent as they waited, hoping to see the Cooper Madison that had dominated professional baseball for the past decade.

They were not disappointed.

The first pitch was a 97 mile per hour fastball on the inside corner to the right-handed batter. The stadium erupted, and the young minor league batter who had drawn the unenviable task of facing Coop was as white as a ghost. He didn't stand a chance and was set down on three straight pitches to end the inning as Coop walked off the field to the sound of more than 20,000 screaming fans.

The next night Coop made another relief appearance and stretched his arm out over two scoreless innings. His official stat line for his two AA appearances included zero hits allowed with only one walk and four strikeouts. His fastball topped out at 98 miles per hour and his slider was unhittable.

The only question at that time was whether or not to bring him up to the majors for an appearance. If they did, he'd be on a strict pitch count of no more than 50 pitches. Since he had two almost perfect outings in Akron, there was an argument to be made that maybe he should just take that into the offseason instead of risking a poor outing in the majors.

The Indians front office decided to leave the decision up to Coop, and for him, there was no hesitation. He wanted to throw, but on one condition: that he started on the mound instead of coming in for a relief appearance. He needed to experience the routine that comes with starting a game on the "bump" again, regardless of pitch count or the fact that he likely wouldn't pitch the minimum five innings required to factor into the decision should they win.

Coop's name was announced as he finished up his pregame warm-up throws in the bullpen and the stadium absolutely exploded. The fans seated in the upper levels of The Jake could feel the stadium concourse below them vibrating. It was a playoff atmosphere with over 42,000 people in attendance, and they all wanted to see Cooper Madison pitch in an Indians uniform.

Amongst the 42,000 plus fans was a small contingent occupying the owner's box suite. Tim "T-Squared" Taylor stood in the middle of the interior part of the suite and encouraged its occupants to move to their seats outside so they could feel the excitement. He gave fist bumps to the guests who Coop had personally invited to witness him pitch as they made their way to their seats, each of whom had a different connection to the star of the evening.

The Westcott Hotel was well-represented by Henry Wilson and Simon Craig, who had never even been to an Indians game before.

Rahul Ansari, who had driven most of the contingent to the stadium in a limousine bus, was also there.

Cara's family was in attendance, and Charlie Knox took in an Indians game with his wife for the first time since the accident. The Indians even made sure that the suite was wheelchair accessible.

Jason sat in between his wife, Erica, and his daughter. Gabby was still giddy with excitement since Coop had arranged for her to meet Slider, the Indians mascot, before the game.

Christopher was next to Lucy Eckert and was awkwardly trying to make small talk to the girl who was oblivious to the crush that he had secretly had on her since she was in high school.

Grace Brooks was seated next to Cara's brother, Johnny, who was trying to convince her to start weight training with him to take her MMA career to the next level.

Stucky was even there. He was seated next to his old friend from his days at the plant, Ed Delaney, and had spent much of the evening catching up with Cara's parents.

The only other two people Coop had insisted on attending were not in the owner's suite, however. Instead, Clarence Walters was seated directly behind home plate. As Coop finished his last warm-up pitch on the mound before the game began he looked past the umpire and met Clarence's gaze. Coop gave a nod and Clarence winked back. In his hand, he held up a shiny gold key pendant that was connected to an equally impressive gold necklace - a gift from Coop the day after their car ride when he first met with the Indians.

Cooper Madison took a deep breath and adjusted his gaze one seat to Clarence's left where his eyes met those of a precocious delivery girl who had come into his life one month earlier. Tears were welled up in Cara Knox's eyes as she blew a kiss to the starting pitcher for the Cleveland Indians and mouthed the words that only they would appreciate.

"Nothing…"

ABOUT THE AUTHOR

Dan Largent was born in Berea, Ohio during the "Blizzard of 1978" to his parents, Jeff and Anne, before spending the majority of his childhood in nearby Strongsville. Prior to starting 9th grade, Dan moved back to his birthplace of Berea and graduated in 1996 from Berea High School.

Dan completed his undergraduate degree in Elementary Education at THE Otterbein University, where he was also a 4-year letterman in football, President of Alpha Sigma Phi fraternity, a DJ on the former 101.5 FM *The Rock*, RA, Assistant Hall Director, and an esteemed member of the Otterbein Food Service Advisory Board (true story).

After a failed attempt to play football professionally, Dan came to his senses and began his true calling as a 7th grade teacher. In addition to teaching, Dan was an assistant football coach and also the Head Baseball Coach at Olmsted Falls High School from 2010-2017. During his first season at the helm, the Bulldogs reached the school's first ever State Final Four and Dan received the Greater Cleveland Division I Coach of the Year award.

In 2013, Dan was honored to receive the PTA Teacher of the Year award for the Olmsted Falls City School District. That same year he was also recognized as the NEOEA Positive Image Award winner for positive contributions to the teaching profession in Northeast Ohio.

Despite those accolades, Dan feels that his greatest accomplishment is being a father to his three children: Brooke, Grace, and Luke.

Dan has been working on a number of novels and children's books over the past decade and is ecstatic that he finally finished the first of what he hopes are many more to come.

Dan resides in Olmsted Township, Ohio with his wife, April, and children Brooke, Grace, and Luke.

91046271R10197

Made in the USA
Lexington, KY
18 June 2018